A LOW BLUE FLAME

A.J. DOWNEY

BOOK THREE

COPYRIGHT

~

ISBN: 978-1-950222-12-4

Edited by Barbara J. Bailey

Book design by Maggie Kern

Cover art by Dar Albert at Wicked Smart Designs

DEDICATION

To Book World, where I drew the inspiration for this one. Not everything is what it seems, context is everything, and words do hurt. Remember that.

PROLOGUE

*L*illi...

I wasn't confident in most things, but as I bounced once, then twice, on the diving board, I knew I had this. I arched through the air and sliced perfectly with minimal splash into the sapphire pool that was as warm as bathwater. I smiled in the depths to myself and fanned my arms out in front of me, dragging myself towards the surface and breaking it, drawing breath to a smattering of applause.

I laughed and turned to my new friends, some of the older kids belonging to dignitaries and the like. Emilio, my new number-one fan, was eleven and sitting on the edge of the pool, feet dangling in the water.

"Show me how!" he called and I laughed, working my way to the edge of the pool, hauling myself up onto the edge to sit beside him and wring the chlorinated water from the ends of my dark blonde hair.

"It takes practice," I told him, and he got up, trotting to the board enthusiastically.

It was the grand opening of the Echelon Tower, the newest, most technologically-efficient building in the Indigo City skyline, and even though I had signed on the dotted line and purchased my apartment – excuse me, condo – I didn't belong here. My bank account said I did, and a small part of my heart agreed, but for the most part, I felt like an intruder. Unlike almost all of the rest of the people who were moving in, I hadn't been born into money. I'd gotten lucky and had become the next big thing in the literary world, and Hollywood had come knocking what felt like only moments later.

I had more money than I knew what to do with and more coming in every day. On top of that, I was blessed with no shortage of ideas on where to go from here when it came to my writing... so I had no idea why I felt so empty.

Yes, you do. You're lonely, and no matter how much money you have, no matter how much you reinvent yourself, you still don't belong here.

I sighed, the ever-present voice of self-doubt slowly deteriorating my good mood.

Stop it. I told myself sternly. *You're here to start over. Reinvent yourself. So stop whining and do just that!*

"Lilli! Like this?"

I looked up to the diving board and called back, "Feet together, don't bend your knees! Okay, go back and remember what I showed you about the hurdle!"

He went back to the beginning of the board, took his steps, bounced and... didn't quite stick it, but he was much closer in execution than he had been the last time. He came up, dark head bobbing above the deep blue water, and I applauded.

"Did I do it?" he asked, grinning, and I told him the truth but tried to remain encouraging.

"Not quite, but you were much, much, closer. Keep practicing!"

I got up and he asked, "Where are you going?"

Truthfully, I needed a bit of adult time, and a hot soak. I was beginning to get chilled sitting on the edge out of the water like that.

"I'm going to head on back over to the grownups," I told him, smiling.

"Yuck! You should just stay here with me!"

I laughed. "Maybe later."

"Will you be here tomorrow?"

"Should be, I like swimming. It's part of why I moved here."

"Okay! I'll see you!"

"See you later, Emilio."

He paddled over to the edge of the pool and the ladder, got out and went to dive again. I pulled my feet from the warmth and left the enclosed pool area, going out to the group of layered and leveled steaming pools of water more geared towards the adult residents of the Echelon.

I slipped into the warmest one with a sigh, around five or six other people already taking up room on the low benches, and crouched on one. I was short, much of my height in my legs, and so, if I were to sit on one of the benches properly, the waterline would reach just below my nose, covering my mouth. *Not cute.*

A handsome man, almost beautiful, sat across from me, his long hair brushing his shoulders. He had a sexy little smile painted on his lips as he looked me over appreciatively, without being slimy or creepy.

"Hi," I murmured shyly, blushing.

"Name is Mark," he said politely. "What's yours?"

"Lillian," I replied, softly.

"Have to say, Lillian, you're a beautiful and unexpected addition to Echelon."

"Aw, thank you!" I said, laughing lightly but not believing a word he said. *Me? Beautiful? Ha!*

"What floor?" he asked, making small talk.

"I'm on forty-four, you?"

"Don't live here," he said. "I'm just a guest, sadly."

"Oh, well, what do you think of the building?" I asked.

He drifted across the steaming pool to me and sat next to me, eyes traveling over me in a way that made me feel electric, appreciated. It was unexpected and charming, and I couldn't have written it any better.

"It's amazing," he said, making direct eye contact.

I smiled and felt my heart flutter. He had an amazing pair of green-blue eyes and his dark hair, swept back from his face, made them all the more startling. His body was trim and fit without being overly musclebound and I liked that. He looked like a man who wore a suit for a living. Someone with a dangerous mind, and I liked that, too.

I lost my balance a bit, crouched on the bench, and he reached out to steady me. I laughed nervously, wondering how, out of all the beautiful people in Echelon, I would be so lucky that he would be talking to, or even interested in, me.

"Steady..." he said, voice low.

"I'm too short," I breathed, and he smiled.

"You're just perfect."

Again with that little flutter in my chest. He pulled me around gently, his hands nowhere out of bounds, the attraction seemingly just as intense on his end as mine. He settled me safely over his lap in the circle of his arms and smiled at me.

"So," he murmured. "Tell me everything there is to know about you..."

Three months later...

1

___

*B*ackdraft...

"Dude, are you even listening to me?" Golden demanded, and I held up a hand. He shut up, and I diverted the rest of my attention fully to the couple at the table nearby.

The dude held her hands in the middle of the table and was talking to her in low and earnest tones but her eyes were too wide, glassy with shock, and I knew the look. I'd felt it myself only a few weeks ago, as one of the guys at the firehouse had told me the same thing that I would bet my last paycheck that this guy was telling her.

Cheater.

"Look, I'm sorry, I... I never expected things to go this far, but being with you... I'm sorry, Lillian; it just showed me how much I love her. Reminded me why I fell in love with her in the first place."

The woman abruptly pulled her hands from his and put them in her lap, those wide, storm-chased blue eyes of hers finally letting loose, twin crystalline tears slipping over the careful makeup she'd put on before their date, tracking mascara down her cheeks.

"I can't believe I'm hearing this," she uttered, her voice hollow, and I knew that feeling, too. I put things together with lightning speed.

This guy was breaking up with his side chick and the side chick had absolutely no idea there even was a main.

Holy shit.

That was a new kind of low, even for me.

"Did I just hear that dude say what I think I did?" Golden demanded, and I held up a hand and waved him off. Aly's face was set in surprise as I abruptly walked away from the table. Yale held his girl practically in his lap, protectively, and I was struck by how this piece of shit should be doing the same to the petite little thing across from him. Instead, he was smashing her heart with a ball-peen hammer, and in one of the most humiliating ways possible, to boot.

The motion of my stalking away from our table caught those devastated blue eyes of hers and she made eye contact with me. I got the full brunt of the pain she was desperately trying to mask and god, wasn't that a familiar ache?

My heart went out to her, and I read clearly the pleading in her eyes for me not to intercede, but chose to misinterpret it. I couldn't ignore what was going on right in front of me. I wouldn't. Some pains were indeed private, but she needed to get the hell away from this guy, like yesterday.

"I'll be back later," I muttered at Golden who'd kept pace with me, and with a shrug, he broke off and went back to his beer. He didn't say a word; neither did Blaze, who I caught out of the corner of my eye, leaning back on his stool. They both knew better.

I stopped next to the woman and eyed the sleazebag. She was pointedly not looking at me, but I had to give her big ups. She wasn't looking at the table, either. She was looking the douche right in his eyes, and I could see the high spots of color on her cheeks, even beneath her muddy makeup. She was angry, and she had every fucking right to be.

Who the fuck did somebody like that?

The guy was trying like hell to remain friends or some shit – I wasn't really paying attention. I was all about the woman. She was staring up at me now, a spark of defiance in her eyes as the man tried to wave me off saying, "We're fine right now; can't you see we're talking?"

"One, I'm not your waiter," I said. "And two, are you all right, ma'am?"

"No," she said, calmly and strongly.

"Is there anything I can do for you?" I asked.

"I would very much like to go home," she said, evenly and politely.

"I think I can help you with that," I said and held down a hand. She stared at it with only a moment's hesitation, then took it, and I helped her to her feet. She dragged her little purse up after her and hung it off her shoulder and the dude's hand flashed out, circling around her slender wrist.

Instant rage flared deep in my chest, just like my damn namesake, even though it wasn't precisely what I was named for. A backdraft is when a fire starts in a sealed room and it damn-near burns itself out, right? Because it's used up all the oxygen as fuel. Then someone, like a firefighter, like me, goes and opens the door. Suddenly, the fire is introduced to all of this oxygen – its main food source– and it flares back to life, explodes, is meaner than it ever was and larger than life.

I felt that. All that pent-up anger and pissed-off at Torrid and what she'd done to me – to us, flared hot and dangerous and threatened to chew through this motherfucker alive.

I did what I did best. I fought the fire, poured reason on it like water, and went very still and controlled.

"Let her go," I said, and I think he picked up on my tone because the cage of his fingers released and I drew her away from him, put her behind me, and squared off, facing the guy, looking down on him from all six-foot-four-inches of my height.

He shrank back in his seat and it was a good call. I raked a hand back through my own light brown hair and said, "You fucked up, tossed her aside, now you've got to live with that," I told him. I heard her suck in a breath behind me and turned. "Come on. I'll get you home."

"Yes, please; thank you."

She turned, back straight and marched for the door in front of me.

"Yo, Backdraft, seriously?" Golden called, and I barked back over my shoulder at him, "Later!"

She reached the front door of the Ten-Thirteen before I did and dragged it open, stepping out fluidly and stopping at the curb. She put her hands on her knees and dragged in breath after breath, as if she was trying very hard not to throw up. I went up to her, stood beside her, and told her, "He's not worth it."

"I know that!" she snapped, and I didn't take it personal. I knew. It was a different sort of thing when you knew.

"I'll get you a cab," I grated and went out to the street, raising a hand, and bellowed "Taxi!" The one I called to rolled right on by, ignoring me completely, and I cursed.

"Lillian!"

"Just leave me alone, Mark!" she barked and I cursed again, under my breath, and went back between the cars to the curb and stepped back up on it.

"Please, just listen to me; don't be like this!" he was saying.

Oh, hell no... like she did something wrong?

"Just. Leave. Me. Alone, Mark." She was shaking but he was going to be persistent, and I finally stepped up, gently took her elbow and said, "Come on, I'll give you a ride myself."

"Thank you," she said over Mark's indignant scoff and she let me tow her to the alley where my bike was waiting, third in line. I went to it, and held out my helmet to her. She took it and put it on without batting an eye.

Okay, we are doing this.

I flung a leg over the front of my Harley and stuck the key in it, giving it a twist and hitting the switch with my thumb to start her up. She chugged to life and Mark, who had followed us, opened his mouth to protest. I had something for his ass, twisting the throttle to make my baby roar.

The woman, Lillian, jumped slightly and I pulled my bike up off her kickstand and heeled it back up into place. I dropped down onto the seat and held out a hand to help Lil up behind me. She got on without hesitation, but wobbled slightly on her heels. She found the footrests and settled in, putting her arms around me.

Mark took a halfhearted step towards us, in his suit that was probably worth more than I made last month, and I didn't let him get any further or in our way. I switched on the headlamp to combat the dark, put my baby in gear, and took us down the alley and to the street, pausing for a break in between the cages rolling by.

Traffic was light this time of night, so I took us out and into the flow of traffic away from the douchebag pretty quickly. As soon as we hit the next stoplight, I turned enough to call out, "Where am I taking you?"

"The Echelon building!"

"What, that big black tower?"

"Yes, the big black tower," she said dispassionately and I gave a shrug. I couldn't tell where her bitterness was coming from; what it was about the building. If I had to guess, maybe it was where they'd met or something. She'd been polite-but-stiff with me to this point, but I got the impression the 'stiff' had to do more with her utter humiliation at the hands of that ass than anything else.

"You're the boss!" I called back to her, and checked between buildings at the skyline to orient myself and figure out what side streets to take in the direction of the obsidian monstrosity that'd been built.

I hated it for a few reasons. One: that they'd built it pretty much solely to cater to the rich and famous. Two: that the city had contracted with the developers that in any kind of emergency, the Indigo City Fire department, which included my ladder, was to go door-to-door checking on residents.

Yeah, at seventy-six floors, anywhere from four to twelve apartments per floor, you do the math. Still, if the woman on the back of my motorcycle lived in the Echelon, I wanted to know, just who was she? That place was reserved for the crème de la crème. Just about everyone and everything the working man could possibly hate about the rich was embodied by that building and those who lived in it. *So who the hell was she?*

I pulled up under the overhang in front of the place to a shocked look from the doorman and some disgusted looks from some of the tower-goers, and got my cheap thrill for the night. The woman, Lillian, got down off the back of my bike and undid the chinstrap on my helmet. She held it out to me and said, "Thank you." She didn't look like a 'Lillian' to me. The name was so stiff and formal, when she didn't give off that entitled sort of vibe.

"Don't mention it," I told her, and before I could ask if she was gonna be okay, she turned and flashed a card on a lanyard at the doorman, who nodded and dragged open the big glass door for her. She clipped across the black marble lobby to the glowing line of fancy optic turnstiles barring the banks of elevators and scanned the card against the black box for it. The LED-lit arrows switched directions, allowing her access, and she walked up to the elevators and pressed her card against the RFID reader below the touchscreen panel. The doors on the nearest car slid open.

She looked back at me over her shoulder, inclined her head, hesitated a moment, but finally stepped into the car, the doors gliding shut, the rectangle of light disappearing, along with her elongated shadow on the expensive, black marble floor. I found myself wondering if our paths would ever cross again.

It wasn't likely. She was guaranteed to be too rich for my blood, clearly, living in a place like this. I shook my head and put on my helmet that was resting forgotten in my hands. I resisted the urge to ask the doorman what her last name was, and took off back into the flow of traffic. I couldn't blame her for just wanting to go home. Suddenly, all I wanted to do was the same.

2

*L*illi...

Rain pattered against the floor-to-ceiling windows of my condo and I sighed. It was storming out there, and Jasper and Marigold, my two cats, were nowhere to be found. The sky rumbled with thunder and I winced, taking another sip from my glass.

I didn't feel like I'd belonged here when I'd first moved in, and the debacle with Mark only proved it to me. However, this was my home, bought and paid for with the royalties from all of my hard work, and I wouldn't give it up. If anything, since the incident weeks ago, I hadn't left it, preferring to spend my days staring at the blinking cursor in an open Word document, each flash of that little black line echoing the throbbing ache of having my heart ripped out.

I closed my eyes and missed the next flash of lightning, but jumped none the less. The inside of my eyelids flared red from the light and before I could even open them the thunder crashed so angrily, I thought it was a direct echo of how I was feeling. Shook. I mean, everything did, my body vibrating from the strength of the cacophony. I opened my eyes just in time to watch the glass in front of my face shudder with the impact of that awful sound and then the lights went out behind me.

I blinked and called out to my home's system, "Alexa?"

Nothing. No response. *Shit.*

I stared out over the rest of the city. There weren't many towers out there taller than the forty-fourth floor I resided on, and none of the ones that did exist were in line to obstruct my view, which reached all the way to the bay. I was disappointed to see that lights continued to twinkle in windows out in the rest of the city, all except for in the windows of the buildings immediately surrounding the Echelon. It looked like just our block, and maybe the next one over, were out. Still, I found myself muttering, "Holy crap."

I had no idea what it would take to knock out the power to a major city's grid or even to just a building like the Echelon, but I imagined that it took some doing. That last lightning strike had really been something else. I wondered for a moment if the Echelon had taken a direct hit because it sure had felt like it. I took another sip of the cool, sweet wine in my glass, which was nearly empty, and sighed.

The power would be back on soon, I hoped. Not that I would write or even keep my laptop on during a storm like this. I hadn't counted on what it would be like this high up during a storm this severe, and I really should have. It felt as if the whole building swayed, which was unnerving as hell.

Not as unnerving as how well and how thoroughly I had been duped by Mark, though.

My thoughts always seemed to circle back to that disaster, even now, weeks on from it. I should have seen it. I should have listened to my instincts. I hadn't, and now I found myself sipping the last of the wine in my glass just to get the taste of bitter regret out of my mouth.

I don't know why my brain insisted on reliving it over and over, but sure, I guessed we could go again. I closed my eyes again, with a heavy sigh as another bolt of lightning forked through the sky.

The first time we'd met had been electric like that. I'd sat in his lap in the hot tub downstairs and it had felt so right and comfortable. Conversation had led to kissing, kissing had led to intimate touching, and before long we were practically having sex right there in the damn tub with something like seven other people around us.

I went to down the rest of my wine and swore. That's right, I was out, time for a refill. Still, my brain insisted on gaily carrying on with my emotional torture.

I'd been so weak not to question it and I blame it on my hormones. I'd been hot for him like you wouldn't believe, and against my better judgment, had invited him up.

"I have a couple of cats..." I'd warned, and when he'd said he'd been allergic, I'd told him I had allergy medicine. I should have seen it for the delay tactic that it was, but I could feel his erection pressed between us. He'd told me only one particular kind of allergy medicine worked for him and what should have been the second red flag had gone up. The third followed directly after when he said he couldn't remember which brand and that he would know it by the box when he went to get some.

I'd been disappointed, but at that point I'd thought that maybe he just wasn't that into me, or maybe I was coming on too strong. I'd shied a little by then and he'd reassured me that he really wanted to, (probably just to spare my feelings), but unfortunately he had to attend his friend's birthday that night. Still, he'd told me that he really, really, hoped there would be a rain check.

I'd let him go and figured I wouldn't see him again, that I'd blown it, that he hadn't been that serious about it and I'd misread and had fucked up. *Stupid, awkward me!* It had stung a little bit. I honestly figured he was giving himself an out and that, again, he just wasn't that into me, but then the knock had fallen at my door later that night. When I'd opened it, he had been standing there looking almost more delicious in a suit than he had been in just a pair of swim trunks in the hot tub downstairs.

He'd pulled his hand out from behind his back and had shook a package of allergy medicine and I'd smiled and let him in.

Impulsive as it had been, it had also turned out to be some of the best sex ever. He'd worn a condom, and had been really good with his hands and I had christened my first night in my brand new condo and said 'Cheers' to new beginnings.

Yeah. What a joke. I was the same girl I'd ever been, just in shiny new digs. *Stupid... worthless...* just like my mother had always told me. Happily-ever-after's didn't exist in the real world. I should have known better. Whirlwind romances without any catches or strings attached only existed between the pages of my books. I had been crazy to think that there was anything good waiting for me in that arena.

I closed my eyes and sucked in a deep, slow breath through my nose, letting it out slowly.

I just needed to do what I did best. Write the damn books, pet the damn cats, and stay locked in my fortress of solitude.

I turned around and shuffled my feet across the plush gray carpet of my living room. I was moving slowly, carefully, so I didn't stub my toes or trip over anything. It was darker than I could have imagined now that the power was out, and eerily silent. The big behemoth of the building I lived in was never as silent as it was now. You really took for granted the white noise of humming electronics and just the sounds of modern life until they were conspicuously absent. It was even worse when it snowed, the quiet, but that was different some-how, peaceful rather than unsettling, like now.

I made it to the kitchen safely, the marble tiles cool beneath my feet as I opened the fridge and carefully felt for the bottle of wine. I pulled it out and closed the fridge and hoped like hell I wouldn't have to haul the contents of it down forty-four stories to be thrown out. I mean, surely the power would be back on before it came to that.

"Not with your luck, Lilli..." I said to the empty dwelling. I worried about poor Jasper and Marigold. Both of them were older and both of them were cowering beneath the furniture. I didn't want to pull them out, fearing it would just be more traumatizing than leaving them where they were, but it was frustrating. I could have used the comfort just then, anything to feel less alone.

I poured another glass of the crisp white wine successfully by sound and by feeling, and let myself feel a little badass for not spilling. I set the bottle down and pressed the cork back into the top but left it out. I wouldn't be able to find the place I'd pulled it from out of the fridge anyway.

I sipped and let the crisp, fruity, sweet Riesling with its delicate peach and citrus notes trickle over my tongue. It was a good wine, and while I was no sommelier, I could still appreciate.

I breathed in and sighed out. I was definitely no sommelier. I was definitely nothing but what I'd always been. A small-town, West-coast girl that had no business making all of this stupid money and had no business pretending like I deserved it, and really had no business trying to date above my station.... Obviously.

This was only my second glass, but I'd drunk the first quick enough that I was getting nicely buzzed, which I would seriously need if this pity party were to continue. Of course, two was my hard limit when it came to drinking, and I almost never touched the hard stuff because no way was I ever going down the road to substance abuse. No, thank you. I'd had a front row seat to that horror show all growing up and I wasn't going to make the same mistakes my mother made.

I thought all the way back to the very beginning as to how I got here, tumbling end-over-end down this particular rabbit hole of thought, plummeting through the layers of my life rather than taking any sort of leisurely stroll down memory lane. Then again, my memory lane looked more like a trip through the haunted wood.

I felt my way out of the kitchen, careful not to slosh the wine in my glass, barely escaping tripping when I transitioned from tile to carpet, just like I barely escaped falling too far into the deathtrap of memories that were the actual growing-up part of my life. I settled on my first major rebirth, instead of going as far back as my actual birth.

While I was Lillian September Banks by that original birth, my pseudonym or *nom de plume* was Timber Philips. Yes, *the* Timber Philips. The one they were billing as the paranormal Nicolas Sparks.

My books had the right formula, you see, and had been picked up by one of the big five publishers a few years ago. I thought I'd had something to be proud of when I'd hit 'New York Times' Bestseller' three books in a row after I'd been picked up – but then Hollywood had come calling. Apparently, I'd had the right formula, visual appeal, and adaptability to my books for them to be made into films. I'd gone for it, because, who wouldn't? And the first movie had earned the studio that had picked it up a lot of money.

Due, in no little part, to my efforts for them not to fuck it up.

No way would I allow Hollywood *carte blanche* to feed one of my works through their meat grinder. I'd made sure there were provisions in that contract to keep me on as a consultant and to assist the screenwriters and I was glad I did. That first movie had been painful to get out there but the readers had loved it. Thankfully, it hadn't seemed to hurt the studio none, having me along for the ride, even if it had been like passing a kidney stone for me. I'd been pretty much invited back to help with the next two, much to my surprise and delight, and the process had become much easier.

Anyway, I went from the girl who self-published her silly little love stories as an unusual and expensive hobby to the girl that was making so much money, she didn't know what to do with it in a little under five years. It'd been one crazy big leap after another and I was both grateful and saddened by it.

I felt like a fraud for so many reasons... but the people around me in the business both promised and assured me I was not. I had to believe them, even though I wrestled with the idea of it every single day. Yup. I had a major case of impostor syndrome.

I returned to watching lightning flash through the clouds, my traitorous brain finally satisfied and calming way the hell down, with the second glass of wine going down even easier than the first. I don't know how long I stood there, thinking about my life, my books, my mother and her super-destructive alcoholic ways, and of course, Mark, but the edge was certainly taken off. *Self-medication for the win, this time.*

I was roused from my bitter and dark musings by a knock on my door and I blinked at my faint reflection in the window glass.

"Who on earth..?" I murmured, and moved carefully across the room. The knock came again, more insistent this time, just as I reached the door. There shouldn't be anyone up here. It was a secured building. A really secure building.

I opened the door to reveal two tall firemen in their thick canvas fire suits.

"Is there a fire?" I asked, with apprehension.

The two of them looked at each other and laughed slightly.

"No, ma'am," one of them said and turned slightly, letting the emergency light in the hall fall on me. The other, the one on my right, sucked in a breath.

I looked up at him sharply and echoed the sentiment.

"Oh, hi, it's you," I breathed, and he smiled, pleased that I'd remembered him.

"Hi, back," he said with a slight laugh. "It's me." He had a bright white smile and it set off a flurry of butterflies in my stomach. I didn't know how to feel about that. This was definitely a new plot-twist in the story of my life.

"What can I do for you gentlemen?" I asked, politely.

3

*B*ackdraft...

I took back every fucking curse word, bitch, and gripe I'd uttered dragging my ass up forty-four stories worth of fucking stairs.

Blaze and I were from different houses, but it took more than one house to canvas every occupied apartment or condo that this building had, with over seventy-six goddamn floors. I'd let Blaze have the list, I hadn't even thought to check for her name... Lillian.

Like I would ever forget it.

Blaze wasn't a dumbass and could see there was something telegraphing between me and the woman. He kept his mouth shut, and I didn't know whether I wanted to kiss him or curse him.

"What can I do for you gentleman?" she asked politely.

"Oh, nothing," I said, caught off-guard by the question, really just bowled over by how beautiful she was. My memory hadn't done her justice. She looked amused and I realized I was acting like a starstruck idiot.

"I'm confused, if there isn't a fire, then what are you doing here?" she asked.

"Safety protocol, ma'am. Your building has a contract with the city," Blaze explained, but she didn't move her eyes off of mine.

"Oh," she said, simply.

"You doing okay?" I asked softly and I wasn't asking as a matter of safety protocol. She leaned a shoulder against the doorjamb and took a sip out of what was probably not her first glass of wine, and, if I had to guess, wouldn't be her last tonight, either.

"As well as can be expected," she said, with a rueful smile.

"Sorry to ask, ma'am..." Blaze said politely with an 'aw shucks' tone. "I wouldn't happen to be able to use your facilities, would I? It's been an awfully long climb and there hasn't exactly been an opportunity."

"Absolutely, sure, go ahead." She stepped aside to let him through and he handed me the clipboard. He shone his light at her delicately painted toes; she had one foot crossed over the other beneath the hem of her satin nightgown and robe, like a child caught out of bed with her hand in the cookie jar. It was adorable, and I guess adorable was maybe what I heartily needed a dose of after Tori. *The fucking bitch.*

Blaze went down her hall and disappeared into her bathroom, shutting the door so it was just me and her.

"I never got your name," she said softly and I smiled.

"Friends call me Backdraft," I said and she held out her hand. I took it gently and shook it. *Could she be any cuter?*

"Lillian, Lillian Banks."

"Nice to meet you again, Lil."

"You too, Backdraft." She blushed in my headlamp over the way I shortened her name and laughed slightly over the unusual awkwardness of mine and I smiled.

"Emmet, if you prefer something a little more normal," I said. "Emmet Calder."

"Oh! No, if Backdraft is the name you prefer, than that is what I shall call you. It wouldn't feel right otherwise."

She's sweet. Not entitled, I thought. *Definitely rich, and totally not a bitch.* I liked what I was seeing.

I let her small, soft hand go and she took it back. Silence engulfed us and I felt the need to say something, anything before Blaze got back, so I blurted the first thing that came to mind.

"Been thinking about you. You know, since that night."

"Oh! Um, me too..."

"Yeah?"

"Yeah, I don't think I ever properly thanked you... I'm sorry if I didn't. I mean, I don't remember saying 'Thank you'."

I took the opportunity that presented itself and said, "You can, you know... Thank me."

She looked startled and I laughed, I hadn't meant it that way, but she'd suddenly turned me into some kind of awkward teenage boy that didn't know what to say about anything. I swallowed and tried to backpedal.

"I didn't mean for that to come out near as creepy as it just did. I only meant that I'd um, I'd really like to take you out to dinner, or for a drink, or something."

She smiled bravely and looked me up and down before saying, "As long as you promise that you don't have a wife or a girlfriend... I, um... I could stand to get out of the apartment for a while."

I looked behind her and said, "I always kind of wondered what a place like this would rent for."

She closed her eyes and shook her head, "I just called it an apartment again, didn't I?"

"Ah, this one of the condos?"

"Yeah, I um, I bought it before the building was even finished."

"Oh, yeah?"

"Yeah." She blushed and named off a figure.

I gave a long, low whistle. "Wow."

And I'd just asked her out. *Go me.* This woman was way out of my league... *Except she'd said yes... what does that mean?*

Well, not like I would know until I got to know her, and the only way to get to know her would be to take her out, so...

She was looking at me as if she was trying to decide something, and I gave a shrug and asked, "Did you ever get to try the food at the Ten-Thirteen?"

"I'm sorry?"

"Oh, shit, no, I'm sorry. The Cormorant. The place where we met the first time. We call it the 10-13."

"Oh. No." She shook her head. "Why do you call it that?"

"It's a nickname, a couple of reasons for it." I didn't back down. "Would love to tell you over some food or a drink there, say on Saturday night?" I knew I was pushing it, but I really, really wanted her to say 'Yes' already.

She bit her bottom lip slightly and finally nodded, asking, "What time?"

"Around six?"

"Okay, I'll meet you there at six."

I smiled, "Sure you don't want me to pick you up?"

She smiled back and it made her go from beautiful to stunning. She said, "I'll take a car, no big deal."

"Okay, The Cormorant on Saturday at six."

"I'll be there," she said softly as Blaze had come back out of her bathroom and was coming up the hall of her condo towards us. She stepped aside and let him by.

"Have a good night, Ms. Banks," I said with a wink and Blaze smiled.

"Yes, thank you so much for letting me use your restroom."

She smiled graciously and said, "You're welcome. I'll, uh, see you then, Backdraft," before closing the door.

We stepped off, walking a little bit up the corridor before he said, "Well? 'See you then?' Come on, man, don't make me beg for it."

"Saturday at six at the Ten-Thirteen."

"Nice!" he hissed and held out a fist.

"Yeah, well, you know... we'll see." I knocked my fist into his and sighed, and we kept moving.

I couldn't stop thinking about those gorgeous, stormy eyes of hers. She'd probably been tipsy to agree to go out with me, but for some reason I would take it. I was curious. I saw a matched pain in her that

I still felt pretty keenly. I didn't think I was looking for a relationship right now, but a friendship? Sure.

Okay, to be honest, I was kicking myself and demanding to know what the fuck I'd been thinking. I was nervous, which was completely goddamn ridiculous. I tried to thrust every thought of her out of my head as we finished our assigned floors, but at the same time, I was suddenly grateful that I'd drawn the short straw of having been on tonight.

I'd be lying if I said I hadn't wondered, hadn't hoped against hope, that'd I'd be the one lucky enough to knock on her door. Apartment 4403. Well, condo... but they were the same damn thing really.

Lillian Banks.

It felt good to have a full name, too. Now, I just had to hope again. Hope that she wouldn't stand me up and that I would get the chance to learn more.

"Bro, get your head off the girl, and back in the game. I don't want to pay out to those two assclowns." We'd bet we'd get our floors done before Cowan and Rizzo from Blaze's house.

I looked up and grinned at Blaze, "Yeah, sorry."

He laughed, "Don't blame you. She's hot, seems nice..." he trailed off and I nodded some.

"Different from Torrid, that's for sure." I said it so he didn't have to.

"Yeah. You need that," he said, sounding relieved. I figured he was dying to make the observation.

"Yeah," I agreed, my thoughts far away and back on the woman. I thought Lillian maybe needed different, too. The sadness in those eyes of hers was still kind of haunting me.

4

Lilli...

I got out of the sleek black towncar and the driver closed the door. I stared dubiously at the shingle hanging outside, above the door, like some old-fashioned inn. The sky was clear but the pavement wet from another harsh thunderstorm earlier in the day. I worried my bottom lip between my teeth, grateful I'd put on a lipstick that was like Teflon and that could withstand even my most nervous of habits.

Everything in me was screaming this was a massive mistake; that I shouldn't have agreed to this, that I should get back in the car. The car that, of course, was pulling away from the curb right as I thought about retreating. I sighed and squared my shoulders as the door to the restaurant opened and the man himself stepped out, smiling.

"Hey," he said, and I was struck by how handsome he was. Vastly different from Mark, for sure. He was over a foot taller than me, for one, where Mark had only been around eight to nine inches taller. He was also built much different: broader through the shoulders and powerfully-muscled. Where Mark was fit in a runner's build sort of way, Backdraft was more built to work, which, as a firefighter, I'm sure he did. I looked him over and silently appreciated. He wore his leather biker jacket open over a soft-looking, broken-in gray Henley that hugged his chest. Over the jacket was the vest full of patches and I swallowed hard, unsure about that part, but a little late to go back now; he was walking towards me.

"Hi," I murmured back as he came out to stand with me, thrusting his hands in his jeans pockets the way I had mine thrust into my coats.

"You found the place," he said with a warm grin, and I do believe he was as nervous as I was, which honestly didn't help me feel any less awkward. Not in the slightest. *Damnit.*

"Look, I, uh... I really am thinking that this might have been a bad idea. I'm sure you're a very nice man, Backdraft. In fact, I know you're a very nice man, giving me a ride home like that, but I just don't know that I'm ready to do this, I mean, date, anyone." I shifted on my feet, squirming under his gaze as his smile grew wider.

"Oh, you thought I was asking you on a date?"

I froze and felt my face set into stone, my natural reflex when I thought I was about to take a hit on an emotional level that I just wasn't prepared for. He put up his hands as if to ward something off, and he cried, "No! Shit! Bad joke! That didn't come out right at all. That totally didn't come out like I meant it to, I'm seriously just trying to say I'm not ready to date either. Please don't take that the way it sounded, I'm begging you. I'm serious, I just invited you out to get to know you better. I was hoping we could, literally, just be friends."

I sucked in a deep breath and when I let it out, it plumed in the cooling air. I took my eyes off of him and turned my head to stare up the sidewalk, trying to decide if he were being genuine or not or if this was a setup for a laugh at the rich bitch's expense.

The more things change, the more they stay the same. I thought to myself. Five years ago, I would have said it was for a laugh at the poor girl's expense. Truthfully, money didn't change a whole hell of a lot.

"I really screwed that up, didn't I?" he asked and he sounded genuinely rueful.

I looked back at him and sighed out. "No, I'm just having a really hard time trusting anyone right now." I put a hand to my forehead and nearly drowned in my frustration and apprehension.

"Let's try this again," he suggested, walking our encounter back. "Hey, Lillian. Glad you could make it. This place has some really great food and I was hoping to get to know you better, you know, as just friends." He even stuck out his hand, it was kind of adorable. I couldn't help but smile.

I debated for several heartbeats and lowered my fingertips from my forehead where I'd looked at him past my hand. I took his offered hand, giving it a shake and said, "Hi, Backdraft, I'm glad I could make it, too." I laughed nervously. "I could really use a glass of wine, do they have anything good here?"

He grinned broadly, his hazel eyes sparkling under the streetlight. He let go of my hand and turned, giving me the 'after you' gesture, hand palm-up in front of his body. I went to the door and he stepped up first, pushing it open for me. We stopped at the 'Please Wait to Be Seated' sign and he caught the bartender's attention and held up two fingers. The bartender, a man in his fifties but still in good shape, with a thick head of salt-and-pepper hair and matching beard, craned his head on his neck to sweep the restaurant floor with his gaze. He held up seven fingers in return and Backdraft gave a nod.

He took me gently by the elbow and said, "Come on, this way."

I followed him around to the other side of the 'L' shaped bar, behind the back wall of it that held the liquor. There was a row of booths behind that wall, and there was a narrow hall leading back to the bathrooms. Backdraft pulled me past him where he'd been leading the way, and I took a moment to examine the back of his leather jacket. A large silver shield was embroidered there, a knight's chess piece in profile picked out in indigo thread. There was a white ribbon or banner over it with 'Indigo Knights' in the same dark blue thread as the chess piece and another that curved the opposite direction on the bottom proclaiming 'Nomad.'

I was afraid I didn't know what any of it meant, but I could always ask. It was probably a safe-enough topic to get a conversation going and might help me stave off the general question of 'What do you do?' that I knew was coming.

I stopped before sliding into the little two-person booth and unbuttoned my coat. Backdraft, apparently a gentleman, took the garment from me and hung it on the brass hook provided between our booth and the next one over. My purse, I kept a hold of, and set it on the seat before sliding in, trapping it between my hip and the wall.

He took off his jacket, but rather than hang it with mine, he did the same thing with it that I'd done with my purse, guarding it as if it were something of value, and maybe it was. I mean, it could very well be holding his wallet.

"You're sure it's all right to sit here? That we shouldn't have waited for the hostess?" I asked.

"Ah, yeah. Bartender is Skids, he owns the place with Reflash. They're the president and vice-president of the same club." He gestured toward his coat and the colorful patch facing out.

"I really don't want to sound rude or ignorant," I said. "But aren't all motorcycle gangs dangerous?"

He grinned and said, "Well, outlaw ones can be, sure. We aren't a gang, though. We're a club. The Indigo Knights was started by a bunch of cops, way back in the day. Gradually they started adopting a bunch of other first responders. Now we have not only cops, but firefighters, paramedics, and even a lawyer."

"Oh," I said. "You're a firefighter, obviously," I stammered, blushing. *So dumb! I sounded so dumb!*

"That I am," he said with a broad grin. "Blaze, the other guy that was with me at your place, he's one of the club, too. He's not with my ladder, though. It was just a onetime thing that we partnered up that night."

I nodded and was sort of at a loss for anything to say. I didn't want to come off sounding any dumber than I'd already managed. Of course, that opened me up for the dreaded question.

"So, uh, what do you do?"

I licked my lips and rolled them together. The gloss layer of my lip-color felt tacky by now, but I had faith it still looked okay. This stuff really was bulletproof.

"Um, I write. I'm a writer," I said, nodding, but I didn't elaborate. Everyone who asked me anymore pretty much had to drag it out of me.

Backdraft smiled and laughed a little bit. "You must be a damn good one to afford a place like that in the Echelon."

I nodded and said, breath held, "A lot of people seem to think so, but I don't see it."

"Well, you are your own worst critic."

I felt myself smile. "I always say that, too."

"Hey, look at that, something in common after all," he teased lightly.

"Oh, I wasn't always rich," I said, waving the implied notion away.

"No?"

I shook my head. "It's a relatively new thing and I'm afraid I'm not handling it super well. Everyone treats me so different and I just don't really feel any different. You know? I mean, in some ways I'm less stressed, but in other ways, it's more. It's really like I just traded one type for another."

He nodded and really seemed to be listening to me. Finally he said, "I could see that."

"Yeah?" I asked skeptically.

"Yeah."

The waitress came by and dropped a couple of menus saying, "Sorry Backdraft, it's a little crazy in here. Do you know what you want to drink?"

I picked up the little wine menu at the edge of the table and gave it a quick sweep while he answered, "Yeah, Kristy. I'll have a Coke."

"And I'll have a white Zinfandel, thank you," I told her.

"No problem, I'll be right back with those."

She swept off in the direction of the bar and I asked, "So what's good here?"

He grinned and said, "Everything, and I do mean everything. Reflash is a world-class cook."

I smiled, my comfort level rising ever so slowly and asked, "Where do you get such interesting names?"

"Uh, they're road names, given to you by the club when you get your colors."

I raised my eyebrows over my menu and he smiled again heading me off saying, "That's to say when you get the big center patch here on your vest." He pointed to the back of his coat and I nodded my understanding.

"Sounds very structured," I said.

"It is, but a lot of guys gravitate to that sort of thing."

"I can see it," I remarked. He wasn't even looking at his menu, just sitting, sleeves of his Henley rucked back over his muscular forearms, hands folded neatly on the table in front of him.

I made a selection of the crab-stuffed rockfish and set my menu down. He asked me what I liked to do when I wasn't writing and I told him, and the conversation was easy for a moment, but of course, he circled back to what he didn't know but was an easy thing for most people to talk about – my job.

"So what do you write?" he asked.

I felt myself blush and mumbled, "I always hate it when people ask me that." Of course, I had grown to almost hate it more when they didn't have to.

"Why?" he asked, and that smile of his was entirely too disarming and really, really nice to look at.

"I write romance novels," I said and tried not to slouch. It was just such a mixed bag on how people responded to that bit of information.

"Huh, that's cool. You write under your name or…?" he left the question hanging, but his reaction had me sighing inwardly with relief. There was no laughter, no judgment on his face or in the set of his shoulders.

"A pen name," I said evenly, but I didn't volunteer it. You pretty much had to be living under a rock to not know who Timber Philips was anymore. *Please don't push it, please don't push it, please don't push it…* I silently begged.

"Which is...?" He smiled and I had to smile back, despite my inner voice saying, *Crap.*

"You have to promise to be cool," I said because I really didn't want any super uncomfortable displays of excitement drawing a whole bunch of unwanted attention.

"I promise," he said and held up two fingers in a Scout's Honor.

"I write under the name 'Timber Philips'," I answered, and his first reaction was to frown.

"I know that name, but I'm really sorry, I can't place it," he said and he sounded genuinely apologetic.

I felt the tension in my shoulders and back ease some. The waitress was coming this way and I looked her direction and held up what I hoped was a subtle finger at him to beg a moment before I told him anything more. His mouth turned down and he gave a knowing look and nod. She set down our glasses and took our food orders, asked if we needed anything else in the meantime, and when we declined, left with a cheerful smile and nod.

"Um, one of my books, *Hallowed Be Thy Light*, was made into a movie. It's supposed to premiere just before Halloween in New York."

His head jerked back in surprise. He cocked it to one side and gave a nervous laugh.

"It's all right if you don't believe me," I said with a smile. It wasn't a common reaction but it wasn't one I'd never had before. "You can take a second to look it up on your phone, if you'd like. The name might not be real but I can't switch bodies so easily; my picture is all over the internet." I gave a shrug.

He said, "You really wouldn't mind if I looked it up right now, would you?" It was my turn to grin and give a little laugh.

"Why should I mind? I get it," I shrugged. "It's a pretty outlandish claim. It's not a common reaction I get, but it's still a legitimate one."

He rooted through his coat and pulled out his phone, eyeing me carefully to make sure that I really didn't mind. I sat stoically and waited patiently.

"Philips only has one 'L'," I said, helpfully.

He laughed a little and looked it up; when the page, or whatever rendered, he gave a low whistle.

"Holy shit, you're pretty goddamned famous," he said. I laughed and it felt good.

"Never quite had it put that way before, but I have to say, it's kind of nice."

"What is?" he asked.

"You, not making a big deal out of it."

He shrugged and put his phone away, saying, "I get it, I guess. Being famous isn't all it's cracked up to be sometimes."

"You know someone else famous?" I asked. His responses were curious to me.

"Sort of, not really. One of our guys, Youngblood, is a homicide detective– Wait, how long have you been in Indigo City?"

"A few months," I confessed.

"Ah, so before your time, for sure. You probably missed it, so I'll explain. Youngblood's woman, Chrissy, was a defense attorney. Ever hear of Skip Maguire?"

"Vaguely, I would have to look him up."

"Baseball legend here. Really popular guy. Apparently he liked to pop his wife when he'd been drinking."

"Ah, that's right. Didn't his wife kill him in self-defense? I remember hearing something about it, even across the country."

"Oh yeah? Where you from?"

"Oregon, originally."

"Okay, and yeah, she killed him, but she ended up charged with his murder. Chrissy was her lawyer and got her off and his fan base went ape-shit. Next thing Youngblood knows, he's being called over to her apartment for a double homicide. Someone had kicked in Chrissy's front door, shot her and her best friend."

"Oh, my god, that's awful." I was appalled but enthralled with his story.

"Well, not as awful as everyone first thought, turned out Chrissy wasn't dead, but her friend was. She ended up first in the hospital and then in protective custody. Media about hounded her to death, which wouldn't have been so bad except Skip's douchebag following wasn't about to give it up. It was a real shit-show and took forever for them to get it sorted out."

"I'm glad she's okay," I said honestly. I watched how some of the real celebrities who played my characters on the silver screen were treated and was glad that type of scrutiny was almost never turned on the author. People could be animals and had no concept of privacy anymore. I hadn't encountered even a tenth of what some of the actors and actresses attached to my work had, and I was grateful for it. Still, let me just say, I'd had some moments before.

"Yeah, she's okay now," Backdraft was saying. "Quit being a defense attorney and went over to the side of the angels. She works for the DA's office now, moved out of her place and in with Young-blood. They're good, but yeah, I was there for a taste of that bullshit, Youngblood's my best friend, and just from that taste I can't imagine living it twenty-four/seven."

"It's not so bad, really," I said. "I mean, I've gotten pretty big and I have readers everywhere, but I still get to enjoy quite a bit of anonymity. I'm still not all the way used to being recognized when it happens, though. I'm pretty much an introvert, and so it's always a little jarring and unexpected when it happens, you know?"

"I could see that," he said affably.

"I don't mind it," I told him. "I love my readers to death. I mean, I wouldn't be here without them. It just gets awkward sometimes. People can get incredibly bold! Like they think they know me and some of them *do* know all about me to the point it can get creepy. But, for the most part, my experiences have been good. I just have to be careful being in the public eye, you know? It's like the world is just waiting for a scandal sometimes and when they don't get it right away, they're willing to make up just anything anymore to manufacture some drama." I'd seen it with some of the poor actresses portraying my characters and thought regularly that if it ever happened to me, I wouldn't be half so cool about it. They laughed it off; I would be a crying, anxiety-riddled mess.

He nodded and said, "Okay, so tell me something, creepiest fan experience so far?"

I twisted my lips. "You know, that's really hard," I said.

"First one that comes to mind."

"The girl that showed up at my house when I first hit it big and didn't know any better. I guess my address was on some people-finder site and I didn't do as good a job as I should have protecting my given name. That one was definitely unnerving."

"So, what happened?"

"Well, um, you're going to think I'm crazy, but I made her a cup of coffee and we talked about it and the poor thing was in absolute tears but I was really lucky. That was as far as things got. My publisher had me moved into a secured building by the next week."

"Wow. I don't know how I would have handled a fangirl just showing up at my house like that. You didn't even think to call the cops?"

I blushed with embarrassment.

"I was probably exceptionally naïve at the time. You see, I didn't go the direct traditional publishing route."

"You didn't?"

"No," I said, laughing a little. I had been sipping on the crisp wine from time to time and I took another now. It was really good.

"Then how did you do it?"

"I uh, I self-published first. With the advent of e-readers, it kind of opened some doors. I treated it like an expensive hobby in the beginning."

He frowned. "Okay now, explain that."

He seemed genuinely interested and he was incredibly easy to talk to. So much so, that I found myself enthusiastically explaining.

"Well, when you're on your own, you have to pay for things like your own editing and cover art and both of those things can get really expensive. Especially on a regular-joe salary."

"How expensive?" he asked.

"Um, depending on manuscript size, most editors – at least for one of my books – ran anywhere between seven hundred to a thousand dollars."

"Jesus Christ!" he exclaimed. I laughed.

"Yeah, well, cover art for me started at about a hundred dollars a cover, but when I started buying exclusive imagery, that went up to seven-hundred-and-seventy-five dollars apiece."

"What! Why so expensive?" he asked.

The waitress set our plates in front of us and I took a moment to exclaim over how everything looked so good and to ask for a glass of ice water. I was feeling a touch flushed from the glass of wine and maybe needed to back off just a little bit. I confess to being a total lightweight, so much so that usually I had two glasses max and I was buzzed enough to want to be done.

Kristy went and got my water right away, and with an exchange of a few final words, it was just me and Backdraft again.

"Where was I?" I asked.

"Some seriously expensive-ass cover art."

I laughed, "Oh, right!"

I explained about covers and their different components. About the difference between stock photos and exclusive photos through photographers, as well as the added cost of design. I tended to go with photo-manipulation for my covers, but I even went as far as to discuss the finer points of the varying types of other commissioned artwork authors sometimes used. The thing was, he was actually interested, absorbing everything I told him like a sponge. I couldn't ever remember any other man doing that who wasn't an author themselves.

"Wow," he said, finally, our plates empty or nearly so in front of us. I was absolutely stuffed to the gills, and all of it had been amazing.

"Yeah, it's a lot," I agreed.

He let out a breath, blowing out his cheeks, and shook his head, eyes wide in that incredulous, mind-blown look.

"Don't even get me started on marketing as an indie," I joked.

"Shit, publishers do a lot of shit people take for granted, don't they?"

I nodded slowly and said, "Yes, but they also take a way-bigger chunk of the proceeds, too. Nothing is free, it's just a matter of whether you want to pay up front or on the back end."

His head bobbed slowly as he processed all of the information I had dumped in his head. I ran a finger around the rim of my nearly-empty wineglass absently while I waited for him to say something.

Finally I had to ask, "So what's it like being a fireman?"

"Probably eighty-five percent boring and the other fifteen percent shit-your-pants terrifying," he said and winked.

I laughed and he grinned broadly.

"If it's terrifying, then why do you do it?"

"Ahhhh." He leaned back and rubbed his fingertips lightly over his chest, looking both full and considering. "For me? Because I'm an adrenaline junkie and I always wanted to be a real-life superhero."

I felt my own face split into a stupid grin. That was both the most honest and, at the same time, adorable answer he could have given me.

He sighed and I felt it too, our evening was definitely winding down to an end. I was surprised to feel regret about that. I almost didn't want it to end at all. I was enjoying Backdraft's company immensely.

"I got a shift over the next four days," he said.

"Four days?" I asked.

He nodded, "Four days on, three days off. That's how we do it right now."

"Wow."

"Yeah."

"What time are you off?" I asked out of curiosity.

"Naw, it's not like that. It's literally four days on staying at the station, then three days off at home."

I felt my mouth drop open, "That sounds awful! I can't imagine."

He laughed a little and said, "Well, if it helps, I can't imagine living the high-life walking from my bedroom in my boxers to the office across the hall and working whenever I want. That's gotta be real nice."

"It is," I confessed, but now I was trying really, really hard to banish the image of this beautiful man in just his boxer shorts out of my brain. That was precisely how I let myself get into trouble with Mark in the first place, thinking with my libido rather than my brain.

"Let me give you a ride home?" he asked and I smiled and shook my head.

"I've already texted for a car," I said and set my phone down on the table.

"Fair enough," he said and flagged Kristy, our waitress, down.

"Oh, I've got it," I said reaching for my purse.

"No way," he said. "I asked you here, remember?"

I felt my mouth drop open and was about to protest but he handed Kristy his card. I waited until she walked away and said, "But I thought I was supposed to be thanking you for the night we met?"

He shook his head and smiled, "I just wanted you to talk to me. You said thank you several times that night. It was pretty sweet, actually, given what you were going through."

"Fine, then at least let me get the tip."

He nodded and said, "That's fair enough, you know, on account of this isn't a date and all."

I bowed my head, smiling and blushing at our awkward exchange out front of the restaurant, and glad the ice had been broken enough that we could both laugh about it now.

I didn't even bother asking how much the bill was. I waited until she returned and he'd signed the slip, and then handed Kristy some folded bills that I knew was way more than the total bill had even amounted to. I remembered what it was like to struggle, and again, I had more money than I knew what to do with and I didn't often spend it. I was happy to pay my blessings forward.

My phone buzzed against the table and I looked.

"My car is here already, that was fast." I didn't bother keeping the disappointment out of my voice. His smile broadened and he got up, taking down my coat and holding it open for me so that I could shrug into it. I reached across the booth and grabbed my purse and snatched my phone off the table.

He grabbed his receipt and scribbled his number on the back and handed it to me saying, "Here's my number. I'd really like to hang out more. I really enjoyed our talk. It was good to learn some new things."

"I'd like that too," I said, settling my purse across my chest. "I've got to go."

"Really looking forward to hearing from you," he said.

I smiled and said, "Goodnight, Backdraft. Thank you for a lovely meal."

"You're welcome, Lil, it was nice talking to you; I mean that."

I left, reluctantly, and got into the back of the waiting towncar, trying to catch a glimpse of him through the front window. I immediately programmed his number into my phone so I wouldn't lose it and shot him a text message.

Me: It's Lilli, I wanted you to have my number, too. Thanks again.

He texted back a moment later.

Backdraft: Thanks Lil, shoot me another text to let me know you got home okay. Okay?

That was really sweet.

Me: I will.

I settled back for the rest of the car ride home and smiled like an idiot at the passing scenery thinking all the while: *I made a new friend. Yay!*

5

*B*ackdraft...

"What up, Hose Boys?"

"Oh, you think your real damn funny, don't you, Oz?" Ripley demanded.

I cracked up but was busy wrapping my wrist. Oz dropped his gym bag and said, "Oh, I know I am, I'm fuckin' hilarious, just ask anybody."

"How's life at the ol' gray bar motel?" the Captain called out from over by one of the trucks, checking off his inspection report.

"Same shit, different day."

Oz dropped onto one of the weight benches and flipped open the top on his shaker bottle, taking a slug of his pre-workout. He swallowed and made a face, pulling back his head and letting out a belch.

"Dude, that's disgusting," Ripley complained.

"Pussy," Oz said flatly, and I laughed again. His brand of humor took some getting used to, with the dry sarcasm, but he could be funny as hell.

"Speaking of," Oz said by way of lead-in, "Who was the girl you was with at the 10-13 Saturday night?"

"How'd you know about that?" I asked.

"Psht, Kristy asked if I knew who she was."

"Oh yeah, why?" I asked, taking a drink of my own pre-workout.

"She gave her like a four-hundred-dollar tip," Oz said flatly, and I choked, pre-workout coming out of my nose.

"Jesus Christ, man! Y'okay?" Ripley pounded on my back while I coughed, eyes streaming. Oz threw me a towel to mop up my front and wipe down the garage's cement floor.

"You're mopping that up. Soap and bucket," the Captain called, without even turning around to look.

"You fucking kidding me?" I demanded, ignoring him.

Oz looked amused. "Do I look like I'm fuckin' joking?"

"Four hundred bucks. You're sure?"

"Did I fuckin' stutter, man? I told you, that's what Kristy told me. Now she's trying to figure out who your girlfriend is."

"She's not my girlfriend," I corrected immediately. "She's just this girl I know, you remember the one."

"If I did, now, I wouldn't be asking you, would I?"

"She was the one I gave a ride home to from the 10-13, that one night."

Oz was looking at me like I was nuts and I shook my head, muttering, "Just never mind."

"Whatever, man, you keep your secrets for now. Headphones on, motherfuckers, let's grind this out. I got other shit to do today."

He sounded irritated as fuck but that was just Oz. He honestly didn't care. It took a few years of knowing the guy to know the difference, though. We worked our backs and tri's, and by the time we were done, the subject had gotten the hell off of Lil, which was a good thing. I kind of felt like if I told anybody who she was, it would be like I was diming her out. It was like the woman had a secret identity or some shit. I just didn't feel right giving it away.

I thought about her some more in the shower, which probably wasn't the wisest idea at the house where any of the other guys could walk in. She was a tiny thing, but curvy in all the right places. A real woman with an hourglass shape. Her eyes were deep and soulful and reminded me of the Chesapeake on a stormy day. An almost slate gray-blue with this darker ring of leaden sky at the outer edge of her irises that turned the whole of her eyes stunning. Honey-wheat-blonde hair fell to the middle of her back and I knew that from the first time I'd met her. The night we'd had our dinner, though, she'd kept it neatly pinned up with a clip. Not fancy, but still elegant.

She was beautiful, and didn't it suck that I'd automatically friend-zoned myself just a little bit? Well, a lot a bit, but it made sense. I mean, I wasn't more than three months out of a relationship with Torrid, and Lil's escape was even closer from the douchebag that'd dropped her like yesterday's garbage.

One man's trash is another man's treasure. I thought to myself and it was true.

She'd texted that she was safely home and I texted back a short good deal and goodnight, letting things go. I was playing it cool, but it'd been a couple of days of fighting myself not to text her. I didn't want to seem too eager, but I was. I wanted to spend more time in her company. She seemed smart and driven for all that she was shy and had a tough time trusting, and who could blame her for that?

"Yo, Calder!" one of the guys called out and I yelled back, "Yeah, what?"

"You coming to the store, man?"

Shit, it was my night to cook. I stuck my head under the spray and shook my face back and forth in it to rinse off.

"Yeah!" I shouted back after a second, and whoever it was, I think it was Barnaby, yelled back, "Well, then, hurry your ass up!"

"Yeah, yeah, keep your panties on," I grumbled.

"I heard that!"

I smirked and shut off the water, mind still on Lil and as far away as it could get from what the hell I was supposed to cook tonight.

We took the rig like we always did in case we got a call while at the store. I wasn't really there with the guys, letting myself be distracted, replaying bits of conversation in my head from last Saturday, fists buried in the dark blue pockets of my uniform pants as a bunch of the guys horsed around in the aisles, tossing snacks into the cart.

We did our customary stop in the magazine aisle but I found myself drifting more towards the books. Sure enough, there was a copy of one of hers on the rack. Pretty prominently displayed, too. *Hallowed Be Thy Light* emblazoned in gold foil low on the cover, a gold seal proclaiming *Soon To Be a Major Motion Picture* off to one side. I studied the cover and recognized the actors on it as these young up-and-comings, surprised that one of them had gotten the time away from that big fantasy-epic series of his to shoot for Lil's project.

I shook my head, still in disbelief that I'd asked a world-renowned author to dinner. I mean, things just didn't happen like that in real life, did they? Wasn't she supposed to have body guards or some shit? Like an entire security detail? I guess not, when it came to day-to-day life. Maybe at events, though. Kind of boggled my mind a little that as a romance writer she got rooked by that guy. I mean, wasn't that kind of thing part and parcel for the trade or whatever?

I guess not, the more I thought about it.

"Dude, seriously? You lookin' at romance novels now? You must be really bored."

I snapped out of my daze and said, "Nah, man, I'm like a million miles away, wasn't really looking at what I was staring at. Got a lot on my mind."

"Oh, yeah, like what?" Brody demanded, arcing a loaf of bread through the air and into the cart like he was the next Kobe Bryant or some shit.

"None ya business," I declared.

"You sure about that?" Ripley asked. "You've been distracted all morning."

He had a right to be worried. We all did when a dude was off-kilter. That was bad juju on a call and we reserved the right to check in with each other if a guy was acting too far off his base, considering it was all our asses on the line.

"Yeah, just thinking about this girl I met."

"Oh God," Brody said rolling his eyes. "Please tell me she's not like Tori."

I laughed a little and said, "Actually, she's nothing like Tori. It's also not like that, we're just friends."

"Yeah, sure, that's what they all say, right up 'til the two-am booty calls start." Ripley said, flipping through a copy of *Guns & Ammo*. I shook my head.

"No, really. She just got out of a bad relationship, I'm not exactly a prize winner on that front, either; we're keeping it 'just friends'."

"Shit yeah, you won the prize!" Barnaby called. "There were an Olympics for bad ideas, you took the fuckin' gold with Tori."

I flipped him off, but he wasn't exactly wrong. I wasn't missing the two-am phone calls and the screaming matches. I'd tried to forgive her when I'd caught her cheating the first time. Heard her out, agreed that yeah, maybe it was my fault. That I hadn't been 'present' enough with how the city was working us all like dogs through this hiring freeze, but when the guys had come to me and ratted her out and come to find out she was fucking a guy in my house, on my shift? Yeah, no. She was done. I was done and had no more interest in any of her bullshit excuses or playing her blame game.

"Seriously," I said, eyes drifting back over the cover of Lil's book. "Just friends."

"Whatever you say, man. Just get her off the brain if shit gets real." I looked over at Brody and frowned.

"I said I'm cool."

"All right, all right," Captain Walden said coming up the aisle to dump some produce into the cart. "Both you girls are pretty, stop pickin' on each other."

Brody put up his hands and walked backwards up the aisle, turning at the end and disappearing. I shook my head and when the rest of the boys weren't looking, picked up Lil's book.

Of course, I chickened out and set it down on a different random aisle when I realized there was no fucking way I would get through checkout without one of the guys seeing. I would get shit for days if they caught me with it and I just plain didn't want to explain or deal with it.

On the ride back to the house, I pulled out my phone and shot her a text.

Me: Hey.

Lil: Hey, you. :) I was wondering when I would hear from you again.

Nice. She'd been thinking about me, too. I kind of felt stupid all of a sudden for not texting sooner. Wasn't like I didn't have a whole lot of free time. It'd been the 'Q' word around the house the last couple of days.

Me: Yeah, it's been busy on my end. I wanted to see if you were up for a local adventure this weekend.

It took a minute or two for her reply to come back and when it did, I had to smile.

Lil: An adventure, huh? Okay, you have me intrigued. What kind of adventure?

Me: The Saturday Market at Bayside Park? It's in Old Town a few blocks from the 10-13.

Lil: What, like a Farmer's Market?

Me: Yeah. Is that dumb? That's a dumb idea, isn't it?

Lil: LOL no, not at all. I actually love those kinds of things. I didn't know the city had one.

Me: Sure does. Can I pick you up? Say around 7:30?

Lil: Oh, gee, from when to when does it run? I've been up late nights lately and that's a little early.

I started typing another message but another text came through before I could finish.

Lil: You know what, how about I just meet you there around 8:00?

I deleted everything I'd typed and hit her back.

Me: That sounds great. I'll see you there, Bayside Park at eight o'clock. I'll even have a hot cup of coffee waiting for you. What do you like?

Lil: LOL, you don't have to do that.

Me: Least I can do for disrupting your nocturnal ways.

There was a long pause, the indicator that she was typing back crawling across the screen for what seemed like forever.

Lil: I like White Mochas or Caramel Macchiatos (sp?)

Me: What's (sp?)?

Lil: Oh, that means I'm not sure if I got the spelling right on the word I messaged just before I put (sp?) there. Maybe that's just a writer or a west coast thing.

Me: Always the writer, huh?

She sent a blushing little emoji and sent back: Sorry, just habit I guess.

Me: You don't ever have to apologize for that. Look at you! Teaching me yet another something new. I like it. I'll try to remember it. Seems pretty useful.

She sent back a smiley and then: Sorry, I've got to go, my publicist is supposed to call me about the HBTL premier. I both love and loathe the premiers in equal measure.

Me: Oh, I'm going to have to know why that is.

Lil: Love to see the finished movie made out of my book, it never gets old. Hate the social aspect of it. They're exhausting for an introvert like me.

Me: Makes sense. I'll let you get back to it. See you on Saturday.

Lil: See you then!

Rock on. I would get to see her again. That was awesome. I went through the rest of my day on cloud nine. If there were a cloud higher, I would have hit that too, after we pulled off saving a mom and her kid from a car fire on the Ellis St. on-ramp.

Just a day in the life of Indigo City's true finest. The ICFD.

6

—————

*L*illi...

The fall day was crisp as I got out of the towncar at the curb by Bayside Park. I thanked the driver and handed him a decent tip. He tipped his smart-looking uniform cap that I had no name for and said, "Always a pleasure, Ms. Banks. Just give us a call or text if and when you need picked up."

I smiled warmly and said, "Thank you, Antonio."

He smiled tightly and gave a nod, and went back around to the driver's side. He pulled away from the curb, leaving me to scan the park. I stood at the top of some broad stone steps that led down into a wide, flat cement courtyard of sorts. The park was built out into an observation platform that doubled as a jetty. The Chesapeake Bay lapped at the stone platform it was built out over.

In the center of this cement expanse was a fountain, a bronze statue of Poseidon and his trident in the center, mermaids and fish carved into the stone comprising the fountain basin.

There were aisles and rows of pop-up tents off to my left, and beyond them the roofs of food trucks and a bunch of tables set up for people to eat. Past that were the park's trails and grass; trees with falling leaves dotted it here and there, while people meandered.

I scanned the people milling around the fountain for Backdraft and laughed when I saw him approaching with a cup of coffee in each hand. I descended the steps and reached out for the one he held out to me.

"Right on time," he said. "I like it."

"I hate being late. I'm the kind of person who will show up an hour early for something and wait around just so I'm never late. I swear to God, it's almost a phobia."

He laughed. "I don't know that I'm quite that bad, but yeah. On-time is just polite; don't be wasting people's time."

I smiled and took a tentative sip of the coffee, it was good and sweet, just the way I liked it, and the perfect drinking temperature. I felt my lips curl in pleasure around the plastic lid and Backdraft smiled at me around his.

"Shall we?" he asked and jerked his head in the direction of the tents.

"Absolutely, we shall," I said laughing and was surprised at just how giddy I was feeling, how excited I was to see him.

We moved in that direction and he asked "So, how'd your week go?"

I said, "Okay. Busier than I'd like. I didn't get much writing done when all I wanted to do was write. There's a lot going on with the back end of things. They want to option a few more of my books for film and the screenwriters have been in touch. They're surprisingly really great at asking for my input now. They don't always take what I have to say into consideration, but they always explain the 'why' of it, you know? Like why it won't work, or why it has to be the way they want to do it, so that's nice. I was really surprised about that, especially after the first movie." I rolled my eyes and he laughed.

"Yeah, the way it comes across sometimes, it's like once you sell the rights for something like that, it's theirs to do whatever the hell they want to do with it."

I perked up and felt another surge of excitement, "That's exactly what I thought, too, for the first one and I was like 'Oh, hell no!' With how much of a bear it was in the contractual stage to get me in as a consult, I was very surprised that they were so willing to have me there when it came to the writing. Still was really hard for me for the first film. Honestly, what I've found, is that a lot gets filmed and everything is fine right up until the editors get a hold of it." I made a face. "That's where things can really go sideways. I've seen a full-on screaming match between a director and a film's editors. It was pretty wild and uncomfortable."

"Wow, sounds like," he said and took a drink. "Uncomfortable because a bunch of grown-ass adults acting like toddlers or...?"

"Ah, you caught that, huh?" I asked. "No, it was mostly because the director was freaking out about them ruining quote unquote 'his vision' all the while I'm standing there thinking to myself, *Really*? I mean, really?" I gave Backdraft a cross-eyed look and he laughed.

"It was a movie out of your book!"

"Oh, my god, right? That's what I thought, but apparently, this guy was like once he took it on it was all his, and I didn't matter anymore. Working on that project was the worst. So stressful. We went back and drove some even harder bargains when the studio wanted to pick up more of my books. It was hard, too. There's so many good books and stories out there waiting to be told that they could have easily at any time been like '*Um, no*' and dropped us like a hot potato but lucky for us, that didn't happen; they were just as over that director as we were."

He laughed and said, "Good deal, good deal. Sounds like maybe you and your team or whatever got a bit of firefighter in you, too."

I laughed and blushed, suddenly embarrassed about being such a chatterbox but this was the first time I'd gone out since our dinner and had interaction with another adult. The kids down at the pool in my building didn't count.

He'd provided me the perfect segue, though, and I took it, asking, "What about you? How did your week go?"

"Ahhh, I try to leave work back at work," he said. "It was a pretty good week, though. We won more than we lost, so there's that."

I nodded and pressed my lips together, bowing my head some as my heart went out to him. I think I was one of the few that even though I didn't walk the walk, I could talk the talk, so to speak. I couldn't imagine doing his job, but at the same time, I could. Imagination was sort of my job, so there was that.

I said, "I imagine it's a tough thing, more than any of you guys let on, you know, when you lose some." I took in a cleansing breath and let it out. "I want to say I couldn't imagine what you do, but it's kind of my thing." I wrinkled my nose a little and he smiled big.

"Yeah, I guess that's a good way of looking at it. I guess it's like you get it without ever getting the full brunt of it. That's a mixed bag for sure." I smiled faintly and swallowed a bit of my coffee as we slow-walked.

"Thanks for that," I said shyly, cautiously.

"For what?" he asked, his forehead wrinkling.

"For not just blowing me off and saying how I can't possibly get it. You'd be surprised at how often I get that from people."

"Wow, yeah, condescending much?" he asked.

I wrinkled my nose and murmured, "Welcome to basically what it is to be a romance author to like half to three-quarters of the population. Especially to men."

"Again," he said nodding. "I could see it. I mean, we were out at the grocery store the other day and some of the guys gave me a ration of shit for even looking at one of your books on the shelf. Can't imagine what they'd say if they actually saw me with it in my hand."

I looked at him and said, "Why didn't you just tell them you knew me?" I asked. "I bet that would have shut them up."

He kind of frowned a little and said, "I didn't want to. After our conversation the other night, it kind of felt like I'd be diming you out, you know? Like I'd be blowing your cover or something. I didn't want to do that to you."

I stopped in my tracks and stared at him, a little wide-eyed. That was quite possibly the sweetest and most considerate thing anyone had ever done for, or said to me.

I said as much. "That's really very sweet of you, Backdraft, but I honestly don't hide it at all. I just typically don't go around shouting it from the rooftops. If it would save you some grief, you're more than welcome to impart that information."

He'd stopped with me and smiled that brilliant and disarming smile that made my heart trip in my chest. I smiled back, suffused more with warmth from that smile of his than I was from the coffee I held in my hand.

"I'll keep that in mind, Lil. I'll keep that in mind," he said and we resumed our walk, reaching the edge of the tents. "Where do you want to start?" he asked.

"Um, how about this end?" I pointed the way of the produce and he gave a nod.

It was a beautiful fall day, the sun high in the wide blue sky despite the weather report calling for afternoon rain.

We perused the stalls slowly, and I ran my gaze over every color and just tried to absorb every sight, sound, and interaction between people like a sponge. Eventually, Backdraft asked about the night we met, but surprisingly, it didn't hurt or sting like I expected it to. Likewise, I expected to feel overwhelmed with humiliation or embarrassment, but neither of those really reared their ugly heads, either.

I sighed uncertainly, I didn't really want to tell the story but I supposed it needed telling so I said, "I met Mark the day I moved in to the Echelon."

I told him about that first night and how things went over the next few months, and the humiliation started to creep in the further along in the story I got. How did I account for ignoring the warning signs? The missed dates, the quick phone calls that were far quicker than they should have been if he were really as into me as he said he was? The answer was, now that I looked back on it, that I couldn't and that was, more than anything, the source for my embarrassment now.

Backdraft nodded, "You're not the only one," he confessed. "Happens to the best of us; it really does. My ex, Torrid, suckered me but good. Was even doing one of the guys in my own firehouse."

He shook his head and tossed his empty coffee into one of the trash cans at the intersection of one of the next squares of pop-ups in the Market's grid. He held out a hand for mine and gave me a questioning look to ask if I was done. I drained the last sweet dregs in a big mouthful and handed my cup over. He tossed it for me.

I felt my forehead wrinkle and asked him, "What kind of name is Torrid?"

"Ah, that would be her road name. Her real name is Victoria or Tori for short."

"Sounds like she was maybe a bit of a wild child?" I hazarded a guess.

He laughed, "Was? Yeah no, try is. None of my brothers really liked her, either. My dumping her ass isn't about to slow her down." He sighed and shook his head and my heart echoed the look of hurt that flickered through his eyes and mirrored the disappointment on his face. We were two of a kind, so it seemed, when it came to cheaters and broken hearts.

"Brothers as in the firehouse or the motorcycle club?" I asked, as much for clarification as to steer towards a change of subject.

He laughed again and said, "Both sets of bros, actually. Well, except for Ackley, who was the assclown on my shift that was boning her behind my back."

I winced and said, "That's almost worse, her cheating with someone you worked with and that person knowing and hiding it from you. I mean, ugh! Just ugh."

"Yeah, I know, right?"

"I'm sorry that happened to you," I murmured, and he looked me over and nodded.

"You know, you're a cool chick, Lil. I'm sorry that guy, Mark, took advantage of you like he did. We both deserved better than what we got when it came to all that."

I said dryly, "There's certainly no shortage of assholes in the world; is there?"

He laughed and nodded, and said, "You've got that right."

A voice called out from down the aisle, "Yo, Backdraft!"

Both of us turned our heads at the same time. A much smaller man, with brown hair and a matching, trim beard, waved at us from down the way. He had on a leather jacket and vest that was a match for Backdraft's and I had to smile.

"I'd ask if he was a friend of yours, but it seems kind of obvious," I said.

Backdraft laughed, "That would be Yale. He's one of the city's ADA's."

"I see, the attorney you mentioned."

"Yeah," he said with a grin, like he was pleased I'd paid attention, which, why wouldn't I?

Yale turned and said something to an equally small blonde woman who was bent over and looking at some handmade funky jewelry at a stall. She straightened and said something back and Yale raised a hand in our direction. She looked our way, smiled at Backdraft, and waved.

"That's Aly Cat. She's Yale's girlfriend," Backdraft told me, but then her eyes fixed on me and widened.

"Uh-oh," I said with a smile, and sure enough, the next thing anyone knew there was this squealing girl jumping up and down excitedly in their midst, apparently going a little batty for no apparent reason.

"Woah, busted," Backdraft remarked coolly, watching Aly's antics with mild interest.

She gripped Yale's shoulder excitedly and babbled in a rush as they walked this way, but by the expression on his face, he wasn't getting even half of what she was spilling in his ear. To be fair, she was talking really fast.

"I have to call Dawnie! Can I call Dawnie?" she asked and Yale blinked at her, bewildered.

"You never have to ask permission to call your best friend, Pet. I keep telling you that," he said, but they'd reached us, and she was back to squealing enthusiastically, and all I could do was smile.

"Yes, hi. Backdraft tells me your name is Aly," I said, laughing and holding out my hand, taking hers and shaking it. She was so overwhelmed her hand just sort of hung limp from mine, like she forgot what she was supposed to do with it.

Awwww! I thought when it was apparent she was so excited she was tearing up and unable to speak for a moment. There were people looking at us now and I felt my cheeks heat. I hated being the center of attention, but her enthusiasm was taking the edge off of that. It sometimes helped when they were this excited. It was the sort of excitement that was infectious and made me just as happy to meet a reader as they were to meet me. Her emotion spilling through me via our conjoined hands meant that I was starting to get teary-eyed!

"I am so sorry," Yale said. "I have no idea what's gotten into her; I've never seen her like this."

"It's okay, I understand, it happens sometimes," I told him.

"Baby," Aly said, and her tears began to fall, "She's *Timber Philips!*"

Yale's look went blank as he tried to access the memory that would tell him who that was, but I could see he was coming up blank.

"That's me," I said sheepishly, and Backdraft looked on amused.

He finally helped his club brother out and said, "She writes romance novels."

Understanding dawned on Yale's face and he gave an enlightened nod. He held out a hand to me, his other arm going around Aly and hugging her comfortingly into his side as she tried to get her overwhelmed tears under control. I let her limp hand go so that I could shake Yale's proffered one and it was like she regained the use of them. Both of them flew to her mouth as she tried to curb her enthusiasm, at least just enough so that people would quit staring at her like she'd gone completely mad.

"Damien Parnell, nice to meet you, Timber," he said. "This is my girlfriend, Aly. As you can tell, she is somewhat of a super-fan of your books."

I laughed a bit, relieved as the crowd around us began to disperse and I said, "Pleased to meet you, and it's Lillian, actually. Timber is just my pen name, not my given one."

"I have to call Dawnie, she'll never forgive me if I don't." Aly's hands had come down and she had reached into her pockets and was already in the process of dialing her phone.

"How did you two meet?" Yale asked, looking between me and Backdraft.

"Oh, um..." I faltered and Backdraft came to the rescue. *But of course he would.* I thought with a smile. *That's what he does, after all.*

"You were there, you gomer. Remember the woman I gave a ride home to from the 10-13, that one night? It was a few weeks back, maybe a month or more."

Yale frowned and then that enlightened look crossed his face again. He nodded and said, "Ah, yes, that was you."

Aly's voice cut in and she said into her phone, "Oh my god, Dawnie! You'll never guess who I am standing here with."

I smiled and Backdraft nudged my arm with his elbow and gave me a look that asked *Is it always like this?* I kind of rolled my eyes a little bit and gave a half-shrug. Not always, but sometimes. Not always this intense but some iteration of the same. I smiled, and Aly's rushed chatter filled the air and she held out her phone.

"Will you say something to her?" she asked hopefully.

"Oh, are you sure you don't just want to send her a picture?" I asked.

"Wouldn't help," Yale said. I frowned slightly, puzzled.

"Dawnie's blind," Aly said by way of explanation.

"Oh," I said hollowly, the wind knocked out of my sails a bit and the moment suddenly taking on far more gravity for me, more weight.

I took the phone without hesitation. "Hello, Dawnie?" I said.

"Holy shit, it is you," I heard on the other end. "You've got to be freaking kidding me!"

I laughed nervously and said, "It's me, but I've gotta ask, how do you know?"

"I only listen to like every interview you've ever given ever! Holy crap, this is really happening! I'm really talking to Timber Philips on the phone!"

I laughed again and said, "Well, it would be really nice to meet you, some time. It's a small city, so I am sure it will happen eventually."

There were several heartbeats worth of silence as I looked at Aly and Yale, who were both looking at me with very different expressions, Yale's almost apologetically embarrassed and Aly's ecstatic.

Finally Dawnie said, "Wait, you live here?"

"I do, just moved here over the summer," I said.

"Oh my god, this is the coolest thing ever!" Dawnie cried. "You gotta tell me, did my best friend totally act like a dork? I'm really hoping she totally acted like a dork."

I laughed and said, "I'm going to hand her back now. It was nice talking with you, Dawnie."

"Holy shit, this is like the best day of my life! I mean, it was nice talking to you, too."

"Bye for now," I said smiling and handed Aly the phone. She and Dawnie squealed all over again and some of the people around us even laughed. I could see a couple of girls with pieces of paper and pens in their hands standing off to the side with a mix of eagerness and dread on their faces, and I smiled warmly at them.

"Just a second," I murmured to Backdraft.

"Not at all, duty calls, I get it," he said affably.

I waved them over, determined to remain humble. Of course, the attention like this always got worse during a new book release or close to a movie's premier. I was still getting used to it being the new normal, though. I was also determined to stay humble. These ladies, after all, were the reason I could afford to even be here, living this life. I owed them everything.

The two girls I motioned over to me broke into excited smiles and came forward, and I took my time to chat with them and sign their papers. Alas, the Timber Philips signature came more naturally to me than my own anymore. I can't tell you how many binding legal documents I had screwed up and had to have reprinted so that I could re-sign them with the correct name.

I finished up with a few more signatures and turned back to Aly, Backdraft, and Yale. Aly had her hands over her mouth again, her eyes wide while Yale whispered in her ear.

"I'm sorry," she squeaked. "You were just trying to have a nice morning out and I totally blew it for you, didn't I?" She looked like she was about to cry for a totally different reason now, and I couldn't have that.

"Oh, no! No, no, no!" I said laughing. "Don't you worry about a thing," I assured her. She was so sweet and looked so fragile that I went over and hugged her, which was something I almost never did. She hugged me back and she was so overwhelmed by it all she was shaking, trembling finely.

"Still, I'm sorry, but you don't understand. Dawnie and I have been reading your books since the very first one ever."

"Wow!" That was a long time and a lot of books ago. "I am super honored to meet you, then," and I was. I didn't often get to meet someone who started reading me way back in my indie days anymore.

I stepped back and Backdraft asked, "You wanna grab lunch at the 10-13?" He looked at me as he asked, a suggestion more than a question in my case, and I thought it sounded like the perfect idea. It would get me out of the crowded public space and give Aly a little time to calm down.

"That sounds like a great idea," I said. "Would you two like to join us?"

"You're serious?" Aly asked, her look blank, as if I had just put her on overload.

"Of course, I am."

"Can we?" she asked Yale, and her voice was brittle. Judging by the way his dark eyes swept over her, the answer was an unequivocal 'Yes.' That man was so in love with this girl, I couldn't see him denying her anything.

What I wouldn't give for a man to look at me like that someday. The thought came naturally but unbidden, and with it, a crushing sadness swept my soul. Still, it was like a cloud scudding over the sun. The light dimmed but didn't go out, and as soon as the cloud passed the light was as strong as ever. It'd been a good long while since I'd been in such a good mood.

"Of course, we can," Yale said with a smile, and Aly threw her arms around him and hugged him tight, giggling.

"If you don't mind," I said. "I'd like to go back and buy some of the honey that was being sold back there. I'm one of those 'look at everything before you buy' kind of people."

I was met with a chorus of "Sure," "Absolutely," and "No problem."

"Can I call Dawnie back and have her join us?" Aly asked, her bottom lip captured between her teeth, and I smiled.

"That sounds like a fine idea; I would really like that," I said.

7

*B*ackdraft...

"What're you reading?" Barnaby asked, pulling himself into the top bunk above mine.

"A book," I answered honestly, but I was only half paying attention to what he'd asked. I was actually sucked in to this thing.

Back on Saturday, we'd walked over to the 10-13, met up with Dawnie getting out of a cab, and had lunch – the five of us. We'd had a pretty good time. I didn't get to hang much with Yale, and it'd been kind of nice to connect with that brother. Truthfully, the brothers I spent the most time around were Youngblood, Blaze, and Oz. The first, because he was my best friend; the second, because we ran into each other often enough while on the job, and he helped me work on my brownstone; and the third, because he came by the firehouse once a week to lift with us. A change of pace, he called it, from his regular gym routine, which in and of itself, had become a regular gym routine for him.

I'd given Lil a ride home after lunch, which had ended right around when dinner was supposed to get started. She'd pouted a bit and had said she wished she could, when I asked if I could take her for a ride, but she had work to get back to. I thought she maybe worked too much, but I couldn't throw stones, living in a glass house. I was here four days a week and the other two I was retrofitting and renovating the busted-ass fixer-upper brownstone that I lived in.

Technically, I should be working the fire house on a much different schedule, but we were short, a hiring freeze was in place city-wide, and that made the department hard up enough that they were handing out mandatory overtime like fuckin' candy. Still, it didn't amount to much in the long run, though. Firefighters were paid shit.

"Huh, no shit? A book? Really." Barnaby said and shook the whole damn bunk as he settled in.

"Yeah, as in none of your fuckin' business, Barn. Now shut up, I'm trying to read this," I shot back.

One of the other guys started cracking up across the room and clapping and I frowned, redoubling my efforts to read the print on the page. I was so into it, I couldn't be bothered to turn on the fucking light in my bunk despite the increasing gloom.

After I'd dropped Lil off, I'd had to go to the grocery store for some TP for my place. I'd found myself back on the magazine aisle staring at the cover of her book. Aly's reaction had been something else. Dawnie's expression of awestruck wonder behind her hippie glasses had been priceless, too. That girl was a tough nut to crack, but Lil's presence had done it. Aly's blind best friend practically glowed and was as cracked wide open as I'd ever seen her.

Lil was the true superstar of the day, though. She'd been patient, kind, and free with her time to every person who had come to her with a pen and paper, or even a story idea of their own. She'd patiently coaxed out details and had encouraged every person that their book needed to be a thing, that the world needed their story.

We'd been stopped no less than five times between the market and the 10-13. Once she'd been made, iIt was like the super-fangirl set came out of the woodwork. Likely, someone had posted her last-known-location as the market because, no joke, when we'd ridden by it on our way to take her home, there were women and girls all over the park toting books under their arm and talking in excited clumps, all of them looking at their phones even though the tents had all come down and the food trucks had all started pulling away.

For me, though, it was Lil herself. Her selflessness and the fact the whole morning into the early afternoon had played out the way that it did... that's what sold me on picking up the book for myself. I was super surprised to find that I was glad that I did. There was a whole lot more to her writing than a love story. There was intrigue and a little danger to it, too.

She knew how to tell a story and I was suddenly kind of ashamed of passing the whole genre off as a load of crap all this time. Of course, to be fair to myself, a stereotype became a stereotype for a reason. Usually because there was some truth to it. Unfortunately, it was how we tended to unfairly apply stereotypes that was the problem. Not necessarily the fact that they existed in the first place.

Damn this woman made me think. She challenged me, and I liked it. Count me grateful to have made a friend of her.

Her book got snatched out of my hand.

"What the fuck, Barn?"

"I wanna know what you're reading!" he cried, laughing and I pounded a fist into the bunk above me, bouncing him on his mattress.

"Give it back, asshole!" Too late, Barnaby was fucking howling with laughter.

"You're reading a fucking romance novel?" he mocked.

"It's not like that," I said and hated that it sounded defensive. I mean, what the fuck did I have to be defensive about? Other than their macho bullshit.

"Oh, then what is it like?" he demanded.

"None for your fucking busi – " The alarm sounded, red lights flashing, the grating sound drowning all else out.

"Time to go to work!" Captain Walden shouted.

"Yeah, you two can finish your lovers' spat later," Ripley joked. I got out of my bunk and ripped my book out of Barnaby's hands and dropped it on my rumpled blanket.

Barnaby's eyes glittered with tears he was laughing so hard. I struggled not to pop him in the mouth. Arrogant prick.

We slid down the pole and suited up, half of us dragging our gear to finish suiting up in the truck on the way.

"What have we got?" Brody asked over the headset.

"Structure fire, no occupants that we know of. Looks like abandoned building." Captain Walden briefed us.

"Squatters?" I asked.

"Could be, so look alive."

When we reached the structure fire we realized it was at the old Indigo Moon Brewhouse which was derelict and given up for dead despite being on a prime chunk of real estate at the edge of the city. The old industrial area had been undergoing a gentrification and revival. Artists had pretty much taken over the neighborhood and it was full of the granola set. Galleries, artist's lofts, vegan eateries, and coffee shops had taken over a lot of the smaller brick buildings and they were in a fight to the death with a historical society over what to do with the old brewery, which had a beautiful, original-brick façade.

The main consensus was to turn it into lofts and apartments, but the historical society wanted to preserve the building as much as possible to its original state. Negotiations took place, diplomacy was deployed, but eventually, the talks broke down and a volley of lawsuits were launched. The whole thing had been tied up for the better part of a year and in that time, a decent sized chunk of the city's homeless had peeled back the construction fence and moved right on in.

Like most of the homeless population across the country, it was rife with people who had lost their way, homeless as a direct result of the opioid epidemic. I couldn't tell you how many burned-up junkies we'd had to deal with as a result of them cooking up their poison and passing out in their drugged-out fugue with candles lit, touching off a blaze. It was especially difficult when they burned out several neighbors in the process, leaving hardworking but poor families with no place else to go but the streets, themselves.

This blaze could be either be a junkie fire or a campfire gone awry. With how gutted the building was, I somehow doubted it was an electrical fire. In any case, the only people likely to be left homeless were folks that'd started out that way, this time. Still didn't keep it from being a damn shame.

We'd already responded here once, not for a fire, but for an overdose. That guy had been three or four days gone by the time we'd got here so we'd packed it in and left the coroner's office to take over and do their job. It was sad. It was even sadder that this had become the new normal, but it was what it was. This was the job. Lately, we seemed to lose four for every one we saved, two of them easily to OD. It'd been a hard year across the damn board for emergency-service types and it was taking its toll by way of suicides. A lot of guys could only internalize so much pain and heartache before it chewed them up from the inside out.

"Shit, we got visible flames, she's lit up like a fuckin' Christmas tree." Ripley said and I shook my head and crossed myself, shooting up the too-often-uttered prayer of: *Please, no bodies tonight.*

We pulled up, the sirens died on the smoke-choked air and all of us jumped out. I made sure my gauntlets were a good fit, flexing my hands before I opened the cabinet on the side of the truck and shrugged into the rest of my gear through the canvas straps and metal clasps. The tank was heavy, but I was used to it. I checked my pressure, got my mask on, and dropped my helmet on my head. Brody raised a fist and we knocked them together as Captain Walden snipped through the construction fence with bolt cutters, opening up a path for us to get to the boarded-up ground-level windows.

As a ladder company, it was our job to blaze a trail, open things up to vent so the engine company could get the water where it needed to go. We were a fire-fight's toolbox, carrying axes and bolt-cutters, our trucks equipped with ladders and the Jaws of Life. I hefted down my fire-axe from its holder on the side of our rig and we trooped up the sidewalk to where the Captain held the fence aside for us.

"After you, gentleman! Watch your asses in there!" he yelled.

I shot him a salute and said over the radio from inside my mask, "Aye, aye, Captain."

"Do it, Calder!" came over the headset and I hauled back with the axe and heaved it into the plywood in front of us. Handholds achieved, Brody got in there with me and we put our backs into it, ripping it out of the old wood window frames it'd been nailed into.

Most of the glass was already busted out, but Ripley got in there with a steel pry bar and busted out the rest. I ducked and stepped through. It was smoky down here, but not too bad, not yet.

"Get that ladder in the air! Start hosing it down from the top!" I didn't recognize the voice over the radio but we weren't worried about it.

"Yeah, it's a little bit of smoke but it's not too bad down here," Ripley reported.

"Get to the second floor, but watch your asses."

"You got more to worry about out there than we do in here," I said. "Watch that brick façade."

"You don't need to say it, Calder," Brody said unhappily. "We all know."

"Yes, the fuck he does." Captain Walden shut him down. He softened his hard-assed tone some by saying, "Safety first, boys. We learn from our mistakes."

It was a bigger fight than expected and ended up being a first-alarm, all-hands-on-deck box assignment. Truthfully, I was surprised they didn't rank it up higher than that. When all was said and done we'd found one DOA, but we couldn't get him out. By the time we reached him, he was a crispy fucking critter and there had been drug paraphernalia surrounding the body.

I sat on the end of one of the trucks, one of our guys on safety duty pouring water over my head to cool me down. Angel stood nearby monitoring, portable oxygen in his hands if I needed it. I waved him off.

"Hell of a fight," he said looking up at the smoking and steaming building.

"How long we been at it?" I asked.

"Something like nine hours," he said. I shook my head.

"Felt like three."

"Adrenaline," he said casually.

"Yo, Backdraft! You good?" I looked over and jerked my head in a nod. Blaze raised a hand and gave me a wave. He went back to what he was doing, which was working hoses. He'd come in with engine number forty-nine.

"You boys did good," Captain Walden said. "No injuries. Gotta like that."

"Hear, hear."

"Shit," Ripley muttered.

"Must be a slow news day," Barnaby said.

I looked over behind the line at the reporters trying to crowd it.

"How long do you think before you can get in there and retrieve the body?" someone asked, and thrust a microphone into a guy from Blaze's team's face.

"Fuck you," he grated, and hefted a loop of hose over his shoulder and walked it forward.

"Fan-fucking-tastic," Captain Walden griped under his breath.

"How the fuck they know about that shit already?" Barnaby asked, leaning back and taking a slug out of the half-empty bottle of brand-name water in his hand.

"Cops are here," Angel said mildly.

"Better not be a leak on our end," the Captain muttered and stalked off in that direction.

I shook my head. After what happened with Tony and Chrissy, there was absolutely no love for the press in this town. The cops blue-walled them into oblivion and the ripples had been so far-reaching, we red-lined them right along with them. ICPD and ICFD had a good relationship, unlike most cities who, for some reason, had major animosity going between the two departments. We liked to give each other a ration of shit, but there never was anything meant by it other than good-natured ribbing.

We had our boxing matches, basketball games, and hockey teams, and faced off for charity and shit, but whatever brawls came of it, that shit got left on the ice or in the ring. It never carried over. We didn't understand why it'd kept up in other cities. It just didn't make sense to us. We all played for the same team in the end.

We ended up staying longer, which was typical. Eventually, another ladder and engine came to swap us out. This was one of those blazes that was going to need watched and need a crew or two standing by to knock down hot spots and flare-ups.

"Come on, boys. Let's get out of here." Captain Walden sounded tired and annoyed. Welcome to dealing with the Indigo City press.

"I don't know why they even bother trying to interview any of us," Ripley said dryly. "They make up their own shit anyway."

Some of us laughed in that unspoken 'You've got that right' way.

The ride back to the firehouse was a sober, quiet one, and thankfully Barnaby was either too tired or had forgotten completely about Lil's book. When we got back, I made sure to shower up and get out of the locker room first. I hid the book, which was right where I'd left it on my bunk, and laid down. I pulled out my phone from the bracket we'd put on the wall for it and lit up the screen.

I was going to call her, I kind of wanted to hear her friendly voice and scrub the image of that burning corpse out of my mind but she'd already beat me to it. I had two missed calls from her. I smiled and hit the voicemail icon to play what she'd left.

The automated voice told me, *"You have one new message. To play message, press one."*

"Hey, Backdraft, I saw you on the news this morning and I wanted to make sure you were okay. There was a paramedic standing near you with an oxygen tank and it made me worried. You didn't get too much smoke, did you? Anyway, I'm up and I'll be getting to work here soon. My day is mostly clear. Give me a text or a call back, okay? Talk to you later. Bye."

I saved the message, I don't know why, before I called her back. She picked up on the first ring.

"Hello?"

"Hey, yeah, I'm fine," I said. "Angel was just there as a precaution."

"Oh, good. I'm so relieved," she said, laughing nervously.

"Thanks for checking up on me," I said. "It's kind of nice."

"The news said somebody died in that fire," she said softly. "I'm sorry you had to see that."

"Thanks," I said quietly. "They were gone before we got there. Overdose."

"Oh, my God. That's so sad."

"And common, unfortunately," I said but I didn't want to dwell on it. Dwelling on it is how this job got to you, how it ate at you until you drowned yourself in a bottle or worse. I flipped the script.

"I don't want to dwell on it too hard, tell me about your day. What have you got planned?"

She sighed and it was a gusty, long suffering sound. I smiled, figuring it couldn't be that bad.

"Well, I've been up since four-thirty. So far I've written a couple of thousand words, had something like three different calls with Veronica, she's my personal assistant, and I have to say, I am ready to tear my hair out." She sounded unhappy and I frowned.

"What's wrong?"

"I'm just frustrated. Typical flaky industry types changing things willy-nilly and every time I try to write, my phone is ringing again with another change or a 'Oh and one more thing' and I'm totally being a diva right now, aren't I?"

I laughed, "I don't know," I said. "Is consistency really too much to ask for?"

"Oh my god, right?"

"So what do they keep changing on you?" I asked.

"Transportation to New York. First they want me to take a commercial flight, then they want to charter one, then they want me to charter one. I have to be there Thursday, no, Friday, but no later than Friday morning! The only thing that hasn't changed is the hotel."

"It's in NYC?"

"Yeah."

I shrugged, "So how about fuck 'em all? Take a ride with me. I have Thursday, Friday, and Saturday off and I've got no plans. We can take the bike, it's supposed to be nice. You can do your thing and I can find something to do."

"Would you be interested in attending a movie premier?" she asked. "I mean, it's a romance movie, obviously, but at the same time, you could check that whole experience off your bucket list."

"For real?"

"I wrote the book," she said, laughing. "I get a plus-one."

"Yeah," I said, nodding. "I'm down."

"Want to know the stupid part?" she asked.

"Sure."

"It's not even this weekend, it's next."

"Wait, so how many times are they planning on changing things between this week and next, then?"

"Well, they're not, now. You're really sure you want to do this?"

"Yeah. You really sure you're up for a ride that long?"

"Yeah," she said and giggled a bit, which went straight to my dick. I told it *Down boy!* and smiled.

"Look, I hate to cut this short, but I'm beat and need to grab some sleep. I meant it, though; thanks for checking up on me. It was sweet."

"No problem, seriously. You, um, maybe up for doing something this weekend, too?" she asked and it was almost shy, like she expected me to shoot her down or something. Considering she'd become the highlight of my week, that wasn't happening.

"Yeah, I'd like that. I've got my Friday night, free. Want to do something then?"

"I could really use something low-key," she said.

"Dinner and Netflix?" I suggested.

"As long as it's the original slang definition of 'chill' and not the new one," she said laughing at her own joke.

I rolled my eyes. "I'm pretty sure we're like the definition of 'old', the fact that just made me roll my eyes."

She laughed and said, "Kids these days, what will they come up with next?"

"Who the fuck knows, but just so you know, you're safe with me."

"Thanks," she said softly and I yawned.

"Try to have a better rest of your day."

"You, too. Get some sleep and sweet dreams."

"Thanks."

We ended the call and I dropped my phone on my chest and sighed. The guys started coming in to find their own bunks. Barnaby pulled himself up into the top one above mine, and thankfully, still didn't say anything about the damn book. I wanted to read some more, but at the same time, I didn't want a big deal made out of it.

Shit. If I was going to see this damn movie, I needed to finish the book. I put my phone back where it belonged and closed my eyes. I was so exhausted, I was out inside of a minute.

8

____

*L*illi...

"Marco!" I called, eyes closed, lightly treading water in the warmth of my building's pool.

"Polo!" several young, giggling voices called back. I swam in their direction and called out again.

"Marco!"

"Polo!" But this time, a familiar, warm, and rich masculine voice called out from the edge of the pool behind me. I opened my eyes and turned and a bunch of the kids were turned that way, too.

"Hi!" I called. "You're early!"

"Yeah, well, somebody told me that for certain appointments, it was a good idea to show up an hour early just to make sure you wouldn't be late."

I laughed and Emilio, sounding disappointed, said, "Does this mean you have to go, Lilli?"

"Aww, no!" Backdraft said. "I'd hate to interrupt such a fun time."

"They have loaner suits," I called.

"You're kidding me," he said. I grinned and shook my head.

"Just go to the front desk and tell them you need one. Give them my apartment number, forty-four-oh-three."

"Yes, ma'am," he said with a salute and walked back towards the lobby.

"Who's that?" Rosario, Emilio's little sister, asked.

"That's my friend, Backdraft," I said.

"He's a biker?" Emilio asked.

I laughed, "And a fireman."

"Really?" another boy from the building exclaimed. "That's so cool!"

I smiled, laughed, and closed my eyes spinning around in the water three times and calling, "Marco!"

Three enthusiastic cries of "Polo!" met me and I surged in their direction to a bunch of squealing laughter.

"Marco!"

"Polo!"

"Annnnd gotcha!" I tagged someone and opened my eyes. The older boy, maybe thirteen or fourteen, laughed and waded a few feet away.

"Right, okay." Backdraft came out of the locker room, running his hand back through his hair which was much darker when wet. His borrowed pair of black swim shorts were... short, and left very little to the imagination. Of course, with how he was built, the material sort of strained around his muscular thighs but my brain had gone out to dinner without me because... abs.

I'd spent a lot of time browsing through cover model photos for my covers, but Backdraft had them beat. I blushed and averted my gaze as he trotted alongside the pool to where it was deep enough, and threw himself in.

"Lilli says you're a fireman!" Emilio said and Backdraft smoothed back his hair. He was head and shoulders above the water and my arms and legs were getting tired from treading.

I moved closer to the shallow end, bristling with jealousy, while Backdraft smiled at my young friend and said, "Yep, I am."

"That's way cool," the older boy, whose name I think was Neil, said.

"How do I become a fireman, too?" Emilio asked.

Backdraft said, "Well, first off, what's your grades look like?" and I felt my face split into a wide grin.

Rosario rolled her eyes. "Terrible," she said. "Our tutor is so boring. Emilio falls asleep."

He didn't even bother to deny it, just looked sulky, and said, "Yeah."

"You've got to stay awake," I said. "I'm afraid it's only more of the same the older you get."

"Now, hold up, Lil," Backdraft said, and he asked Emilio, "Why is it boring?"

"I already know all the stuff! She never tries to teach me anything new."

"It's true, Emilio just doesn't do his work. He passes every test, though."

"Have you tried talking to your father?" I asked gravely.

"Pfft! He doesn't listen!" Emilio said bitterly.

Backdraft and I exchanged a look.

"Tell you what, you do the work anyway, even if it's boring, and get three good report cards in a row, I'll take you on a personal tour of the firehouse."

"Really!? Like the whole thing. You'd show me everything?"

"Scout's Honor." He even held up two fingers, which was absolutely adorable.

We played with the kids and swam for the better part of an hour before I declared I needed a break; that I was starving.

Watching Backdraft haul himself out of the pool was a treat, and I committed it to memory, words flowing through my brain like the water down his muscular back. Purely for research purposes, of course. I was definitely not ready to jump into another relationship after what had happened with Mark. In fact, I had made certain Veronica knew that my friendship with Backdraft was strictly platonic and that we either had to have a hotel room with two beds, or two separate hotel rooms altogether.

She'd sworn to me on a stack of Bibles that it would be so, but still asked me double that stack of times if I was sure. I was lucky to have her in my corner. She was more of a friend to me than an employee, and I wished we lived closer. Alas, she called New York home and I was here in Indigo City. I was super excited to see her next weekend, though.

I went into the women's locker room and pressed my thumb against the scanner on the face of the locker that'd I'd put my things in. It beeped twice, flashed green, and popped open. I still got giddy and thought it was the coolest thing. The front doors to the condos had the same biometric locks. It was super convenient when my arms were loaded with groceries.

I ditched my towel in the hamper. It was another amenity of the building. They had a full laundry service, no need to bring your own towel, or even your own robe, down to the pool. They also had both a trash and a laundry chute on every floor, and even though they were clearly labeled, we'd already had several electronic notifications not to confuse the two. I think it was a lot less stupidity and a lot more carelessness on some tenant's part.

I grabbed my key card to the turnstiles and the elevator from inside the locker, and I was ready to go. I went out into the pool area in a borrowed robe to wait for Backdraft, and watched the kids who were still splashing and playing.

"Lilli! Thank you for introducing us to your friend, he was a lot of fun!" Rosario said and I smiled.

"Yeah! You should have him come around more often," Emilio said.

Backdraft had repeatedly ducked under the water and let the kids stand on his shoulders. He would then stand up and launch them into the deeper water of the pool, and it had looked like a ridiculous amount of fun. They'd all tried to get me to do it, but I was too shy. I mean, I weighed a lot more than skinny little nine and eleven-year-olds.

The hero of the hour came out of the men's locker a few minutes later, running a hand back through his damp hair, his jacket with its colorful vest hanging from one hand. His heather-gray tee shirt had a faded blue Ford logo on it, and hugged his chest invitingly. The sleeves were tight around his muscular biceps and it was draped over a worn and comfortable-looking pair of jeans, the frayed cuffs over a pair of well-worn but still serviceable motorcycle boots, the kind with the buckle peeking at the outside of his ankle.

"You okay?" he asked.

"Yeah," I said and gave him a tight-lipped smile, trying not to flame with embarrassment at having been caught looking.

I'm just having some seriously impure thoughts and that's not okay since I was the one to set down the 'just friends' rule, I thought to myself.

"You're a shit liar," he said, laughing, and touched my shoulder to turn me in the direction of the lobby. He steered me out of the pool area and I waved to the security and concierge at the front desk. They both smiled and waved back and I scanned my card at the turnstile, waving Backdraft through. I scanned it again and stepped through it.

"Fancy," he said.

"That's right, the last time you were here, the power was out."

"Ah, yeah, skipped leg day that week." He raised his eyebrows and stretched out his bottom lip and I laughed, scanning my card again at the reader by the elevator's touchscreen.

"Fully locked and loaded, isn't it?" he asked.

"It's kind of silly, how much this building does for its tenants," I answered, rolling my eyes. We got onto the elevator when the doors opened and he looked from me to the panel, his brows crushing down as the doors slid shut, forty-four flashed on the screen and we were whisked away.

He kind of shuddered, and I asked, "Don't like elevators?"

"Respond to enough elevator entrapments, and you wouldn't either," he said and I nodded.

"No, I can't imagine I would."

"Trust me, you'd never want to ride an elevator again if you ever saw that movie *Devil* by that director guy with the name I can't pronounce. The one that did *The Sixth Sense*."

"Never seen it, I really don't like scary movies."

"Comedy?"

"More of a drama, thriller, action, and romance girl, just to name a few."

"Ooo! Be still my heart." He winked at me and I seriously felt like I glowed from it. "I think we can both agree on action."

I smiled and the elevator opened up onto my floor. I went to my door and pressed my thumb to the little mechanism on the handle and two beeps later, you could hear the automated lock roll back and I pushed the door open.

"Okay, this place is way cool."

I laughed and stepped inside, standing aside so he could enter and said, "Oh! I have cats, I can't remember if I told you. Not allergic, are you?"

"Nope, and you did. It's all good." I shut the door and he said, "Wow; that view never gets old."

"No, it doesn't," I agreed and called out, "Alexa, turn on the lights at fifty percent, please?"

Alexa responded, "*Lights, fifty percent,*" and the lights came up, but not so bright as to either blind us or spoil the view.

"Thank you," I called.

"You're even polite to the artificial intelligence, which has no feelings," he said and he had this charmed look in his hazel eyes.

"You can never be too polite, the world could use a lot more of it, don't you think?"

"I agree," he said and then shook himself as if waking from a dream. "Right, I'm going to hit the kitchen while you go do what you need to do." He made a shooing motion with his hands and I laughed at him.

"I was just going to order a pizza," I said and he gave me a flat look.

"Hell, naw, I'm cooking."

I made an impressed face and said, "I have no idea what's in there or what's still edible."

"I'll make it work," he replied looking into my fridge. "You've got a lot of stuff here."

"I'm going to grab a shower and get dressed. Twenty minutes, tops," I promised, walking backwards up the hall.

"Pajamas!" he called after me. "You're supposed to relax, so act like it. Do comfortable!"

"I have some really embarrassing sets of PJ's," I said.

"Do it! Sponge Bob slippers all the way."

I laughed all the way up the rest of the hall at the ridiculous image.

"I do not, nor will I ever, own Sponge Bob anything," I corrected him before passing into my bedroom and he laughed, a rich, wild sound that felt like I could wear it like a lush fur. I really loved his laugh. It was the kind of laugh that inspired you to not only smile, but to live. Like, live life to its fullest, take risks and all of that.

I padded across the room toward my bathroom, completely comfortable having him in my home. I didn't feel like everything needed to look perfect, or like I needed to rush so that I could get into the kitchen and do whatever. There was no pressure to be this immaculate hostess or anything like that.

I couldn't ever remember a time any man had made me feel like that: completely at ease.

9

———————

*B*ackdraft...

She had a fully-stocked fridge for living all by herself. It was kind of nice, actually. A fireman's utopian paradise of fresh veggies and a freezer full of vacuum-sealed meat perfectly portioned for a single person.

She had a little bit of everything and I had some ideas of where to go with it. I pulled out some chicken and got some water going in the sink to rapid-thaw it. She had another, what looked like a mini-fridge, at one end of her kitchen and curious, I opened it up. It was a climate controlled mini-wine cellar and for some reason, I wasn't surprised she favored whites over reds. Worked for me. I selected a chardonnay and decided to wait a little bit longer to open it, until either she got out of the shower or I needed it for the sauce I had planned.

I wasn't big on carbs, but one of her cabinets had an assortment of pasta and that pretty much clinched it. Chicken in a white wine sauce was easy enough and she had everything for it, including shallots, which I found tucked away in one of her crisper drawers. I had planned on making do with onions, but that was a fantastic find.

I set to work peeling and chopping, getting everything prepped that I would need. She was taking a long time, but I resisted the urge to go check on her. It was totally cool if she wanted to run on girl-time. Nothing could be worse than Torrid's version of it. I honestly hated how late that woman had made me to more than a few things, and I was talking like a minimum of an hour late, each time.

I shook my head and banished all thoughts of my ex. That was over and done. I was also lying to myself about being cool with the 'just friends' with Lil. I mean, I was cool with it for now, and if she wasn't interested, for always, but I really hoped she was interested, too. That at some point, things could and would, evolve.

Soon would be nice, before your dick falls off from spanking it. I chuckled to myself, twisting the knob on her cooktop to get the pan heating.

"Wow, smells really good," she said and I smiled, concentration on the butter, shallots, and garlic in the pan.

"If it's one thing fire guys know how to do, it's cook. This is going to be a total cheat meal but worth it."

She laughed and said, "I didn't know you were watching your girlish figure." I looked up as she went to move around me and damn near had a heart attack. She was beautiful and her version of 'comfortable' knocked it out of the park.

She had on this light peachy-pink, satin nightie-thing, edged in cream lace under a long satin cream robe and it did fabulous things around her figure, clinging to her lush curves; her nipples were erect and pressed tight against the thin cloth. She brought the two sides of the robe together and overlapped them, belting it at her waist, and I caught her blushing.

"Sorry," I said and put my eyes back in my head.

"Told you my pajamas were, um, embarrassing."

"Not how I'd describe them," I said with a smile and ladled some of the juices from the bottom of the pan over the chicken breasts I'd laid inside. I'd turned on the oven a minute ago and was waiting for it to preheat. It looked like, from the display that it was just about there.

"Good to know," she murmured and I wasn't about to press it. *So, she liked to wear pretty things that made her feel good, what was so embar-*

rassing about that? I filed the question away for later. It was one that I for sure wanted to try and get an answer to eventually.

"I'm surprised Jaspar and Marigold haven't come out of their hiding place to bug you. You're in the kitchen."

"Haven't seen them yet," I confessed. "Can you grab me the bottle of Chardonnay on the top right? Is it one you mind opening?"

She went to the wine-cooler-thing and opened the door, selecting the bottle I'd picked.

"Good choice, how much you need?"

"Half a cup or so."

She opened it, brought down a couple of glasses and measured me out some in one of her measuring cups. I added it to the pan, steam billowing and the wine sizzling.

"You really have this stuff down. I would have burnt myself by now, having you watch me. I'm a nervous cook."

"How come?" I asked.

She hesitated, and finally took a deep breath and spit it out, "Alcoholic perfectionist mother."

I winced. "Perfectionist or narcissist?" I asked and she blinked at me, startled. *Nailed it.* It explained the confidence issues.

"Nailed it," she said, a straight echo of what I'd been thinking. *Great minds think alike.* She asked, "How did you guess?"

I shook my head, "Seen it myself. Best friend growing up had a dad that was the same way."

"Youngblood?" she asked, and I shook my head and got quiet for a second. She'd showed me hers; I could show her mine. I took a deep breath and spilled.

"Youngblood is my best friend now. A couple years back it was another guy. He and I grew up together, joined the fire department together, but for some reason, the good lord didn't see fit that we die together."

Her face crumbled into lines of deep sympathy and she said, "I'm so sorry. If you don't mind me asking..." She trailed off and I finished for her.

"What happened?" She nodded and I put the chicken in the oven and set the timer. "We were working a fire. The brick façade of the building came down. A bunch of us managed to get out of the way. He didn't. Neither did another one of our guys; got burned real bad in that fire, took a spinal injury and had to give up firefighting. It was a total shit-show."

I tried to banish the haunting image of Corbin's face as we'd pelted back from the falling bricks. He'd been right beside me, and yet somehow, I'd gotten clear and he hadn't. I'll never forget it. Watching him, seeing him there, then all those falling bricks and then – nothing, he was gone. That look of sheer panic and terror on his face in that one split second was burned into my fucking brain forever. The last moment I saw my best friend alive.

She nodded and said, "Thank you for telling me. I won't pry anymore. I can tell you don't like talking about it."

I tried to breathe through the heavy somber pall that descended in her kitchen, and tried to haul it back in, end-over-end, like one of our hoses, saying, "I don't, but it's good, you know? Something I should do every once in a while."

"Is that the tattoo on your side?" she asked. The mood was beginning to ease up and lighten again, slowly but surely.

"Yeah, he died on his birthday, so I got his name and the date."

She made this face somewhere between a grimace and a wince. "Oh his birthday? Really?" I nodded. She sighed and the sadness on her face made me adore her even more. She had a real gift for empathy. It didn't surprise me in the slightest that she was an introvert. That shit had to be exhausting, feeling everything from everyone around you, as they were feeling it. I couldn't do it, but some people, like Lil, didn't seem to have a choice. She wore the burden like a pair of wings, though, graceful and pure. She said, "I didn't get a good look at it in the pool."

I turned into the light cascading from the recessed portals in the ceiling and lifted my tee all the way up on that side, turning so she could see it.

Corbin

9-27

She lightly touched the edge of it and I jumped, her stormy blue eyes flicking from the ink to mine as gooseflesh swept out from her fingertips and across my chest. I felt my nipple harden and I fought down the image of her running her mouth over every inch of my chest and stomach, of those pouty lips of hers going around my – *get a fucking grip, buddy!*

She traced the lower edge, the curve of the flames and smoke around my dead best friend's name and I shivered, then forced a laugh.

"Ticklish," I lied and she smiled, taking her fingers away.

"Sorry," she murmured shyly and picked up her wineglass from the counter, taking a generous swallow. I followed suit. I needed the fortitude to keep my hands and mouth to myself, repeating *just friends, just friends, just friends,* over and over again like a mantra in my head.

"Smells really good," she said, changing the subject.

"Yeah, super easy," I said. "You had everything for it, too. Including the heavy cream."

She smiled. "I like it in my coffee in the morning, better than half-and-half. Makes it richer, smoother."

"Coffee addict, huh?"

"Guilty," she said, with a little smile that echoed the sentiment.

"Kind of had to expect it," I said. "The whole 'writer' thing maybe tipped me off."

She laughed a little and asked, "Is there anything I can do to help?"

"Nope, I've got it. You could cue up the Netflix, though. Find us something to watch."

"Okay." She took her wine and went around the counter, past the dining table and down the step into the sunken living room. I watched her move and watched the echoing reflection of her in the darkened glass of the floor-to-ceiling windows beyond her. She picked up the remote from the modern glass coffee table, switching on the flat-panel TV bolted to the wall across from the overstuffed plush sofa.

She cued up the streaming service and I went back to dinner, dumping linguini into the boiling water and checking on the chicken in the oven. It looked ready to go, so I brought it back out onto the stove top. I removed the chicken and set it aside before adding the heavy cream and grated cheese, stirring it slowly, bringing up the sauce to a simmer, being careful to make sure it thickened without breaking – err, the oil separating out from it.

I got the broccoli steaming and pretty much lost sight of her momentarily as everything on my end came together and when I looked again, she'd quietly moved around me in the kitchen, staying out of my way, to retrieve dishes and silverware and set one end of the table for the both of us.

I liked that, that we could occupy the same space and move in perfect sync without once getting in each other's way. It wasn't often you found people you jived with that completely, so it was really nice that we did.

She brought down a serving dish for me and I dumped the drained pasta into it, threw in the perfectly-steamed broccoli, cubed the chicken and dropped it in and doused the whole mess generously with sauce. A few tosses with some tongs and it was good to go.

"Voilà," I said and she giggled. "What?"

"That's French, not Italian."

"So?"

"So in Italian, I think that's 'ecco'."

"I don't know what either means," I said truthfully, and she smiled wide, blushing.

"They mean 'here', as in 'here you go,'" she said.

"You speak both, don't you?" I asked.

She laughed outright and said, "No, well, a little of both. I took French in high school but I know a little Italian because I had a character speak it once and had to find someone who was fluent in it to get it right."

"Oh, yeah?"

"Yeah, Google translate isn't actually all that reliable. Single words here or there, sure, but entire sentences?" She made a face, like a scared grimace almost, but comical. "I made that mistake –once. Turned out, I had a few readers in the country of origin and I got it all wrong. They weren't happy, and rightfully so. I was both lucky and blessed that they were willing to help me fix it so it read correctly. I pulled that book from publication, fixed every bit of it according to a local to the language, and we all lived happily ever after."

We'd taken our seats at the table and I laughed at how she put it. It was absolutely fucking adorable.

"I think the world needs a whole lot more 'happily ever after' in it."

"I one-hundred-percent agree," she said, and raised her glass.

"To 'happily ever after's," I said.

"To 'happily ever after's," she murmured and we clicked our glasses, which rang a little too clear to be glass. My guess was, it was probably crystal. Another thing I liked about Lil, she had expensive tastes but it didn't seem to really mean much to her in the long run. Like she'd just as happily trade it all just to make someone happy. Like the smiles were far more important to her than the cash. That wasn't something you found in a lot of rich people. At least, not the way the media portrayed them. Lil was probably the first actual rich person I knew but she was just so down-to-earth it was like all this money wasn't even there.

We each sipped our wine from the perfectly pitched and sparkling crystal, (that probably cost more than my last paycheck for the one glass,) and tucked into our food.

"Hmm," she hummed out in pleasure, closing her eyes and chewing slowly, savoring the bite of broccoli she'd put in her mouth. "This is amazing."

I smiled, "Glad you think so."

The conversation was smooth and natural, flowing back and forth between us like water in a tidal basin. I gleaned little bits of information from her here and there about her life. She didn't have a good relationship with her mother, though she was too embarrassed to talk about it. Her cheeks flushed all through the topic and she couldn't look at me. Instead, she studiously fixed her eyes very solidly on her plate and the food she pushed around on it. We moved to the topic of my parents; I'd had the all-American-boy upbringing and a good relationship with both my mom and dad who lived nearby and were contemplating retiring to Florida. She had no siblings, I had one asshole brother.

Her cats finally came out to visit just as we were clearing our plates from the table, I now knew why she'd shuffled a couple of small chunks of chicken to the edge of her plate. Before she rinsed her plate at the sink and put it in the dishwasher, she took it over to the end of the kitchen where the kitties' food bowls rested and knocked a piece of chicken each into their waiting wet food dishes.

"This is Jaspar," she said, scratching the behind of a white cat with washed-out tabby blotches on his coat. "And this is Marigold," she said giving the striped ginger kitty some lovin's. "Jaspar's my good boy and Marigold's my special girl."

I smiled. "Looks like the perfect 'crazy cat lady starter set' to me." She scoffed and I laughed. "What, I thought it was some kind of rule that if you're a writer or author that it at least required two to start."

"Let me guess," she said, narrowing her eyes in suspicion, "You're one of those dreaded dog people."

"'Dreaded!' Dreaded? Oh, *I* see how it is." I turned back to the sink to hide my stupid smile and rinsed the pan I'd used to make the chicken, mumbling, "Dreaded, ha!"

"Well, I won't be explaining to these two your reasoning, that's all you."

"Okay, okay, I see how it is," I said and we finished up cleaning the kitchen together, laughing.

"What do you feel like watching?" she asked.

"Let's see what they got listed."

We went over to the couch which was easily long enough to seat, like, seven people and I was pleased she was comfortable enough to sit close. I took off my boots and crossed my feet at the ankle on the chaise end of things, tucking myself into the corner while Lil curled up like a cat, her legs up under her, next to me. She spoke into the remote, bringing up Netflix, and I paid attention to her viewing habits as we scrolled through trying to settle on something.

"You watch a lot of true crime," I remarked.

"I do! I tend to put it on in the office while I am writing as just sort of background noise. I don't always listen to music. Sometimes I need a break from it."

"What did you watch while writing *Hallowed Be Thy Light*?" I asked and she smiled.

"Mostly fantasy movies on repeat."

"Yeah?"

"Yeah, I got attached to a couple of songs from the movies and played those on repeat when I didn't feel like having the TV going."

"Huh, I wonder if that's an author thing or just a 'you' thing."

"I think it's a little bit of both, I've heard of other authors writing to the same song playing over and over for hours on end because it captured the essence of the character or the scene they were working on so well."

"I wonder what my song would be if I were a character in one of your books," I said with a grin and she smiled back.

"I'll get back to you on that, not that I'm writing you into a book, or anything! That would be weird. That –would– be weird, wouldn't it?"

I laughed and nodded, "Maybe just a little weird, but I think I'd be honored if I were romance-novel material."

"'Book boyfriend', that's what we call them. I think you're definitely book boyfriend material." Her face got one of those priceless looks and she said, "Oh, God! That sounded totally corny, didn't it? Like, holy hell; that was really embarrassing!" She covered her flaming face with her hands and shook her head back and forth.

I laughed, I couldn't help it, but I hugged her around the shoulders and said, "No, it wasn't that bad, I promise you."

She shook her head again and took her hands down from her face, which was a brilliant bright pink, and groaned. "Oh, God, please just save me from myself and pick something to watch, already."

I took the remote and asked, "Have you watched this yet?" to make her come out from behind her hands, which she had gone back to hiding behind again. She peeked between her fingers and lowered them, shaking her head.

"No, but I've been meaning to when I haven't had my nose buried in a computer monitor and could actually focus on it."

"Alright, Sci-Fi adventure it is!" I cued up the show and she put her hands onto her cat, Jaspar, who had jumped up into her lap demanding love. Marigold jumped up on her other side and looked at me warily, before curling up against her mama's hip.

We settled in to watch and I couldn't ever remember being this content with Tori, or anyone else for that matter, doing anything so simple. It was super nice and something, hopefully, I could get a lot more of in my life.

10

*L*illi…

I woke up tucked into my bed and couldn't immediately remember how I'd gotten there. I remembered eating a lovely meal cooked by Backdraft and then we watched some of that new show on Netflix, snuggled with the cats, but then? Had I fallen asleep on him? I sat up and breathed deep and blinked, realizing that my stomach was growling and the rich smell of coffee and something sweet was coming in along the air from the hall. I pushed the covers off and put my feet down on the platform my bed was suspended on, digging my toes into the white faux-fur decorative area rug. Jaspar and Marigold were both looking at me like, *'Really mom?'* from where they had been curled up on and snuggled beside my legs. I frowned at them a bit.

"Yes, really," I said, and realized I was still wearing my robe. *That is so weird!*

I turned and put the covers back where they belonged, making up the bed neatly before I descended the two short little flights of glass and cement stairs to the polished cement floor of my bedroom.

The sun glistened along the water of the Chesapeake and I did what I always did first thing in the morning and took in the astounding view I had all the way down to the water. I'd had to move to the opposite coast because of my mother and the need to get away from her influence and crazy, but I couldn't and wouldn't move away from the water completely. It would have been like tearing out a piece of my soul.

I went out into the hall and followed my nose to find a rumpled but delicious looking Backdraft barefoot in my kitchen, flipping pancakes in a skillet, fresh coffee nearby in the French press.

"Ah, hi. Hope you don't mind, I was starving."

"Mind? No, why would I mind?"

He smiled at me and it warmed me all the way to my toes. When I didn't smile back right away, he faltered.

"What's the matter?" he asked.

"I don't remember anything past the second episode," I said, truthfully.

"Ah, yeah, we both fell asleep under a pile of furry purring. I woke up but didn't have the heart to wake you. You looked wiped out, so I just carried you into bed and tucked you in. I didn't want to just leave, so I hope you don't mind. I just racked back out on the couch."

I stood there for what felt like the longest time, just wrapping my head around what he'd just told me. My first thought both did and didn't take me by surprise. *Damn. My first sleepover with him and I didn't even get to sleep next to him. That doesn't seem very fair.*

"You know my bed is, like, eight times the size needed to fit just me and the cats," I said. "You should have taken half of it."

"Just friends, remember?" he said softly.

I rolled my eyes, my lips twisting into a wry smile and said, "I remember, but friends sleep next to each other all the time, I promise." Then I couldn't resist teasing him a little. "Were you afraid your virtue was in danger, what with the big bad romance author and all?"

He laughed and I giggled and he nodded, looking chagrined. "Okay, okay, you got me there and fair enough."

He got the spatula under the pancake he was making and flopped it onto a neat stack of them on a plate nearby.

"Do me a favor and make yourself useful, set the table," he said with a wink.

I laughed and went to oblige, pulling down two more plates and getting the silverware. He opened the oven and I froze as the delicious smell of bacon rolled out, along with a generous cloud of smoky-scented steam.

"Wow, and bacon?" I asked. "I might just have to take you off the market."

He chuckled but didn't comment, but he also didn't look at all uncomfortable with the overt flirt. In fact, dare I say, he looked quite pleased with himself.

While he did some scrambled eggs with cheese, I put the pancakes on the table and went back for the platter of bacon. He stopped me and piled the fluffy eggs on the platter beside the bacon before he'd let me take it and I was struck by just how harmonious things were. Like we were two puzzle pieces that just fit personality-wise and I really loved that. I also had to say, I really loved that he had stayed. Or, rather, that he had felt comfortable enough to stay.

It was nice that the fact I made as much money as I did didn't seem to faze him. Like it was an 'Oh, that's nice' before moving right along to a subject that actually interested him. Those ran the gamut from shows and movies to an awful lot about me. He was a wealth of questions and sometimes it was hard to keep up. I liked it though; nothing he asked me made me uncomfortable and I really loved that he seemed genuinely interested in my work despite the subject matter, even going so far as to enthusiastically get into whatever story I was telling him about, and to even make suggestions.

He let me ask deeply-intimate questions about what it was like for a man to think or feel a certain way and he never hesitated to answer me, always answering perfectly candidly, and I appreciated that so much.

"So, what are your plans for the rest of the day?" I asked when we got through the majority of our meal. I was duly impressed by just how much he managed to put away. He was a large man, very tall and super muscular, but at the same time, very svelte. I didn't think he had enough body fat on him to grease a cake pan. He seemed to be all muscle, at least from what I'd seen down at the pool.

"Mm," he swallowed his mouthful of coffee. "I have a ride with the guys in about an hour I have to get to. You want to go with?"

"Ahhhhh," I hedged. I really did but my inner responsible adult won out. "I'd really, really love to, but I have to get these last few chapters written on this book before I do anything. The deadline might not necessarily be looming, but the sooner I get it done, the sooner I can get to working on the project I really want to be working on right now."

"Lemme guess, got with the publisher and now there's a certain amount of having to write for the man?" He raised his fist and crossed his eyes, and I laughed.

"Pretty much exactly how that goes, yeah. I have to pitch a bunch of story ideas and they pick from them, and it feels like they almost always pick the one that is pretty much –least– near and dear to my heart. So I get what they want done out of my way, then write what I want to write before moving on to the next one they want pitched."

"So what do you do with the ones that you finish that they don't want?" I asked.

"Send them to them anyway," I said sipping my own coffee and smiling around the rim of the mug. "It's a fifty-fifty shot that they take them, and when they don't, I go on to self-publish them under a different pen-name."

"Oh, yeah?" he asked curiously.

"Yeah, she's doing really well, a lot of people say if you love Timber Philips, you'll like her books, too."

He laughed and said, "So you're double-dipping between traditional and independent publishing?"

"Absolutely! Except I don't keep the money from the independently-published books. I donate it to various charities. Partially for the tax write-offs, but more because whatever cause I donate it to is something I'm equally passionate about."

"What's your favorite charity?" he asked, leaning back in his seat.

"Right now? Literacy programs for underprivileged youth."

"Trying to make more readers, huh?"

I smiled and said, "Business feeds itself when you put it that way."

"Best way to do it," he agreed, "but yeah, no, I get it. Reading gives kids places to go. Some kids, we can't imagine the shit they go through."

His face sobered a bit and I knew his mind wandered back to his friend, Corbin, who he'd told me about last night. He'd been how Backdraft had known about narcissistic parents. I reached out without thinking and covered his hand that rested on the edge of the table with my own. His hazel eyes dropped to it and the faint curvature of his lips encouraged me. Still, with what happened with Mark still so fresh, I didn't think it was a good idea if I went there just yet, but with every genuine small act of kindness Backdraft bestowed upon me, he was rather effectively changing my mind.

He gave my fingertips a gentle squeeze between his thumb and the side of his hand and with a sigh that was half-reluctant, half-satisfied, got up from his seat.

"I'm happy to clean up. You cooked."

"Thanks," he said, checking his watch.

"Pick you up bright and early on Thursday morning?" he asked.

"Yeah," I said softly. "I'm looking forward to it."

He laughed lightly and picked up his jacket from the back of the couch, swinging it around and sliding his arms through.

"Might not be saying that by the end of the ride, but we'll see."

I smiled; he'd warned me about the potential of becoming saddle-sore, said it always happened from a long ride, but to what degree was a very individual thing. I was willing to try and could always fly back if need be, I'd told him. He'd said good point and I knew that he was giving me one last chance, here and now, to change my mind.

Not on your life, I thought, but what I said was, "I'll be ready."

"Okay, I'll see you then."

"Be safe," I told him and his look softened. He nodded and I knew he took it seriously. I also knew that nothing in life was guaranteed and that something similar to what had happened to his friend could just as easily happen to Backdraft. That was the way life really worked.

I saw him out and held my breath at the door that he might just bend down and kiss me. I wanted him to, and I suppose I could have been the brave one and initiated, but I wasn't. I watched his broad back, the wide expanse of leather emblazoned with its shield and the indigo knight chess piece and hoped I hadn't bitten off more than I could chew with such a long first real ride, all the way from Maryland to New York.

I guess I would find out in a few days. He gave me a wave and stepped onto the waiting elevator and I sighed, holding back my curious boy Jaspar with my foot as I closed the door to my apartment. "You don't need to go out there," I declared before I looked back at the table and shouted, "Marigold!" I sighed and she jumped down with her piece of left-over bacon off Backdraft's plate. Jaspar caught on to the fact she had something he didn't, and he took off after her.

"You guys!" I groaned, and shaking my head, gladly went to finish cleaning up. I was grateful for the refreshing change in my daily routine which had become so monotonous lately. I was even more grateful that Backdraft was the reason that routine had been broken up, giving me something to really look forward to.

"What do you guys think? You like him?" I asked, but they were too busy play-fighting in the living room.

I rolled my eyes and finished up the minor chores before heading into my office to write. My sense of romance was renewed and ideas were flowing freely as to where to go with this current piece I was working on. I was hoping for my good morning to carry me through a good writing day. We would see.

11

*B*ackdraft…

"Look at you!" I declared, shutting off my bike, and putting my hands on the tops of my leather-and-denim clad thighs.

"You said to dress for the ride and for the slide. I have to say, I feel really awkward, but the girl at the Harley-Davidson store said this was the best money could buy, so that sounded about right." She wrinkled her nose and looked unsure, blushing with embarrassment, but the girl I'd sent her to, Kathleen, wasn't about to steer her wrong. That's why I'd told her to go there.

"Naw, Kathleen hooked you up, I'm glad to see it. You warm enough?"

She nodded, "Almost too warm."

"Good, you won't be once that wind hits you; hopefully you'll be just right. Where's your bag?"

"Don't need one," she said and smiled. "They literally take care of everything for the red carpet premiere. I just need to show up. Plus – New York–. I already have some things on order to be delivered to the hotel."

"Huh, all right then. What about the rest of it?"

"Veronica said she had it handled and to stop stressing. When

Veronica says she's got it, I believe her."

"Excited to see her?"

"Very," she said, wrinkling her nose in her cute and impish way. I handed her my spare helmet and she put it on.

"Well, then get on, let's get going." I said when she had it on and had dropped her arms to her sides, giving a shrug.

She was a good girl but she did the bad look really, really nicely. The denim of her jeans molded to the curve of her ass, which was outlined by the chaps she'd bought for the ride. The jacket she'd bought was tasteful and elegant, your typical biker fare, but thankfully with none of that stupid fringe that somehow had managed to become popular. What I liked about hers was that she'd chosen one with big rose blooms embroidered in red with bright- and dark-green leaves and vines. The majority of them ran across her shoulders and down her sleeves.

She settled onto the seat behind me and her arms curved around my waist. I started up the bike, which was way loud under the overhang over the curved drive of her building. Even a couple of the valets jumped. I grinned, couldn't help it. It was that little-boy rush, most people would call it compensating for something, but I can assure you, I had no complaints in that department. For myself, I tended to call it 'mechanical masturbation,' which tended to get a few laughs.

I let out the clutch and twisted the throttle gently and moved us smoothly around the bend and to the mouth of the drive. I paused there, hit the signal with my thumb, waited, and pulled into traffic, all but glowing with the pleasure of having a lush, beautiful woman pressed to my back, trusting me to keep her safe.

It was going to be a long fucking ride for someone who wasn't used to it. The GPS said something like three hours and forty minutes. If I were going straight through, it'd be like four to four and a half hours, taking into account a stop for a bathroom break here or there. With Lil, I wanted to stop often enough for her to stretch and walk around some. I figured we could stop for lunch in Philly somewhere and get a good cheesesteak.

"Oh, good!" she called out. "We're taking the bridge!"

"Been on it before?" I called back.

"Once, when I first arrived in Indigo City; had to cross it to get to it from BWI."

"Whole different experience on the back of the bike," I shouted back and slowed just a bit to let her savor it.

She held onto me tighter and her smile in the side view mirror was everything. I was beginning to live for that smile. In the last three or four weeks, Lil had become the last thing I thought about before sleeping and the very first thing on my mind every morning when I woke up. It was intense, and I remembered a time it had been that way with Tori, back in the beginning, but was sad to realize it hadn't been that way with her in a real long time. I almost felt like I had wasted so much time with her which was a sad deal, but I vowed that things would definitely be different with Lil if I ever got the chance to get behind the careful wall that she'd built around herself from being so hurt.

I understood that wall. I had one of my very own, but she'd somehow plucked a brick out of it and had peeked in with those storm-swept blue eyes of hers and it was a shot to the heart. The more time I spent around her, the more smitten I became, and I somehow knew in my very bones that this was something special, something different from any other experience, friendship, or relationship that I'd ever engaged in.

I just clicked with this woman on so many levels and it was awesome, but it deserved a certain amount of caution and care; it was worth taking our time at it, given both our histories.

About an hour and some change into the ride, I pulled off at a rest-stop and Lil perked up a bit. I pulled into one of the spots in front of the outbuilding and killed the engine.

"Figured we could use a break, get up and stretch, use the bathroom if you needed, and take it easy on our bodies."

"I appreciate that, thank you," she said and got down. She pressed her hands to her hips, just below her lower back and pressed, leaning back.

"How you doing?" I asked.

"Good," she declared with a smile. "I didn't realize just how much of your core you used when riding and I have to confess, I have a pretty weak one, too much sitting and typing. I try to swim every day but I haven't been too successful and being sedentary is catching up to me."

I smiled and got up myself, giving my legs a good stretch, pulling my heel to my butt, hand on the top of my boot to get a good stretch through my quad along the top of my thigh. Lil mimicked me and smiled and gave a nod. I chuckled and she sighed out.

"Be right back, I'm going to take the chance to use the restroom."

"I'll walk with you," I said, and I did. I walked her to the bathroom and waited outside for her. I was friends with a bunch of lawyers and cops and was well aware of what a human-trafficking corridor I-95 was.

We were almost out of Maryland and about to cross into Delaware for a hot minute before passing into Jersey. I thought about hanging a left and heading into Pennsylvania to find that cheesesteak, but also thought about skipping it. It wouldn't add to our trip by too much, but honestly, if you wanted a good cheesesteak, you went all the way into Philly itself. I finally decided to stop waffling back and forth on it and just ask her when she got out.

She came out of the restroom and I blurted, "Feel like taking a short detour into Philly for lunch?"

"Sure! Why Philly?"

"Ever had a genuine Philly cheesesteak?"

"No."

I looked at her, aghast. "Okay, now we're totally doing this."

She wrinkled her nose a bit and said, "Doesn't it have green peppers? I don't really like them. They pretty much overpower everything put with them. That might be why I haven't tried one anywhere else."

"Oh, girlfriend, no. The only place to get a Philly cheesesteak is Philly itself. We so gotta do this, now."

She laughed and gave a shrug. "I'm game. What's the worst that can happen? I try it the once and if I don't like it, I never eat it again."

I laughed, "Good attitude."

I asked her to wait for me outside the men's room and to shout if there was any problem. She said 'Sure', but seemed puzzled, and I went in and rushed through my own business. She was right where I'd left her when I came out, and we slow-walked back to the bike.

"Why'd you ask me that?" she asked, when we were halfway there.

"What?"

"To wait for you like that."

"I'm in a club full of cops and a lawyer; sometimes I know too much," I said, not wanting to freak her out. She cocked her head and smiled this charmed little smile.

"Trafficking, right?"

"Yeah," I said and smiled back.

"I watch true crime shows while I write, remember? That and I'm a single woman. We're pretty much trained in fear since birth; always be on guard and expect the worst." A cloud of sadness passed through her gaze as she stared off in the direction of the bike. We'd stopped walking with about a third of the distance left to get to it. "Still, for a lot of us, even being so prepared, even the ones of us that are sharp and look out and think we're able to handle it," her voice softened, "we still get taken by surprise every time."

I had to know and so I asked, "Talking about Mark?" Because I really wanted her to be just talking about him anything else was too terrible to contemplate.

"And my mom," she said and I frowned. She shuddered, almost as if to shake it off.

"We should get going, right? Weren't we leaving so early to beat traffic?"

"Yeah, let me back out before you get on."

"Sure."

I couldn't escape the creeping feeling that I'd stumbled into some sort of emotional landmine for her. It was something I wanted to explore more, because I wanted to know everything there was to know about her eventually, but it was something that could be poked at later, on her own time. I could be patient for the real bad stuff. I didn't want to hurt her by prying.

The somberness of the mood, predictably, was blown away by the rush of the wind in our faces and the pavement beneath the bike's tires as we rode up the interstate, through toll booths, and along the turnpikes up the eastern seaboard, though the water was pretty far out of sight. There were points where I glanced back at Lil who was staring dreamily through her safety glasses, a bit of a Mona Lisa smile on her beautiful lips, and it did my heart some good.

Seemed she liked to ride as much as I did and it had a similar effect on the both of us. The nagging sensation that this girl might very well be the one for me returned and it was voraciously gnawing at my insides. You would think it was annoying when I put it that way, but it was the exact opposite. It gave me this light, effervescent feeling, like my heart rose in the center of my chest, inflated like a balloon, rising with a sense of peace and joy.

Lillian Banks was becoming like a perfect drug for me and I had no complaints. She was probably the healthiest addiction I'd had so far. Adrenaline certainly wasn't the healthiest thing in the world, nor was my relationship with Torrid. That'd felt good at the start but had quickly become toxic as hell. Everything with Lil was different so far. She cared about my feelings and it felt like a fair and equal exchange. I liked that, and I wasn't keen on missing an opportunity to spend any time with her no matter what form it took.

It was like if Youngblood didn't already take my top honor as best friend, Lil could be there. She was certainly becoming a fast runner-up for the position.

I got off the Jersey Turnpike and headed for Philly and Lil seemed pleased as punch, taking in the sights and pointing out things she'd never seen before. It was kind of cool, her excitement over things I'd passed a thousand times and just took for granted as landmarks anymore.

I took her to Sonny's Famous Steaks, which wasn't necessarily the most famous place in Philly to grab one, but it took top honors and was near some famous attractions I thought Lil might like to see. One of them was the Liberty Bell, so we did lunch, which she loved, by the way, and then wandered over that way. It was nice to get the breaks in from the hard freeway riding she wasn't used to, plus, it gave me the added bonus of putting off New York traffic for the time being. It wasn't always fun being a biker in NYC traffic. For one, cabbies just didn't give a fuck. Crazy bastards would just pull out from the curb out of nowhere.

We'd lucked out on the weather. It was overcast but warmer than usual with some pretty frequent sunbreaks. Lil took a bunch of pictures and we even did a few goofy selfies. I thought it was cute that she asked me before posting anything to social media and I said sure, but had her tag my Instagram which, for my end, was mostly bikes, the firehouse, and a fuck of a lot of food pictures.

She added me and tagged me on the spot, my favorite picture by far of us, the selfie in front of the Liberty Bell, me holding up two fingers and Lil laughing, half hiding behind my shoulder. She typed a damn novel in the caption section.

Awesome weather, great fun, even better friends, and my very first time in Philadelphia ever! Thank you @Backdraft_Fireguy for the wild adventure today. Backdraft is driving me to the Hallowed Be Thy Light premier on the back of his motorcycle. Can you believe it? Me! Hope everyone is having a fabulous Thursday. As soon as I get back home, I will carry on writing all the words. Stay tuned for more of my crazy adventures with this guy! #NewBestFriend #ThisGuyIsCrazy #AdrenalineJunkieConvert #TimberPhilips #RomanceAuthor

I chuckled and she wandered back over from where she'd snapped a few other pictures and sighed out. "We should probably get going," she said. "We keep this up, we won't make New York until after dark."

"Ever been?" I asked.

"To New York? A few times." She made a face. "I like cities, but New York is just so big. That's why I picked Indigo City. It was the closest to the cities I am used to on the west coast. Smaller, but with trees and water and green growing things all around and through them."

"New York has Central Park," I pointed out and she smiled with a warm glow.

"I know, that's my absolute favorite part of it."

"Mind if I make one stop on the way to the hotel when we get there?" I asked. I wanted to stop by Ground Zero. As a firefighter, it felt like it was a requisite for visiting NYC. It was before my time coming on the ICFD, but the FDNY had lost three-hundred-and-forty-three of their guys that day, and I didn't feel right not stopping and paying my respects.

"Absolutely, we can stop wherever you want," she said, her smile bright.

"Rock on, let's do it," I said, and she grinned. We went back to the bike and she got on behind me and I took us back in the direction of the turnpike to take us north.

The traffic in the city was pretty much worse than I remembered it, if that were even possible. Lil had a death-grip on me that may or may not have bruised a couple of ribs and I couldn't blame her. When we stopped, I had a habit of resting a hand back on one of her knees, giving it a squeeze. I was pretty sure I hated it just as much as she did. I got stupid lucky and found a spot wide enough to back the bike against the curb between a couple of cars that left them more than enough room to get out without coming close to her. Lil waited patiently on the sidewalk, but her demeanor had sobered and become somber as she stared across the street, the sound of rushing water painting the air over the traffic noise.

I went over and joined her and she didn't say a word, just reached out and took my hand. We crossed at the crosswalk and approached. I took my moment or two of silent introspection and when I turned to Lil, it was to see silent tears slipping down her cheeks while her gaze roamed name after engraved name, as if she was determined to commit every single one of them to memory, like they engraved themselves on a piece of her heart as soon as those stormy gray-blue eyes passed over them.

God, she was so selfless, so beautiful, and so willing to feel everything as the moment called for it. That was a type of brave I had no words for. It made my running into burning buildings look kind of paltry in comparison.

"You okay?" I asked.

"Yeah," she said and sort of hugged my arm, leaning her head against my shoulder.

"Um, excuse me," a light feminine voice called from behind us a minute later, and Lil shot me an apologetic look.

"Yes?" I asked, expecting the same thing she did: a fan looking for an autograph.

"I couldn't help it," the artsy-looking girl with the paint-stained overalls said. "I took this picture of you two standing there and I was wondering if you wanted me to send you a copy."

She turned her phone to reveal this perfectly-lit shot of us from behind, my colors looking pretty proud, Lil with her head on my shoulder with Ground Zero stretching out in front of us. Lil and I exchanged a look.

"Yeah," I said and I gave her my number. She texted it to me and I forwarded it to Lil's phone. "You mind if I post it?" I asked.

"No, not at all! Could you maybe credit me, though? I'm an art student and it could help me if it goes viral or something."

Lil laughed and then covered her mouth with her hand. "Sorry, I'm not laughing at you, not at all!" but she didn't elaborate on how it had a pretty good chance of going viral, at least among her fanbase.

I got the girl's information and posted it to my IG, tagging Lil's Timber account in the process. The girl, Canaday, didn't look too thrilled with Lil, but I got it. She smiled at me and thanked me and I thanked her. It was a stellar image and did my club and colors proud. I even set it as a phone background, I liked it so much.

Lil smiled up at me and we shared a moment of light on the edge of the dark void of somber loss and reflection. This was turning out to be a real good day. Probably one of the best days I'd had in a good long while.

12

*L*illi...

We were late, but I'd kept Veronica up-to-date with regular texts and she was the only person we were technically late for. She kept telling me to stop worrying about it and to have fun, but it was how I was. I was a worrier.

We pulled into the subterranean parking garage of the hotel and stopped at the kiosk to pull a ticket. The attendant at the booth let us know that we just needed to present the ticket when we finished checking in and that they would add the parking to the room charge. I was good with that. I didn't want Backdraft paying anything and by golly, the movie studio could foot the parking bill. He'd just saved them a huge amount of money in airfare, so yeah.

We parked in one of the motorcycle stalls conveniently located near the elevators and Backdraft unlocked and opened up one of the hard-sided saddlebag things, pulling out a heavy black backpack. He slung it over one shoulder after locking up and, helmet dangling from his other hand, gestured for me to go ahead of him.

I'd taken my helmet off too, and tried to smooth down the flyaway hairs in my reflection on the elevator doors. This was a swanky hotel, probably one of the finest in New York, and had been rented in full for the premier.

The elevator dinged and the doors swept open onto a lobby full of brass and dark marble. We clacked our way across the shiny floor, our boot heels making a heavy sound and I smiled. Silly, but it made me feel like a badass.

"Can I help you?" The desk clerk looked disdainfully at our presence and I felt myself blush and shrink a bit. I just wasn't the prima donna type and I still wasn't used to asserting myself, so I tried to remain polite, even though the desk clerk didn't seem to have any interest in even trying.

I wonder what the matter is? I thought as I said, "Yes, I'm Timber Philips and I believe there should be a reservation for me under that name?"

"Right," he said. "Identification?"

I blushed and pulled out my production ID with my author name on it and my given name and handed it and my new Maryland state ID over the counter. He looked at them both like he didn't believe who I was and said, "I'm going to need to see a proper ID with the name 'Timber Philips' on it, Ms..." he checked my license again, "Banks."

"Hey, don't do that, man. She's trying to be polite. There's no need to talk to her that way," Backdraft said, and his tone was gentle but firm.

"And you are...?" the clerk asked and I stiffened taken aback.

"Is there a manager I can speak to, please?" I asked, abruptly. I was pretty done with this guy.

"Timber!" We all turned to the voice that called out and I smiled, my shoulders sinking with relief as Veronica hurried across the lobby in our direction.

"Problem?" she asked.

"Yeah, guy's being a total dick," Backdraft stated flatly, and Veronica gave me a long slow exaggerated blink, her expression saying it all. When she turned, she gave the clerk a pointed look.

"Problem?" she demanded again, and the clerk tugged his jacket down and shook his head.

"This is Timber Philips, I'm officially vouching for her. Now, get her a damn room key," Veronica snapped and I got the distinct impression that this wasn't the first problem she'd had with the hotel.

The clerk did his job but didn't look happy about it, and he held out the room key to Veronica. She snatched it out of his hand, rolled her eyes, and handed it to me. I took it; he said, "Room 1422," in a bored tone, and Backdraft looked like he was about to come unglued. I put my hand on his arm and jerked my head toward the elevator leading up into the rest of the hotel.

We trooped over and called it to the lobby, and when the doors swept open, stepped on board. As soon as the doors shut and the elevator began to lift, Veronica and I squealed like the two excited girls we were, hugged, and bounced up and down.

Backdraft looked surprised and turned a little bit green as he said, "Whoa!" I tried to rein in my excitement, remembering what he'd said about elevators and entrapments before he quickly followed it up with, "Do that again." He grinned, I laughed, and Veronica did too before holding out a slim hand.

"Veronica Preston," she said and arched one auburn brow. "You must be Backdraft."

"Yeah," he said with a slow, sexy grin and I rolled my eyes. *Just friends*, I reminded. *Just friends, you can't be jealous and why wouldn't he flirt? Veronica is beautiful.*

She was, too. Tall and slim, perfectly toned, with long auburn hair swept up into a high ponytail. She wore a perfectly-tailored matching dark-brown suit jacket and pencil skirt with light gold pinstripes and a cream silk blouse underneath. Her high spike heels were a chocolate-brown alligator skin, though I didn't think it was real.

"Nice to meet you, Backdraft."

He looked past her and his eyes landed on me, a questioning look in them as he asked, "Lil didn't introduce me as Emmet?"

"Why would I?" I asked. "That may be your name, but it's not the one you choose to go by. I told you that your preference mattered more than formality."

His mouth drew down into that classic, *I'm impressed* look and he asked, "So, we're here, what's the plan?"

Veronica laughed and said, "I like him."

I grinned. "I told you," I said.

Backdraft paused. "Wait, you told her what, exactly?" Veronica and I exchanged a look and both of us burst out laughing. Backdraft reeled back and said, "Oh, oh-ho, I see how it is!"

The elevator doors opened and we stepped off onto our floor. We found the room and I slid the keycard into the lock. The little light blinked green and I opened the door into a typical hotel room with a single king sized bed in it.

"You've got to be kidding me." Veronica looked like she was fuming. "I'm going to feed that little twerp every brass button off that vest in reverse."

"What does that even mean?" Backdraft asked.

"Up his ass," I explained.

"Come on, we're going to get this fixed," Veronica declared.

Cue over forty-five minutes of arguing with the hotel staff and management over the lack of pre-ordered accommodation as laid out in the initial agreed-upon booking. Or, so Veronica said. She was pretty much to the point that even her unflappable calm was severely damaged. I expected her to lunge over the booking desk at any second and make good on her promise upstairs. Me? I sucked at confrontation. I just wanted everyone to stop fighting and being angry at each other.

Backdraft ended up being the calm to prevail when he stepped in and put his hand on Veronica's shoulder.

"Clearly they aren't willing to compromise," he said. "In the interest of not causing a total scene right now, this room will do, but you know what? There's a thing called Yelp and there's plenty of other social media outlets, so this is what's going to happen. Your hotel is going to comp the room completely, and in exchange, on our end, Lil here isn't going to pick up her pen. Trust me, boys. Her pen is indeed mightier than her sword and she could completely destroy your hotel's reputation." The desk clerk looked down his nose at me and the manager finally took a good look and blanched. Backdraft's smile was pure evil as he said, "That's the compromise, boys. Either take it or you put your head between your legs and kiss your asses goodbye."

I tried to back up Backdraft's threat by calmly looking them back in the eyes like I was already thinking about what to write and how to phrase things. The manager, realizing that I was, indeed, the real Timber Philips, asked us, "Would you like a complimentary breakfast served in your room, or will you be taking it in the restaurant?"

"Attaboy, and in our room, if you please."

The manager looked to me for confirmation and I smiled sweetly. "That would be lovely, thank you," I said calmly, and Veronica gave me a tight-lipped smile with a raised eyebrow.

We left the front desk and went back for the elevator and she said, "Impressive, you two."

"Not really," Backdraft said, tiredly. "Feel like we took the low road."

"We did, but it wasn't any lower than the road they seem to travel on a regular basis," I murmured.

"Right, totally the high road by comparison," Veronica agreed. She gave me some side-eye and asked, "You're going to rake this place over a verbal cheese-grater even after they comped the room, aren't you?" I gave her a tight-lipped smile back and sighed. She knew me so well.

"They comped the studio," I said with a shrug. "We're the ones they insulted."

"That's a good point," Backdraft said. He was looking at me like he was duly impressed.

I sighed, it was a bit of a damper on the trip but I refused to let it get to me. Instead, I changed the topic completely and asked Veronica, "Did you bring them?"

"I will have them brought up, now that we know your room number."

"Thank you."

"Bring what?" Backdraft asked.

"The clothes she ordered, and the designer dress the studio ordered to put her in for the red carpet."

"I don't have any idea how any of this works," he confessed and Veronica smiled.

"That's –my– job, thank you very much," she said.

"Dinner is?" I asked, and Veronica launched into doing what she did best. I smiled at Backdraft and let him be swept along with the Hollywood tide.

13

*B*ackdraft...

This shit was nuts.

Before I knew what was happening, the girls were talking a mile a minute about timelines, and inside ten minutes there was a dude knocking on the hotel room door to take my measurements. By the time he was done, I felt vaguely violated. He'd gotten all up in my junk, supposedly to measure my inseam. I'd been so insecure it'd left Lil and Ronnie howling with laughter and nearly in tears.

If Pasquale could only see me now. I'd thought.

Then it was a delivery of some high-end retail bags and a black, nondescript garment bag. Lil asked a few questions and Veronica told her not to worry, that hair and makeup would be there bright and early, and somehow, that included me.

Next thing was dinner, because the cheesesteaks had long since worn off. That'd been pretty okay, just me, Lil, and Ronnie in the hotel restaurant and bar. They comped it, of course, not that it swayed Lil much. She still had that calculating look and I almost genuinely feared for this hotel. She'd feed their reputation like she fed unwanted pages of one of her manuscripts: through a shredder. I'd read some of her books, I knew she had the writing chops to do it.

Out of everything that'd happened that day, it was finally time for what I'd found myself anticipating the most. I was chilling on one side of the bed in a pair of boxers and one of my favorite, but damn-near worn-out, tees channel surfing, waiting for Lil to get out of the bathroom and come to bed.

She'd taken a long shower after insisting that I go first and just when I thought she'd be out, the hairdryer started up. I smiled to myself and had to wonder if she was putting off the inevitable. Wasn't she the one to say that 'friends slept next to each other all the time'? That it wasn't a big deal?

The hair dryer shut off and the bathroom door opened. She stepped out and I tried to get my admiring sweep in before she looked up and caught me. If I didn't think it'd make her even more nervous, I would have given a low whistle.

She was gorgeous. Her blonde hair foamed around her face, freshly dried. She wore this tiny satin and lace sleep set, black edged in off-white lace, a little cami and pair of short-shorts that put her legs on display. She was a short woman, and I actually liked that about her. There was something about being taller that made me feel all manly or some shit. Sexist as hell, but also true. That being said, she didn't have a pair of legs that most dudes would go for but I liked that about her too. She had thighs I could grab onto and haul her across the bed by, but she wasn't fat, no way. She was muscular from all that swimming she did. Fit and toned, more athlete than model.

Down, down, you need to go down! I thought at my cock, then frantically tried to come up with something that would kill any boner. Thankfully, in my line of work, I had plenty of horror shows to use for backup in situations like this. I also didn't have to tap a single one of them, thankfully. All I had to do was think about Torrid and I was good, boner sufficiently laid to rest. *Rest in peace, buddy.* I thought at it.

"You okay?" she asked nervously, rubbing at a spot on the top of her arm near her elbow with the thumb of her opposite hand.

"Yeah! Yeah, I'm good. What you got going on, though?" I gestured to the arm and she sort of laughed and came around the bed.

"Tendon gets a little angry from so much typing. My back, arms, wrists, and hands can sometimes be a real mess. I do massages regularly but I don't always stretch like I should. Hazard of the job, I'm sure you know how that goes."

"Sure do," I said softly, patting the empty side of the bed. She climbed up and I pushed myself into a sitting position holding out my hands for her arm. She reluctantly handed it over. I put my thumb over the spot she'd been working on and watched her face carefully as I applied pressure. She winced and I backed off just a little and started working it in small circles. The wincing came back and settled into a little grimace, which is right where I wanted it.

No discomfort meant you weren't getting the job done when it came to these types of injuries, but too much discomfort meant you were probably doing more harm than good. The goal was to make her feel better, feel good, not worse. I wanted to fix it, not hurt her more. I ached to do more, though. I ached to make us both feel good, but that's not what we'd agreed to.

Just friends...

"Thanks," she murmured, and took her arm back gently.

"Any time."

"Tired?" she asked.

"Not too bad, figured I'd watch a little bad hotel TV." She looked at Sports Center playing out and made a face. I chuckled.

I eased back down so I could lounge some more and she got up and slipped between the sheets. She laid on her side and tucked her hands under her cheek. I switched off the TV, struck by how tired and somber she seemed all of a sudden and shrank down the bed some, turning on my side with a pillow hugged to my chest so I could face her.

"What's wrong?" I asked.

She gave me a half smile and said, "Don't get me wrong, I love these things, seeing my books come to life on the big screen is always amazing..." She hesitated.

"But?" I gently pried.

"But the politics and the media, all of the attention and flashing lights... what happened with the room and how you're sometimes treated... it can be exhausting."

"Spoken like a true introvert," I said with a smile and she smiled too, pushing down a laugh. I sighed and said, "Let's get some sleep."

"You don't want to watch TV?" she asked.

"Changed my mind," I said when what I was thinking was *Really, I'd rather watch you.* I got up and switched out lights, returning to the bed and sliding under the blankets with her. She huddled on her side on her side of the bed and I asked, "You cold?"

"A little, but you're warm," she inched closer, and I smiled and pulled her over. She turned over and I spooned her, a little sad I couldn't see her face, thinking every boner-killing thought I could scrounge up, and settling her curves into the protective cover of my larger frame. She fit perfectly.

"Better?"

"Better," she said, and her voice was tentative and shy.

We talked softly in the close dark and it was nice, learning more, sharing intimate thoughts. Some hopes, some dreams. We settled into a natural silence, but I lay awake what seemed like a long time after she'd fallen asleep. I closed my eyes and listened to her deep and even breathing and took a liberty for myself. Pressing my lips in a single chaste kiss against the back of her silky-smooth, lightly-scented shoulder. She'd used a lotion on her skin; something exotic and fruity with hints of spicy vanilla.

I settled in and let myself enjoy her closeness and wished like hell it could be something more than what it was currently, but I was too damn scared to push it further. I'd rather have this 'just friends' over 'nothing at all'.

Life with her in it was just too good compared to what it'd been before.

THE NEXT DAY was a total fucking whirlwind of activity for Lil, but for me, not so much. I couldn't believe the amount of shit they put her through for the red carpet that night. She was waxed, buffed, and polished to within an inch of her life and none of it looked pleasant to accomplish. Meanwhile, I sat in the corner and listened, sometimes joining in on the conversation, while everything went on around us.

They'd turned one of the hotel's conference rooms into an impromptu salon, spa, and barber shop and it didn't surprise me when the stylist said, "Your turn, honey."

I found myself thinking that the guy could give Pasquale a run for his money as I sat in his chair. A shave with a hot towel, and a haircut that didn't seem necessary but looked sharp went down; when I was done, Lil had been moved and was nowhere to be seen.

"Don't worry, she'll meet you in the lobby in a bit. Let's get you dressed."

"Seriously?"

"What?"

"I'm pretty sure I've got it, not something I need help with."

He leaned back and gave me that hyper-sober look I was used to getting from Pasquale anytime we told him something he didn't want to hear.

"You know I've seen it all before, right?" he asked. "No need to hide what you might be compensating for with all of the rest of this."

I laughed and just kind of stood there trying to gauge if he was for real. He waved his hand dramatically and stopped in the same exact pose he'd started in. It was a little bit of a standoff.

"Well? What are you standing there for?" he waved his hand at me dramatically again and I sighed. The "Shoo!" put it over the line, though. *Challenge accepted.*

I hauled my shirt over my head and demanded, "Where's this damn monkey suit?"

The stylist walked over to a rack and selected a garment bag off of it and unzipped it. When he turned around, his overly-penciled eyebrows shot up as he swept me from head to toe, lingering on my Jockey boxer-briefs a little longer than was polite.

"I stand corrected, honey," he said, and held out the hanger. I went over and found the pants first.

I pulled them on and realized they hadn't been hemmed. No shit, that guy tailored the hem of those pants and the sleeves on that jacket right then and there. I'd never had a tux fit so damn good in my life. Usually, it was tight in the shoulders and loose in the torso, but I could just get away with it without looking like I was trying to wear my dad's suit.

This was nice: black pants, black shirt, black jacket, with a muted emerald-green necktie and a matching handkerchief for the pocket. He messed with my hair again and nodded at the final result in the mirror.

"Time to wake-up to make-up, honey."

"No way, I didn't sign on for that," I said, laughing, and Martine, pronounced '*Mar-teen*', gave me another flat look.

"You don't and you are going to look like hell on camera. I'm not talking any guyliner or anything like that, baby. I'm talking just the basics. That, and you're here, which means you did sign up for it."

"Shit," I muttered. Lil was gonna owe me. Like 'watching football at the firehouse' owe me. I was going to have to do something hyper-masculine to balance this shit out, but for her I really would do anything at this point, and so, being the good sport that I was, I gritted my teeth and gave a nod.

He put a drape on me and shoved tissue paper into my collar all the way around and got to work. That shit had to be the weirdest feeling, but I had to hand it to him, he was right. He'd snapped a before-and-after pic with his cellphone to prove it and in the first pic I looked like death warmed over; in the second I was alive, so I ate it.

"Thanks, bud, I appreciate your patience with me."

He rolled his eyes and shooed me out of his chair, saying, "You're going to be late; you'd better go."

"I have no idea where the hell I'm supposed to be going."

"Lobby," he sang out, irritated, and I shot him a short salute.

I went down to the lobby in these expensive, shiny, Italian shoes that probably cost more than my brownstone, and Veronica waved me over.

"Okay, so Lilli will be down soon, you'll exit the lobby to the car waiting at the curb. Expect paparazzi, because Nathalie is here, and so is Kit."

"Seriously?"

Veronica laughed and jerked her head, my eyes wandered over and sure enough, there were the lead actress and actor who'd played Quinn and Jack, Lil's characters.

"They're a lot different in person," I said, surprisingly underwhelmed, and Veronica smiled a secretive smile.

"They usually are, people tend to forget they're human beings, and when they're humble, like those two, you can totally miss being in the same room with them."

"I'll tell you what I can't miss," I said, eyes glued to the top of the stairs where they'd gotten stuck on Lil.

"Ah," Veronica said, pleased. "There she is."

She was beautiful, radiant in this form-fitting, simple yet elegant satin gown with just the right amount of shimmer to the cloth. It was a deep, emerald green, the perfect match to my tie and handkerchief, and I somehow didn't think that was any kind of coincidence. At the same time, I didn't care.

In this moment, I burned for her; a low, blue flame that rose higher and higher with every step she took down those stairs.

Her satin pumps were the perfect match to the gown. It was perfect for her, a halter-style with a plunging neckline that flared at her chest, dipped with the perfect amount of curve to follow the natural flow of her hourglass figure before flaring outward again to flow down her hips and near straight to the ground. It gave a last little flare at the floor into the smallest train and she was gorgeous in it. Her throat was adorned with a gold necklace in the perfect 'Y' shape; dangling from the end was a teardrop emerald. Her earrings matched, simple gold, delicate chains with smaller teardrop emeralds, dangling from her ears. Her golden wheat-blonde hair was swept into one of those classy twists where it was all tucked into itself, a long gold comb set with more emeralds pinning it at the seam, winking in the overhead lights as she turned her head to ask something of the man escorting her down the stairs.

I squashed the flare of jealousy pretty damn quick. He looked old enough to be her dad, but come to think of it, she and I had never talked about him – her dad, I mean. There was still so much about her that I didn't know, and I wanted to know everything.

She caught sight of me and her perfectly-glossed, shell-pink lips parted in the most beautiful smile; I think my heart cracked from the pressure of it swelling so big. She reached the bottom of the stairs and I smiled down at her as she reached me.

"You're so beautiful it hurts," I told her honestly, and I heard her suck in a breath, but then Veronica was doing her thing and we were supposed to play follow-the-leader and smile for the cameras.

"Here we go," Lil said lightly, and I could hear the static electricity of her anxiety crackle across the surface of her words. I tucked her hand into the crook of my arm all gentlemanly and tried for the life of me to figure out how to be her shield, how to make this easier for her in any way possible.

Like I said, I was pretty much smitten and ready to do anything for her, whether she asked it of me or not.

14

*L*illi...

    The first gauntlet of paparazzi wasn't so bad. They were mostly here for the stars and could care less about me, which was helpful. We strode down the entryway carpet of the hotel and slid smoothly into the back of the waiting limo with no problems and I breathed a sigh of relief. Backdraft kept staring at me and I couldn't quite read the look on his face; what he was thinking was a mystery to me.

"You look really good yourself," I said and smiled.

"Hey, that's all that Martine guy."

"He's quite the fashionista," I agreed, laughing.

"Reminds me of Pasquale, back home."

"Who's that?"

He told me about the Trinity General nurse who had basically attached himself to the club. He sounded just like Martine, only funnier. I couldn't wait to meet him. I hoped that Backdraft would want to keep me around long enough that I got the chance. Depending on how the rest of the night went, it could go either way. I was a little worried, he was already looking a little shell-shocked but I was also a worrier. That's what I did. I was a world-class worrier.

The car stopped and started, moving slowly through Manhattan traffic and we sat mostly in silence.

"You ready?" I asked softly when we pulled up to the curb and he smiled the most reassuring smile. Still, before he could say anything, the door opened and he was out, his hand reaching down to help me. I took it, and no matter how many times you think you're prepared, you aren't.

I stepped out of the protective confines of the limo into the maelstrom of strobing and flashing lights and a cacophony of shouts and shouting. I clung to Backdraft's arm and let him guide me down the carpet in the slow, timed walk Veronica had reminded us must be maintained, behind some of the lesser stars of the movie.

I would be grateful when Nathalie and Kit exited their cars because it would be sure to draw the attention off of me. I know, selfish, but true none the less.

We stopped at regular intervals for still-photo opportunities along the carpeted walkway leading into the theater, and for the most part ignored the questions shouted at us, just smiling instead. The transition from still photos to video was a gradual one and eventually we couldn't dodge any more questions when a microphone was thrust into my face.

"Ms. Philips, how are you tonight?"

I put on my best smile and went to work, stepping into my Timber Philips persona and acting for the camera.

"Oh, I'm really excited!" I answered. "I don't think this will ever get old."

"This is your third work made into a movie so far, how do you feel about that?"

"Oh, blessed." I put my hand to my chest and declared the truth. "I am so incredibly grateful to all of my readers out there for making the movies of my books as successful as the books themselves, and to the people who haven't read my books but are enjoying the films? I can't even tell you how happy that makes me that I get to welcome a whole new group of people into my worlds. The studios have done a phenomenal job bringing my worlds to life and I really couldn't have asked for a better cast. I could gush on for days, but I think they're expecting us further down the carpet."

"Well, thank you for your time!"

"You bet!"

I moved Backdraft and I to the next set of cameras to field the next question, "Timber! Who are you wearing tonight?" I laughed and they clarified, "The dress, of course!"

I gave them the designer's name that I'd been asked to memorize, and then they asked, "And who are you?" thrusting the microphone at Backdraft.

"Oh, uh..."

"Oh, he's shy!" I covered for him. "He's honestly just a friend," I said, giving Veronica, up the carpet, the surreptitious hand signal. She sent a man in a tux with a clipboard and a headset our way and made it seem like we needed to keep moving. We moved off camera after a half-second more banter and had one more interview to go through, but there was already blood in the water and the sharks were circling.

"Timber, who's your new man?"

Shit.

"Backdraft is just a good friend," I said and kept it at that.

"How good?" she asked and I plastered a smile on my face.

Backdraft leaned in and gave her a wink, "When it comes to real life, Timber doesn't kiss and tell."

"Oh!" the gossip-show's hostess laughed and we moved on before she could do or say anything else that could pry or be potentially embarrassing.

"Nicely done," I murmured close to his ear.

He leaned down and said into mine, "It's the media, they'll find some way for it to bite us in the ass later."

I laughed and said, "You're not wrong," and we made the door and were safely whisked inside and out of the limelight.

"That was exhausting," he declared, flatly.

"Now you see why I hate these things."

He grunted in agreement and my smile returned as several of the executives that made *Hallowed Be Thy Light* come off the page wandered our way.

I felt bad, but I had warned him that it would be this way. Still, Backdraft listened, standing at my side, and did a fair impression of not being bored out of his skull while I talked business and did the professional banter as was required of these stuffed shirt functions.

Pretty soon, drinks from the full bar in hand, we were led to our theater seats by one of the ushers and left, for a moment, to our own devices.

"Jesus, I don't know how you do it," he said softly and I smiled genuinely. My face hurt from all the forced artificial smiles.

"I don't know either, sometimes. I know it sounds awful and ungrateful, but I really wish I could just write the books and interact with my readers and, well, now, viewers, versus all of these Hollywood types. I'm just not cut out for all of this corporate crazy-making."

"Well, you could have fooled me. You do extremely well at it."

"Not always," I murmured quickly as a few of the lower-level producers and representatives from my publisher took nearby seats.

I took a sparing sip from my champagne flute and we all settled. A few moments later, the lights lowered, the theater darkened and became more intimate, and the movie began.

I sighed, and tight muscles eased as Backdraft slid his fingers through mine and gave my hand a reassuring squeeze. I held on and didn't want to let go, and he smiled faintly and left his hand entwined with mine. I couldn't tell you how grateful I was for the silent support and comfort. I genuinely didn't deserve a man as good as he was to be here with me tonight. I really didn't.

The movie played all the way through, everyone politely sitting through the rolling end credits to the little bit at the end and there was my character Mags, a sudden surprise at the very end of the credits standing like Yoda on the little bar stool by Quinn's drawing table, her hands resting atop her shillelagh as she stared at the camera.

"Don't you be leaving a mess, now," she scolded, leaning forward imperiously. She winked and leaned back, cackling. "Now, off wit ye!"

The music finished out and she disappeared in a sparkle, and the curtains closed over the screen to a chorus of light chuckles from the audience. I felt my eyes mist. The whole production had been just perfect.

"Don't do that," Backdraft whispered. "Your makeup will run and I really don't want to face Martine again so soon."

I laughed and stood and he followed suit, letting my hand go reluctantly. We filed out into the lobby and after-party and Veronica found us.

"Want me to rescue him?" she asked.

Backdraft looked at me amused, and I smiled up at him.

"This next part is going to bore you to death. I have it set up that when it gets to be too much, Veronica will rescue you by way of needing a big strong man to get the swag bags and gift baskets back to the hotel. Lame, but all I could think of. I don't want you feeling like nothing more that arm candy."

He nodded carefully and smiled. "I appreciate that," he said genuinely. "A lot of these guys, the way they talk at you like you're stupid, I don't want to smart off and wreck something for you. I think I'm good for about half an hour to an hour, though."

"Good deal," Veronica said and did what she did best. Melted back into the crowd to handle some bit of drama or business or other.

"You're sure?" I asked.

"I'm sure. Whatever makes your life easier, I mea – "

"Ah! There she is."

Backdraft was interrupted by the director and several producers wandering over.

"I'm dying to know, Ms. Philips. What did you think of my vision where your work is concerned?"

"Oh, my, I was so very impressed!"

"Truly?"

"Oh yes, it was like you were inside my head! You did beautifully, the actors were perfect and their performance nuanced. I'm afraid I may have teared up at the end."

"Excellent, excellent! And what about you, good sir? What did you think?"

"Honestly, I was skeptical about cutting the part with Quinn's conversation with Doan in the Summerland, but I understand why you did it. I thought for sure it would leave anyone who hadn't read the books in the dark on what Lil – I mean Timber had going when it came to Fae history, but it was a good call and you and your team made up for it in other ways."

I stared up at Backdraft in shock.

"You read my book?" I asked, incredulously.

"Well... yeah," he said.

I stared at him, stunned, and he stared right back. The moment was heavy as I tried to process how monumental this was to me. I mean, no one I had ever seen had actually read one. It had always been some excuse or another. *'Reading's not my thing'*, or *'I don't have the time'*, or even *'You really expect me to read a romance novel?'*

It had gotten to the point that I didn't even ask anymore and here this man was, and he'd read my book without any expectation, or pressure, or –anything–.

"You read my book," I said softly, and the director and the producers standing with us all chuckled, and with a few exchanged pleasantries wandered away.

"Well, yeah, Lil. They're your whole life. I wanted to know everything about you, and I thought they were a good place to start."

I fell in love with him, completely and totally, right then and there.

He chuckled and leaned down, whispering in my ear, "I'm going to stop distracting you and let you take care of business. I'll see you back at the hotel and we can talk about it, if you'd like."

I nodded dumbly and he laid a light butterfly kiss on my cheek.

"I'll see you later."

"Okay."

I watched him leave, dumbfounded, and didn't know what to say.

He found Veronica and she smiled and enthusiastically helped him gather the gift-basket-things that were a thing at every premiere and celebrity event.

I moved through the rest of the evening in a bit of a fog, but it was an elevated one. I don't know why it affected me so much, that he had actually read my book, but it did. Oh, lord, did it ever.

15

*B*ackdraft...

I brought up her gift baskets, chuckling at the contents of some of them. One had condoms in it, which made me smile as I set it on the bedside table.

I missed Lil, like a fractured ache in my chest, but that was probably because the revelation that I'd read her book. Goddamn, I'd never been so in tune with another woman in my life. The look on her face. I knew I'd done something unexpectedly profound, but I had never seen someone fall completely in love and had that look trained on me. That was exactly what I'd seen, though, and it affected me like nothing else ever had.

She'd looked at me the way Chrissy looked at Youngblood, the way Aly looked at Yale, and I had craved it like a drowning man craved air. I'd been a little sad to realize I had never seen a look like that on Torrid, but at the same time, I could honestly say, I'd loved her but not in the way I was falling for Lil. This was something so deep, so profound, that if I were drowning? Well, if this was what drowning in another human being was? I'd die a happy man and I hadn't even gotten to so much as kiss her yet.

I showered and when I got out, I lay on my back on my side of the bed mindlessly channel-surfing in a pair of my boxer-briefs. I had nothing else to do while I waited on Lil to come back to me. I had to say, it was a special kind of torture. I didn't see or hear a goddamned thing playing out over the hotel's TV set. All I kept seeing was that look she'd given me; all I could hear was that stunned dream-like quality to her voice. *"You read my book?"*

Such an innocuous sentence, but one that changed me forever, soul deep. I shut off the TV and sat up when I heard her key card in the lock, leaping to my feet when the door handle depressed. I waited, my heart damn near in my throat, as she rounded the corner and stopped just a few feet from me.

She looked up at me, those storm-swept gray-blue eyes of hers calling me home, like some sort of siren and I slowly closed the gap between us. I cradled her face in my hands and just drank her in by silent sight for several moments. It was the first time that I'd ever been with a woman where literally nothing needed to be said. Instead, I let my body do the talking and my lips do the walking as I lowered my face to hers.

Her breath, sweet with champagne, fanned over my lips as she let out a relieved little gasp and then we were kissing. Slow and sensual, neither one of us wanting to be rushed, her skin smooth as silk under my hands as I smoothed them down her graceful neck and over her shoulders, leaping from her arms to her ribs to caress that hourglass shape through her gown.

She let out a light little sigh of relief and I let my hands sweep to her back to find the hidden zipper there, lowering it, even as her hands fluttered lightly onto my heated skin, slightly cool to the touch and setting me further aflame from it.

Her hands slipped down the back of my boxer-briefs, nails biting slightly into my ass as she gripped it, pressing our bodies tightly together and I groaned into her mouth. She was a fantastic kisser, her tongue taking its time to explore the inside of my mouth as much I took the time with mine to caress the inside of hers.

I rucked the long, heavy, flowing skirt of her gown into my hands, inching it up to give her enough slack to lift the halter over her head.

She broke the kiss and moved with me, bowing her head, lifting it over, before peeling the front of the dress off of her skin. I chuckled and had to kind of figure that she had some sort of adhesive holding things in place, there was no way it would have stayed covering her perfect breasts with that plunging neckline without a little help.

She let the dress drop into a puddle at her feet and pressed her body back up against mine. My arms went back around her, holding her to me, as she boldly shoved my underwear off and captured my throbbing cock, stroking it between us with one small hand.

Our mouths tangled like wildfire caught in the wind, the flames swirling high and higher, twining and twisting, rolling together beautifully as my hands found the globes of her ass and pressed her even tighter against me. She had on these black lace panties that rode high on her ass and I had half a handful of them and half of her smooth and perfect skin. It was an amazing and alluring contrast in textures as I lifted her bodily right out of her heels.

She let me go, her hand leaving my cock so she could put both arms around my shoulders and twine those muscular legs, which were easily half of her short height, around my hips. I was made instantly aware of just how much she wanted me. Her wetness was soaking through her panties and pressing against my cock, the scent of her arousal suddenly permeating the air and driving me all sorts of wild. I turned us both so I could lay her on the bed and she tore her mouth from mine so that she could lay back and look.

I snatched a condom out of the damn gift basket on the bedside table and she smiled, her hands running over every bit of me that she could reach, as I tore it open. She laid back, taking her hands from my skin and ran them over her own, cupping her breasts like low-hanging fruit just begging for my mouth to be on them.

I stared at her, rolling the black, slippery latex over the head of my dick and down my shaft and the naked want and need in her eyes as she grasped her bottom lip between her teeth made me throb. A surge of pleasure pulsed out from my balls and through my bloodstream so intensely I thought for a second that I fucking came before I could even get inside her.

I knelt on the bed between her thighs, stroking myself and letting my eyes rove down her, from those gorgeous eyes of hers, over her beautiful breasts, down her flat stomach to her adorable navel, to the light little pooch of her lower belly. I hooked my fingers into the waistband of her black panties and revealed the rest of her, whisking the scrap of material away from her glistening sex over her strong legs covered in black, thigh-high stockings, which were so hot on her I had every intention of leaving them right where they were.

God, she was beautiful, that classic sense of timeless beauty. Full-figured, like Marilyn Monroe. A total blonde bombshell on par with Scarlett Johannsen, and she was giving herself to me completely.

Mine for tonight, and if I had anything to say about it, for all eternity after. Her spirit was a pure shining gold, resonating with my own on such a deep sub-level I wondered how I'd ever made it work with anyone else up to this point.

I was loving how she was giving herself completely over to the act of sex with me right now, too, like all of her inhibitions had gone out the fucking window. She lay there, looking up at me, her hands traveling over her skin, gripping her breasts, pinching her nipples, smoothing over her stomach and thighs as her hips lifted unbidden from the plush pillow-top mattress in invitation for me to take her.

She wasn't putting on a show, she was genuinely immersed completely in both me and the moment, and it was the hottest fucking thing I'd ever seen in my life. Her eyes dilated with her passion, heavy-lidded with her wanting and lust. I let myself fall forward and caught myself with a firm hand above her shoulder; with the other I kept up the rhythmic stroking of my cock, pressing it at her opening, lifting it to stroke her wetness over her pussy lips and against her clit.

She gasped and moaned, writhing under me impatiently while I teased her with my cock until I couldn't stand it anymore.

I was about to ask her to open her eyes, to look me in mine as I slid my way into her hungry waiting pussy, but I didn't have to. She fixed me with her gaze, dark passion radiating from it, and I slipped my way inside her, sexy and slow, inch by agonizing inch, lowering myself on top of her, until our bodies were pressed close and I could kiss her again.

Jesus Christ, I needed a minute like this, deep in her, tongues warring, my body pressed to hers while I struggled to hold off. To not come, not yet, but damn, it was a near thing, a losing battle. I wasn't sure I was going to last. How could I with a woman like her underneath me?

16

*L*illi...

  I slid my hands along his warm, warm, skin and hugged him with my thighs as he moved with purpose inside me. He smoothed his thumbs along the side of my cheek as if to move my hair but really, it was a protective, covetous touch that made me grip him harder with my pussy. I wanted him inside me, deep and deeper still, and there would be no way that I could get enough.

I was madly, deeply, and totally in love with a man named Backdraft and it brought me such happiness I couldn't even begin to express it. For once, the author had no words, and so, I tried to tell him via a different route.

I kissed him with passion, I gripped him with fervor, I touched every smooth and chiseled inch of him that I could put my hands on and I felt like it was still woefully inadequate to express how I felt. I had never had a man *set me on fire* the way that he did.

I giggled against his mouth, I couldn't help it, and he pulled back from our kiss and searched my face, a smile of his own touching his lips.

"What?" he asked in a gentle whisper, but he didn't stop moving his hips. If anything, pushing himself up like he had, had driven him deeper, the way I wanted. I felt my eyes flutter shut and I moaned. I remembered I owed him an explanation and fought my way through the fog of bliss to give it to him.

"Mm, I thought it was your job to put out fires. Not to start them."

He chuckled deeply, darkly, and put his lips next to my ear and whispered in a sexy growl, "Well, let me introduce you to a controlled burn, baby."

The way he said it, so intense, so low and sincere, made me shudder beneath him. I put my hands to his face and my mouth to his, the intensity turned up between us as we kissed like our very survival depended on it.

He reared up, and hooked an arm beneath one of my knees, laying my leg along his chest, resting my calf on his shoulder, his hand smoothing up and down over the silk of my stocking as he seated himself impossibly deep inside me and stilled for the time being. His other hand he used to trail fingertips across my chest in a feather-light touch, drawing an ever-tightening spiral around one nipple before pinching it with slowly increasing pressure until I threw back my head and gasped. He kept things just like that, where it just felt so good and didn't spill over into pain.

He jerked his hips thrusting himself into me, our bodies already tight together, rocking inside of me, touching off gentle waves of pleasure that swept up from my core to be met from the waves cascading down from my chest. They met in a swirl of euphoria in the very depths of my being and I moaned, this gasping little pathetic thing that was choked down on a strangled cry when his other hand smoothed down my leg, his thumb finding my clit to tease it with a gentle and fine pressure.

"Oh, sweet Jesus!" I cried and gripped the covers with one hand while I stuffed the other against my mouth to keep from crying out too loudly.

He smiled down at me and turned his head, pressing a kiss against my leg as he slowly began to draw his hips back, adding to the rolling motion, finding that spot inside me, teasing it from the inside at the same time he teased it from the outside with his thumb.

I cried out and it sounded like I whined a little but I couldn't tell if it was because I was on the edge and I was whining for more, or if the intense feelings he wrought were getting to be too much and I needed him to stop. He smiled just a little, and a dark passion filled his eyes as he encouraged me, "That's it, baby. Come for me, come around my dick. You're almost there, you got this."

I panted, feeling like he drew me tight and tighter, my body bowing, shivering with the tension as if I were a rubber band stretched to the breaking point, only when I snapped, it was the best thing to have ever happened to me.

I spasmed and jerked against him, my voice dragged from me as the intensity of the orgasm reached a point where it almost scared me. I wasn't one to typically cede that much control, but I let him take it and I trusted him, and when the point came that the attention to my clit was far too much, that I was far too sensitive, and I was about to wrap both my hands around his wrist to pull it away, he let go. He moved his hand away from it and back to the top of my thigh, hugging my leg to him as he rode out the last waves of my orgasm, thrusting slowly but surely, his eyes closed as if listening to fine music.

Maybe he was. Maybe he was listening to me. To the little feral whimpers and moans, to my gasping and panting as the sensations he brought out in me plateaued and miraculously began to slowly build all over again.

I didn't know if I could take anymore, but I wanted to find out. I lay for a moment and stared up at him, dazed. He looked down at me and smiled, bowing over me to place his lips against mine again and I was certain that this was everything; that this was what heaven must be like. To love and be loved, to feel it so completely you didn't have to speak the words.

I wrapped my arms around him and held close to him. He cradled my head in his hand, his arms slipping around my body to hold me in his protective embrace and I felt so whole, so safe and wanted. It was all I had ever desired and he gave it to me so freely I nearly wept. Yet still he moved inside me as if he had all the time, stamina, and energy in the world.

I gasped, low and slow, even as that sweet sensation suffused me, growing in intensity as the dawn, until that moment where the universe held its breath and all of that light and life burst over my horizon and I cried out, holding tightly to him, his voice rough and ragged in my ear as he cried out too, "Oh, God, Lil!" and his cock throbbed in counterpoint to the pulsating pleasure emanating from the center of my very being.

We came back to each other, me cradled carefully against his chest; him, holding himself protectively over the top of me; both of us, our breathing ragged and uneven. We stared each other in the eyes, wonder shaping our expressions as we stared at one another in disbelief.

I don't think it had felt that amazing to either of us with anyone else. It was written in our expressions, etched into our hearts and minds and clear as a summer blue sky. We'd just shared something special, something phenomenal, something like neither of us had ever experienced before.

Backdraft said it best when he uttered a single word into the quiet hush of the hotel room.

"Wow."

Wow, indeed.

17

*B*ackdraft...

"Park downstairs, come inside with me," she said and though it wasn't in the form of a question, she was asking, her stormy gray-blue eyes sparkling, yet her mannerisms shy. Her hand was wrapped around two of my fingers and she was swinging our arms back and forth playfully. She didn't want me to say no, and I didn't want to, but I had a club meeting to get to and work the next day.

"I've got a club meet to get to, babe, or believe me I would."

She stuck out her lower lip into a pout and said, "I'll put you on the permanent guest list, all you have to do is show your ID at the front desk and your parking ticket. They'll validate it for you and send you up."

"Full-access pass," I said with a grin. "Guess I gave it to you good."

She laughed and I swear to God, it was one of the best sounds I'd ever heard. I pulled her closer and leaned way over to keep her away from the hot pipes. She let me kiss her and sighed against my mouth like she'd come home; it had nothing to do with the fact we were parked in front of her building, either.

"Fuck," I muttered against her lips. "I'll be back after the meeting. I've got to be at work by one, though."

She leaned back and frowned, "In the morning?"

I laughed a little. "In the afternoon."

She smiled and nodded. "I think I can manage to let you go."

"You're a better person than I am," I told her. She smiled and shook her head.

"Somehow, I really doubt that. You're the real hero, I just write books."

"Have to agree to disagree there, babe."

She glowed a little, thriving with the use of the endearment and it didn't take a rocket scientist to realize that Lil was pretty love-starved. Maybe that's why she wrote it so well. Dream about having something long enough and you become more than an expert at it. It made me sad for her. I could tell by her reluctance to ever talk about it that she hadn't had the easiest time growing up, that there was a little more to it than her proclamation that she'd been raised by her boozer of a mom in a single-parent household.

I didn't pry, though. I didn't want to see the sadness flicker through her eyes like lightning on the horizon because that flicker seemed to take forever to go away once it made an appearance.

Still, despite my best intentions on that front, that flicker was there anyway. The memory of it was hanging around like an old ghost, despite her efforts to hide it as she stepped back after one last kiss to let me fire up my bike to head over to the 10-13. I blew her a kiss and she walked backwards to the lobby door. I waited until she was safely at the security desk, talking with the guard there, before I pulled away.

I breezed into the back room reserved for our meetings and private parties once I reached the bar. For once, it looked like the majority of us were here. Actually, all of us were. That was a rarity due to the conflicting job schedules, and especially rare for Narcos and Driller, yet here they were.

"You're late," Skids declared and I smiled, I couldn't help myself.

"Got a good reason for that; I swear it."

I dropped into the empty seat next to Youngblood who clapped me on the back. Oz leaned back in his chair, tipping the front two legs off the floor, but it was Golden who said what Oz was clearly thinking.

"This, I gotta hear."

"Probably best before y'all see it on the news," I said.

"News?" Reflash asked.

"Yeah, I was up in New York last night attending a movie premier."

"You totally hooked up with that author chick my Aly Cat's nuts for, didn't you?" Yale demanded, grinning.

"Actually," I said, "I don't think it's as blasé as that. I really dig Lil and I think it's going somewhere solid."

"No fucking joke?" Youngblood asked, "How the fuck am I the last one to hear about this shit?"

"You've been busy, man." Which was the god's honest truth. He'd been working a triple homicide, an ugly one.

"Yeah, that," he said dispassionately. "Looks to be a murder-suicide after all. The lab said it's the only trajectory that makes sense for the dad." He shook his head. "Been spending two weeks chasing a fucking ghost."

"Shit, that sucks," Poe said and I agreed.

"Enough time for that later," Skids called from the head of the table, waving us down.

"Whatcha got, Boss?" Driller called down from the end.

"Want to get started on the Christmas run," he said and for a while it was business as usual; spitballing ideas back and forth to make this year's upcoming Christmas toy drive and charity run one to remember. We did it every year, the ICPD and ICFD working together with our club taking point and organizing it. We even cooperated with the Blue Templars. They were another "law-abiding" cop club, and yeah, I put air quotes around 'law-abiding'. They may have been cops, but they were dirty as fuck. Unfortunately, they were also slicker than owl-shit and IAB still hadn't been able to pin those assholes the fuck down.

It was an ongoing bone of contention between our club, the Blue Templars, and the Indigo City police department's higher-ups. The

Blue Templar's bullshit was constantly bringing trouble and scrutiny to our door that we didn't deserve. Then again, all motorcycle clubs were alike, right? Fucking stereotypes.

The meetup wrapped and guys got up to get to work or head off to do whatever, except for Youngblood. He turned to me and raised an eyebrow and I laughed.

"I want to stay and talk about her," I said.

"But?" he asked with a slow grin.

"But I need to get back to her."

"Oh, my man, dinner at my place," he said, pulling out his phone.

I brought out mine, we looked at calendars and set a date a few weeks from now when our schedules looked like they were finally going to match up.

"You seem happy," he said, and I nodded.

"Yeah. Yeah, I am. She's nothing like Torrid, man. She's special. She's everything. I don't really know how to describe it."

Youngblood shrugged and said, "You ain't gotta, I've got Chrissy, remember? I know exactly what you're talking about, Brother."

I smiled and nodded, pushing to my feet.

"You bring her by here in a couple of weeks if you can. Break the ice before Chrissy and I have you over."

I grinned and said, "Barring any disasters, yeah. Should be able to make that work." I held out a hand and he grasped it, arm-wrestle style and pulled me in. We clapped each other on the back and stepped back.

"Don't fuckin' curse yourself, now."

Another exchange of laughter, and to help him through his bout of superstition, I knocked on the tabletop before heading out into the rest of the restaurant and bar. I waved at the guys hanging around and made my way out to a chorus of ribbing. Youngblood had my back and shut them up as I stepped out into the deepening twilight.

I rode back to Lil's and down into the garage, taking a parking ticket. The elevator from the visitor level spilled me out into the lobby and I took the ticket to security and let them know who I was and all that jazz. They let me through the fancy electronic turnstile-thing and scanned a badge against the elevator bank to send me up to Lil's floor.

"Thanks, man," I said, and he handed me back my validated parking ticket. I gave him a little salute with it and stepped onto the elevator, putting the ticket into my wallet.

"Hold that for me, would you please?" a voice called out and I stuck my arm out to keep the doors from closing.

"Thank you," the man said and I looked up, right into the unfortunately-familiar face of the douchebag that'd tricked Lil into being his side chick before humiliating her at the 10-13.

His loss, your treasure, I thought to myself, but it didn't ease my wanting to punch him in his face.

I gave him a tight-lipped smile and said, "No problem."

"Do I know you?" he asked, his eyes narrowing suspiciously.

"Nope." I stuffed my hands in my jeans pockets, shoulders tense under his scrutiny. The doors had finished sliding shut and he scanned a badge on the inside scanner of the car. Floor twenty-one lit up.

"Ah," he said nodding. Good for him, he'd figured it out.

"You live here now?" I asked casually.

"Yes, with my fiancée."

"Lil know?"

"Ah, no. I haven't spoken to her."

"Keep it that way," I said shortly and he blinked, taken aback.

The rest of the ride to his floor went by in a tense silence, and when the doors swished open, he paused, as if he were going to say something. I gave him a cold look and he seemed to think better of whatever it was and stepped off.

I struggled with how I was going to tell her. I mean, she deserved to know rather than to just be blindsided by this asshole in the lobby with his girl. Come to think of it, his girl deserved better than that too, but she wasn't my concern as much as Lil, and I honestly didn't know how to even let his woman know what was up. That was a dilemma in and of itself. Having been on the receiving end of that shit, I knew it didn't feel good, but I was still glad my fire bros had told me.

"What a shit-show," I muttered, and the elevator opened up on Lil's floor. I went to her door and took a deep breath, and knocked.

The smile she opened it with was enough to knock me off my damn feet and just about all thoughts of that asshole disappeared. Hell, I might have even felt something along the lines of a little secret gratitude. She was the one for me, and him fucking it up put us together. So while I still wanted to kill him, I was also kind of grateful, in a fucked-up and twisted sense of ironic fate.

"I missed you," I said and stepped across the threshold, shutting the door before one of the cats could bolt.

"Really?" she asked, like she almost couldn't believe it.

Fuck it. I pulled her close and kissed her soundly until the tension in her body from the sudden action eased and she melted against my chest. I smoothed my hands over the satin of her robe and her arms went around my neck. She pressed her body close to mine and I came unglued, for all the best reasons this time.

"I'm taking you to bed," I growled and she smiled.

"You know where it is." The way she said it, there wasn't anything demure about it.

She yelped and let out a joyous laugh as I picked her up in a fireman's carry and strode down the hall toward her bedroom. The first time I had walked in here she'd been asleep in my arms and I had nearly dropped her, no joke, from how amazing the room was.

Hell, I was turned on just thinking about making love to her in that bed, suspended as it was halfway between floor and ceiling, on its platform. Her bedroom, unlike the rest of the apartment, was two stories and yet remained floor-to-ceiling glass. Her bed, king-sized, was suspended on a cement platform half way between floor and ceiling, two short flights of steel, glass, and cement stairs leading up to it and the two nightstands to either side. The bed itself was a picture in peach and cream satin, a sharp contrast to the cement and steel surrounding it. I carried her up those two flights and set her on her feet in the plush white faux-fur area rug that sprawled beneath the bed.

She laughed and reached up for me to come down, closing the gap between our mouths. I kissed her and she kissed me back and fuck, I was fired up. I made short work of our clothes, hers a hell of a lot easier than mine, that light satin robe and the long satin-and-lace nightgown that clung to her soft curves. She matched the bedroom, I realized, and that made me smile.

She worked so hard at looking so put-together, but I knew that she didn't feel that way. I also knew that feeling, and that she was honestly way more put-together and awesome at holding it together than she gave herself credit for. She was a strong woman, and she needed to be, if this whole thing was going to work. Loving a man in my line of work could be nerve-wracking and hard. I knew she could handle it. She'd already handled so much, given our conversations about her mother and what the douchebag I'd encountered on the elevator had done to her confidence and self-esteem.

I put one arm around her and with the other, flung the comforter back on the bed so I could turn and lay her down.

My beautiful girl thought of everything, there were already condoms on her bedside table. More of them with her author logo on them. I chuckled and didn't go for them immediately. I wanted to taste every inch of her first. I got her onto the bed properly and covered her body with mine, starting with her mouth, her hands holding my face, smoothing down my neck, over my shoulders in a firm, but light, touch.

I loved how she seemed to appreciate my body with those touches. Exploring, but at the same time, each movement reverent, in that exploration raised my skin in goosebumps after their sweep, every hair standing on end. God, the things she did to me, my cock was throbbing and aching to be inside of her but not yet. I didn't anticipate I would last long this first go, so I was determined to make her come with my mouth before I even tried anything that could set me off.

I trailed kisses and light flicks of my tongue all down her body, paying special attention to the pert globes of her breasts, the most perfect natural set of tits I had ever seen on a woman. She was so soft and warm, the satin sheets so slick under my knees as I worked my way closer to the petals of her sex.

Her scent perfumed the air around us, which was another thing; I'd never encountered a woman whose very smell set me off the way hers did. She was absolutely divine, a mix of earthy herbal scent mixed with something floral, almost fruity.

Her skin was petal-soft beneath my hands and lips. All of the contrasting sensations make my cock weep with pre-cum and my body tense as I refused to do what it wanted and instead focused on making her feel everything that I was and then some.

I stared up at her from between her thighs and she stared back. Desire flickered in those stormy gray-blue eyes of hers like heat lightning and I felt a feral smile overtake my lips as I slid a finger inside her hot, wet, and waiting depths. She fell back onto the mattress and let out a throaty moan. I put my tongue against her body and crooked the finger inside her toward her roof and she took off like a shot, hips rising off the bed, writhing against my hand and mouth. I chuckled against her and she gasped and bucked a little harder this time, but that didn't bother me. I just put my free arm over her hips and pressed her back down.

She still tried to writhe but was held suitably still and I continued my attentions, reveling in her bright, clean taste and her soft little whimpering moans.

One of the things I loved about her the most when it came to sex was how much of an enthusiastic participant she was. When things got real and she let down her barriers, she moved, she lost her shyness and the cool, calm front she put on when the clothes were on and was pretty much the definition of 'angel in the streets and a siren in the sheets', or however that phrase went.

She let her hands glide over her skin, her body move, and really got into it, which I loved. When she stiffened, and her body pulled taut as if drawn by strings, it was pure magic for me. Her pussy crushed down around my finger and her orgasm milked it for all it was worth and I loved it. I couldn't get enough of it, and I was pretty excited to see if I could get another one out of her before I got my own.

I let her lay, chest heaving, in the center of her bed, languid, her body loose and liquid, like she was barely contained by her own skin, which honestly, she really wasn't. She almost glowed with real light as she basked in the afterglow and I felt my own chest swell and puff up with more than a little pride that I did that for her. That I was the one here, loving her into such a state, and that I would be the one to do it again – as soon as I got this fucking condom on.

She smiled at me and reached out a hand lazily to draw me back to the bed and I smiled and took it, my cock screaming for some relief, even as my heart nearly burst from a happiness I think was safe to say I'd never really fully immersed myself in before.

"God, you're fucking unreal," I growled and covered her body with my own, her mouth with my own, as she giggled into it and wrapped herself around me. I loved her so much in that moment I wished it could be a permanent thing. Her and me like this, all the air we needed to breathe, the water we needed to drink, the food we needed to eat a thing of the past. I swear, I could subsist on her and her alone. She was that incredible.

18

*L*illi...

"I want to be on top," I whispered into his ear about two or three careful slow thrusts of his in. He kissed the side of my neck and I gasped when he hit that spot that sent shivers down one half of my body. He spent some more time there and rolled us both, his thick, hard length never leaving my body as I suddenly found myself on top, my one thigh aching a bit from the transition. That always happened, but it would be my secret because I never wanted for a moment for Backdraft to think he hurt me in any way.

I slid down him completely, bracing my hands against his chest so that I could sit up, and biting my bottom lip at the depth of penetration and the change in angle. It hit all the right places inside of me, and I was torn between being selfish and grinding to get myself off one more time, and riding him more for his pleasure.

He rolled his hips in that delicious way that decided me for me. I mimicked his movement and carried on with it, stabilizing myself against his chest as his hands found my hips and he ground me back and forth on him. I loved it, that heavy warm glow like sunrise pressing against the horizon starting low in my body. I closed my eyes and tipped my head back, my hair tickling the top of my ass, dipping further down my lower back, the sensation sending prickles along my spine even as he sucked in a breath at the sight of me.

I looked at him, his hazel eyes devouring me from the crown of my head down, stopping at my eyes, a depth of emotion I'd never encountered with anyone else passing between us. That gaze of his swept my body, lingering on my tits with such an intensity I could almost feel the weight of it, and all it did was serve to excite me even more.

I touched the side of my neck which slightly burned with the rub of his stubble on it from earlier and he watched me make the motion. I couldn't help it, with a slight smile I made a show of trailing those fingertips along my own skin, slowly lingering between my breasts as the light inside me intensified. I swept a slow and tantalizing erotic path down my stomach, his eyes trapped by the web of my fingertips and dragging along my skin with them.

I rolled my hips forward and closed my eyes, dipping those same fingers between our bodies and slicking them through the wetness I found there, touching myself lightly as I continued my erotic dance for him.

He groaned, and gasped my name and I could feel he was close, twitching inside me slightly. His eyes closed and such a look of concentration crossed his face. I smiled, knowing damn well the image of me was burned on the insides of his eyelids and good god that gave me such a sense of power.

I loved the sense of power he gave me. One look, one touch, and somehow it was as if I could bring this giant, beautiful man to his knees, and the euphoria and confidence that bestowed on me was another erotic sort of pleasure that I don't think I had ever experienced before with anyone else.

I felt the light inside me surge and I moaned his name softly. He encouraged me, and with a gentle swish of my fingers, that light spilled over my horizon and set me on fire in a beautiful and gentle rush, where fire flowed and imitated water, rippling over my surface like a brook rushing over round stones.

He cried out with me, his big arms going around me as he sat up and crushed me to him, holding me firmly, protectively as our mouths found each other and it was a clash of fire and ice. His steady stillness quenching the fire inside me, the fire inside me bringing him to life to kiss me with a sudden and renewed fervor. I swear to god, the moment was so beautiful, so pure, so everything a tear slipped free.

"Mm, you okay, babe?" he whispered.

I sniffed and smiled down at him, "I'm perfect," I whispered back.

"Good, good," he murmured and brought my lips to his again. I sighed against his mouth and relaxed against him, languid and complete, and he smoothed his hands against my cooling skin, warming me.

"God, that was good," he murmured a moment later.

"Mm hmm," I agreed happily.

"Let me get cleaned up and come back."

"'Kay."

He took himself off the other side of the bed and I rolled onto my stomach, peeking around the headboard as he took himself through the bathroom doorway behind everything on the back wall.

Mm, god, his ass was something perfect, putting Michelangelo's David to shame. I sighed happily and turned onto my back, arching against the satin sheets, enjoying the tactile sensation of the slick, soft fabric against my nude body.

"Jesus Christ," he muttered from the side of the bed, "You're fucking perfect."

I yipped and laughed and he jumped into bed with me, attacking me with tickling kisses and little nibbles against my skin. I laughed and thrashed against the onslaught; I loved this so much.

"Oh, my god, I love you!" I cried and he backed off just enough to see my laughing face. His was so very serious and for a split second I felt a frisson of panic. *Oh, shit! Did I really just say that out loud?*

"Shh, it's okay," he said and bent and placed his lips against mine. My heart calmed and he murmured against them, "When I'm with you, I feel like I've found my true best friend. My soulmate, my perfect match."

"Yeah?" I asked, my voice tight as I held my breath.

"Yeah. I think I loved you the first time we really talked, Lil. You're everything to me."

I swallowed hard and felt those happy tears return. It was everything I had ever wanted a man to say to me and was so raw and genuine I couldn't help but feel something.

He kissed me, and then kissed my tears away, holding me tenderly and sighing, such a content sound. He gathered me up and held me for a long moment before we let the emotions carry us both away into another long slow round of serious love-making.

"I NEED TO TELL YOU SOMETHING," he murmured once we were both sated, the lights were out, and we were both comfortably nestled into bed.

"Mm?" I asked drowsily.

"I ran into that asshole from the 10-13 on the elevator."

I froze. There was only one asshole he could be talking about in relation to us and the 10-13. I groaned and relaxed against him, sighing out my frustration.

"Did he recognize you?" I asked.

"Yeah, he lives on the 21st floor, babe, with his fiancée."

"Shit," I muttered. "I wonder if she even knows he cheated."

"Dunno," I said. "My guess would be no."

"Why's that?" I asked, genuinely curious.

"I know the type of guy," he said. "Hell, my own firehouse mate, a guy on my own shift was banging Torrid behind my back. It was one of the other guys that caught them out and took photos to break it to me. Ackley still tried to fuckin' deny it."

"What happened?" I asked softly.

"He was transferred, the guys at his new house are still giving him the cold shoulder, and the guys from my house are just now starting to talk to him again."

"You don't sound happy about that," I observed.

"Would you be?"

"No. No, I would not," I said with a bitter laugh. He held me a little tighter and kissed the top of my head, sighing. I stared out the glass, far in front of us and out over the twinkling lights of the city at the lights along the Bay Bridge, glittering on the calm surface of the Chesapeake.

"Thank you for telling me," I said softly, after a time.

"You bet," he said, sounding relieved. I'd felt a moment of resentment, but it wasn't aimed at him. It was aimed at Mark. I mean, seriously? How awful and awkward would that have been? Just running into him and his girlfriend or fiancée, or whatever she was to him, in the lobby? It made me angry that he knew I would be too embarrassed, too humiliated, to say anything. God, he'd picked a ripe target in me to have a fling with.

I felt bitter and hurt all over again. Backdraft smoothed a hand up and down my back and I closed my eyes and sighed.

"I'm glad you're here," I whispered.

He chuckled, "No place I'd rather be, babe. No place I'd rather be."

God, I loved him so much. The sting of betrayal was replaced by another kind of hurt – the good kind. I smiled and cuddled close and before I knew it, the sun was waking me and Backdraft was gone – but not without leaving a note.

Dinner, tomorrow night at the firehouse. I want you to meet the other guys.

I laughed gently and laid back, Jaspar jumping up on the bed with a querulous meow.

"You'd better get used to him, guys. I think he's here to stay." My cat head-butted my hand affectionately and I showered him in love. I sighed and looked at the day through brand-new eyes.

19

*B*ackdraft...

"Hey." I helped her out of the back seat of the car in front of the house.

"Hi," she said shyly, and I think she was surprised when I bent down and kissed her. She darted a nervous gaze at the house and I laughed.

"You're not a secret with me, babe. Never again."

She swallowed hard and gave a nod. I still had a way to go, it seemed, when it came to her confidence. I sighed inwardly and smiled outwardly. I wanted to break Junior's dick in two for making her feel like she needed to be kept some dirty little secret. I wanted even more for her to find a happy medium, a balance between who she was out here around everyone else and who she was when she was just with me.

"Oh, um, I brought a bottle of wine," she said. "But looking back on it, I guess that was pretty dumb. I mean, you guys probably can't drink it while on duty, right?"

"Hey, slow down." I stopped her halfway up the driveway to the garage doors and put my hands on her shoulders.

"Sorry," she said taking a shaky breath. "I'm nervous."

"Why?" I asked gently.

She swallowed hard, "These people are your co-workers, they're important not only to you, but to your livelihood. I don't want to be an embarrassment to you."

She was terrified, yet so bravely frank and the contrast was endearing. I massaged her shoulders through her coat and smiled at her.

"There ain't shit you could do, or say, to embarrass me, babes. I love you and I'm so very proud to be walking in there with you to show your sweet ass off." She laughed and yet none of her nervousness diminished. I sighed and asked her, "What's really going on in that gorgeous head of yours?"

She raked her lip between her teeth and sighed, gazing somberly at the firehouse. "I'm afraid it doesn't have much to do with you," she confessed.

"Old ghosts?" I guessed.

"Yeah."

"Your mom?"

"Bingo."

"She's not here, baby. You never have to see her again if you don't want to."

She laughed nervously and nodded saying, "I can't tell you how many times I had to go with her to a work thing of hers and she would get just hammered and when the consequences came? They were never her consequences. Somehow she always made it my fault for letting her drink or whatever."

I nodded somberly and smiled, "You're fine. Everything's gonna be fine."

"So nervous about this and look at me! I bring a bottle of booze."

I chuckled. "Wine, baby. You brought a bottle of wine. It ain't no thing. You don't even gotta bring it out of that purse of yours. No one has to know it's here."

She nodded and I put an arm around her and led her to the man-sized door off to the side of the bay doors. She went with me and I opened it up and held it open for her. She took a deep breath, gave me a grateful look and went through into the garage. I followed her in and took her coat and purse, hanging them on the peg down here by the door.

She glanced around and asked, "Where is everybody?"

"Upstairs, come on."

I led her up the back flight to the second floor. Some of the guys called out enthusiastically and Lil blushed.

"Hey-ey! There she is!" Captain Walden called out from the kitchen.

"Holy shit, you were really for real!" Brody called from where he was setting the table.

"What the hell, you thought he was lying?" Ripley demanded.

"No!" Brody barked back defensively.

Barnaby and Angel cracked up, and Lil said, "Angel, right?"

"Yeah, yeah, nice to meet you! Backdraft has some nice things to say about you," he said and winked. Lil blushed.

"Thanks for looking out for him," she murmured and Angel grinned.

"No sweat."

"Angel's not only an EMT and Paramedic with the house, here, he's also an Indigo Knight, babes."

"Oh, a two for one?" she asked and looked impressed.

Angel laughed and said, "Yeah, something like that."

"Don't let him pull one over on you," I told her. "He has a twin, Golden."

"Hey, I'm not the one to play that game," Angel said throwing a wadded-up paper towel in my direction. I laughed, it was true.

"Yeah," I rolled my eyes, "It's true, Angel is pretty true to his name-sake. Golden is definitely the evil twin."

"I'ma tell him you said that."

Lil laughed but I was on the fence a little, Golden could be unpredictable sometimes. Not in a bad way, but dude had a temper. I think his time overseas had knocked a few screws loose. Still, dude was as loyal as they came and was a damn fine cop and hero.

Lil took in the upstairs. The kitchen was almost loft-like and, along with the living room, looked out over the garage. I pointed out the bathroom up here, the locker room was downstairs closer to where we came in so we could clean up without tracking soot and other shit up here. The bunks were toward the back and the traditional fire-pole dropped us in front of the locker room doors between them and the rigs. I showed her around and introduced her to the rest of the dozen or so guys on shift.

There was Mason and Griggs, along with a few others. Lil was perfect and polite and the more she got to know everyone, the more relaxed she became.

"You seriously write dirty books?" Griggs asked, and she blushed.

"They're um, Paranormal Romance, but yes, they have sex in them." Griggs raised an eyebrow and shot me a look. I shot him a withering one in return for even thinking about it.

"That's cool, that's legit," he said, nodding.

"Come and get it, boys and girls!" Captain Walden called and we all migrated to the table.

Lil smiled warmly at Linden, the only female we had on duty. She was a bull-dyke lesbian and proud of it. She also could whoop any one of our asses at a vast majority of the shit we did, even though she was actually partnered with Angel. She was built for this kind of life, a lot like that blonde giant knight woman on that fantasy epic everyone was crazy about. She kept her hair high and tight except for a long shock of it on top she let fall to one side. She was a natural blonde but dyed her hair brunette, but either color worked on her. She smiled at Lil and nodded back.

Marquez turned down the news on the big-screen mounted to the back wall while we all took a seat and said grace. None of us but the Captain was particularly religious, but we all believed in our higher power and were good with it, so we said our grace and dug in.

"Hell, yeah, Captain! That's what I'm talking about!" Linden declared, dishing out some of the boss's famed mashed potatoes onto her plate.

The meal was good, the company awesome, and Lil fit right it. Everybody loved her, like I knew they would. I had more than one of the guys catch my eye and give me a nod of approval. Considering how much they all just put up with Torrid while secretly pretty much loathing her behind her back, Lil was a breath of fresh air.

She smiled and Brody looked up and choked on his food, swallowed it down and yelled out, "Yo, yo, yo, yo, yo! Our boy's on TV!"

A hush fell over the table and Captain Walden grabbed up the remote and turned it up so we could all hear. Those of us with our backs to the TV, twisted around in our seats to see.

"Backdraft is just a good friend," Lil said from the TV. The microphone disappeared from in front of her face and the voice of the hostess asked,

"How good?"

Lil dazzled with her smile and walked away with me and it cut back to the studio with the blonde chick and her brother-from-another-mother co-host.

"Well, we have it on good authority that life is imitating art when it comes to this particular friendship." Lil and I froze.

"What the hell is that supposed to mean?" Angel asked.

The next image on the screen was devastating. Lil's face fell and I felt my jaw drop open when there we were, in our barely-blurred birthday suits, in Lil's bed. *Drone*, I thought to myself. It had to be.

"What the fuck?" someone demanded, to the sharp clatter of silverware falling from fingers. Lil had a hand on her stomach, the other over her mouth like she was going to be sick.

Then the real nightmare unfolded, the scene cut to an interview seat with fucking Torrid in the shot.

"Now, Victoria, I know this is hard, but who is that man with Timber in the picture to you?"

"He —was— my boyfriend, but not after this," she said tearfully. Images of me and Torrid flashed across the screen as the guys erupted in a fit of rage on my behalf. Lil stood up and looked like she was going to be ill when the shot panned out, revealing Douchebag next to Torrid.

"You dumped that cunt's ass months ago!" Angel cried, appalled.

"I need to go," Lil said, voice breathy. Her hands shook, but she managed to shoot off a text.

"Lil, wait, I had no idea –" The fucking media was tearing her life to shreds on the screen and she looked up at me, humiliation and pain radiating from her in waves.

"It's okay," she said, tears spilling over, "It's not you, it's me... I have to go, I have to get away from you."

"Lil, no, don't do that," I begged but she was already making strides. I went after her and the guys all stood around in stunned, angry silence while Torrid made an ass out of Lil and me on international syndication or whatever. I felt fucking helpless and I didn't want Lil to leave.

"Lil, wait, babes, don't leave, not like this!" I caught up to her at the door. She already had her coat and purse down.

"No, no, don't!" she cried when I tried to pull her in to hold her. She pushed away from me, chest heaving, her heart breaking. Her eyes were wide and so pain-filled as she said to me, "I need some time alone. Please. This could mean my whole career. Just give me some time to sort it out."

Her phone started blowing up and I wanted desperately to fucking shield her from this. I reached for her again but she took a step back into the crash bar on the door and out into the night. I stopped and let the door swing shut in my face at a loss for what to do.

"What the fuck just happened?" I whispered, stunned.

Torrid. Torrid just happened. I seethed and went for my phone ready to call the bitch up, but stopped.

That's exactly what she fucking wants, dude. Don't do it.

"Fuck!" I screamed and threw the goddamn phone against the truck, where it shattered.

I looked up at the loft, all the guys and Linden lined up at the railing looking down at me, all of their expressions a mix of rage and sorrow. I put my hands on my hips, bowed my head, and tried like hell to breathe around this thing. Regret burned the back of my throat with acid as I looked at the shattered pieces of my phone on the ground.

20

*L*illi...

I huddled in the middle of my bed and stroked Jaspar's fur while Marigold huddled miserably at my hip. I stared at my phone on the sheets in front of me, the screen black, and tasted the bitter bite of bile. I was waiting on Veronica to get here, to help me with damage control from the broadcast two nights ago.

I'd tried to call Backdraft after the lawyers and PR firms were mobilized and he hadn't answered. I hadn't left a message. I hated talking to machines and I was sure that this wasn't something to leave a message about. This deserved a conversation. Of course, I may not get the chance. Backdraft may not want to talk to me ever again.

Of course not, you're poison. Everything you touch turns to ash...

Funny, how that derisive voice in my head sounded so much like my mother.

I sniffed and mopped at my eyes with a soggy Kleenex. I had two boxes on the bed, one half-empty; the other half-full of the soggy ruins of the many dead Kleenex that'd gone before.

Everything was on its head. The hate and vitriol pouring in from social media had me shutting down my computer completely and walking away. There were videos out there of readers burning my books and studios were pumping the brakes on further production of any of my works into film for the time being until the media stopped having a total field day.

Veronica had already launched a volley of lawsuits against the paparazzi responsible for the photos of the inside of my bedroom and the show for putting them out there. It was heartbreaking and humiliating on so many levels, and it was all a lie.

I wanted to curl up in Backdraft's arms so badly but I couldn't. I wouldn't. I needed to just stay far away from him. Staying away from him would keep him safe, I hoped, but I knew better. I'd seen the footage of the media and paparazzi camped outside his firehouse and it made me sick for him. I hurt for him more than I even hurt for myself. I was afraid that he blamed me; that he was angry with me and thought I blamed *him* when this was all my fault.

"I'm so sorry you have such a shit mom," I warbled, tears blurring my eyes and wrecking my voice as I spoke to my furbabies, my sole comfort in the total ripping, tearing, shit-storm that had become my life.

I hugged my knees, rocking back and forth, and gave in to the despair eating me alive. What else could I do?

21

$\mathcal{B}$ackdraft...

"Veronica!" I called out, and the tall redhead whirled to tell me off, the rage in her face smoothing out when she realized it was me. I shut off the bike and jogged over to her.

"Why didn't you answer your phone?" she demanded by way of greeting. "She thinks you hate her!"

I cursed and sighed. "I smashed it, right as she left the damn firehouse," I told her. "I went to call Torrid, to ream her a new asshole and I realized that'd be playing right into her hands and I threw the damn phone without thinking. I just got a new one, but I lost Lil's number when I destroyed my old one like an idiot."

"And you didn't try to come here?" she asked.

"Yeah, the security turned me away, said Lil wasn't taking any visitors."

Veronica swore and dug around in her purse saying, "She's a wreck. The lawyers are on it, the PR firm has told her to keep her mouth shut and –"

"Yeah, I know, they called me, told me to keep my mouth shut, too. I been toeing the line, but it's fucking ugly, Ronnie. I mean, I thought Chrissy had it bad, this is... I'm speechless."

"Welcome to the land of celebrity," Veronica said dryly. "It's true what they say, though."

"What?"

"That no publicity is bad publicity." I frowned and she rolled her eyes, clarifying, "That there's no such thing as bad publicity! Her sales are through the roof, she's making bank off the scandal. People are so stupid. They have to buy those books to burn 'em."

"I don't care about money," I seethed. "I care about Lil. She's my fuckin' life and this? Being apart from her? It's killing me!" I swallowed hard and said, "I don't know what to do." She looked at me with sympathy and my voice cracked when I said, "Just tell me what to do... please?"

"Can you prove any of it is a lie?" she asked. I straightened and thought about it for a few. She held out her hands, a pen in one of them, what she'd been digging for in her purse, and I held mine out. She pulled up my sleeve on my jacket and wrote along the inside of my wrist. "Call Lil," she said sternly and when she took her hands away there were two numbers scrawled along my skin. "The second one is mine in case you need it."

"I will, and thanks," I said. "I need to get back to the house. Captain is letting me skate for a little while but I can't leave them a man down for long. I get off the day after tomorrow, in the morning."

"Okay, program those numbers into your phone and don't smash it this time. And if you think up any proof, you call me. We can take it to the PR firm. They'll likely tell us to stuff it and to stay the course, but we can always try."

I didn't like that answer. I swallowed hard and nodded, and she made her way into the obsidian tower holding my princess high and far away from me. I sighed and went back to my bike, cameras snapping away across the street. I gave them the finger and fired up my bike and took my ass back to the station.

The guys had the doors up and stepped aside from where they were washing trucks and rolling hoses for me to park in the back near the locker room doors. Fucking paparazzi motherfuckers had fucked with my bike the night before to get me to come out so they could grill me. As soon as I was parked, I programmed the numbers into my phone.

I shot a text to Lil first thing:

I don't hate you. I love you more than life itself. I'm so sorry.

I didn't have time to do anything other than hit 'send' when the fucking house lit up in a full alarm.

"Structure fire! Let's roll, boys!"

I got off my bike and laid my colors over the back, leaving my phone lying on top. I was in my uniform, had just thrown on my jacket and cut over everything when the Captain had told me to go run my errand, that he'd look the other way for me.

I ran to my gear hanging along the wall and suited up. Brody was pulling on his gear next to me and asked, "How'd it go?" I pressed my lips into a grim line and shook my head.

"Shit," he said. "Sorry, bro."

"Fuck it for right now, we got a fuckin' job to do."

"Right, we do. Let's go be a fuckin' hero," he said. I nodded and marched to our truck, pulling myself up into my seat.

The structure fire was a projects building six blocks away and it was bad. Smoke billowed out of the third-floor windows. The building itself was six stories tall.

"Going down from the top!" I yelled and the ladder was already moving into position. I shouldered my tank and put my mask over my face. I bundled up, making sure my jacket was secure and my gauntlets were in place. The smell of campfire was strong and cloying, the harsh overtones of burning plastic riding the air and stinging the eyes. I made sure I had airflow, that comms was working with a swift radio check, and I moved my ass, hauling balls up the ladder with more of our guys on my six.

"Watch yourself, Calder!" The Captain came over the radio.

"Copy that. Brody, you with me?"

"On your six, Calder. Let's do this."

I cleared the ledge of the roof and strode across the tar-paper roof. I tried the door to the emergency stairwell, but it was locked.

"Ram!" I called and Brody thumped me on the shoulder. I set

aside my axe and took up the other side of the battering ram. We hauled back on it and it took two-and-a-half tries for the door to bust loose.

"Goddamnit!" Brody cried when some of the folks from the units stumbled out onto the roof.

"Barnaby, get these people out of here! Brody and I are going in." I took up my fire axe.

"Copy that!" Barnaby's voice came over the radio as he helped people out of the stairwell. Smoke roiled out against the deepening twilight, and I took one last look up into the sky. I spied a star or two starting to come out and then I couldn't see shit. I let the respirator do its job and pushed past bodies until suddenly, there was no more resistance from the press of people attempting to flee.

We plunged down the stairs to the first landing and started kicking doors, pushing people, coughing and choking, towards the stairs, creating a human chain with the few who stubbornly wanted to stay put despite the blaring alarm and faint wink of the emergency lights through the smoke.

We pounded on doors and made our way, floor to floor, until we reached the inferno chewing through the third floor.

"Brody! Here!" I shouted. I could hear someone coughing, someone crying, even through the chaos and rage of the flames.

"It's bad in here, Boss," I heard over the radio. "Fully engulfed, out into the hallway." I almost didn't recognize my own voice, the adrenaline surging, my blood rushing through my ears even as the fire roared up the hall. I kicked, and kicked again, the screaming and crying getting louder, forming words in thickly-accented English.

"Help! Help us!"

"One, two, three!" Brody kicked out with me in unison and the door gave, flying into the apartment.

An older woman was coughing and wheezing, choking something out in Spanish, a little girl nearby clutching a doll or something to her chest, crying. Brody went for the old woman; I dove for the kid and scooped her up. She screamed and wailed in terror, coughing and hacking, making these little mewling sounds between. Brody went first, the old woman screaming, probably for her granddaughter. I couldn't make it out and honestly, I didn't care. I had a job to do, get them out alive.

It was pitch black except for the heat and angry glow off to our left.

"Down!" Brody shouted over the radio and I turned my back on the flames. The heat was so intense that I could feel it even through my gear. I hugged the little girl close and bolted for the stairwell, moving down and nearly crashing into the rescue crew coming up from the bottom. They about-faced and we hauled ass down the stairs.

The kid went limp by the second floor and was totally fucking out by the first. I burst out onto the sidewalk and pelted for Angel, my mask so dirty with soot I could still barely see. The little girl roused and asked, "Mr. Mittens?" and I passed her off to Angel, who put oxygen on her.

"Here!" Lind passed a limp kitten and another mask off to me. I knocked off my helmet and ripped off my mask and put the oxygen on the cat, coughing the stench of the fire out of my own fuckin' lungs. Still, I had to work on the kitten, because if that little girl lost her cat I'd feel fuckin' terrible.

"Come on, little man!" I urged, rubbing his tiny limp body with my fingers, shoving his whole face into the mask. I swore to myself, soft and full of heat, angry, wanting to just save one fuckin' thing. If it wasn't my relationship with Lil, let it be this girl and cat.

Brody poured a bottle of water over the little ball of fur to cool him down and with an indignant cry, his little eyes rolled back into focus and he writhed in my hand, mewling up a storm. I grinned and let out a laugh and looked up and over to Angel and felt the fuckin' smile die on my lips.

His shoulders were slumped and he wasn't knuckle-dragging against the girl's sternum trying to get her to open her eyes anymore. Lind looked like she'd taken a hit to her lady-balls too, and was pulling a sheet out of the back of their bus.

"No," I said, and he shook his head and reached out to Lind to take hold of the sheet to cover the little girl. "No, no, no, no, no! Man, no!" I yelled. "You have to keep trying."

Angel shook his head and looked like even he was close to tears and said, voice cracking, "Man, I can't. It's too late, she's gone."

"This is bullshit!" I screamed at him and threw my helmet off the top of my head onto the ground. "You've got to be fucking kidding me!" I screamed at no one. "The girl fucking dies but the goddamn cat lives?"

I shook my head, my rage suddenly fueled by the unfairness of everything! The girl fucking dies but the cat fucking lives. Lil gets fucking cheated on but her life gets turned upside down and inside out and I'm just supposed to sit here, her man, and not do a goddamned thing!

They weren't even close to one another but it still tore at my soul, ate me alive, and was destroying me from the inside out. I looked down at the crying, mewling cat in Barnaby's hands where I'd thrust it and bowed my head. Helpless to do anything, I just stood in the rush of activity around us as Lind looked at me with the same horror in her eyes that I felt.

The girl fucking dies but the cat fucking lives.

This was some seriously fucked-up shit.

All. Of. It.

22

*L*illi...

I'd stared at the text message on my screen and chewed my lip for the better part of an hour. I'd missed the text by two. I sighed and bowed my head, feeling so uncertain as to how to respond to something so profound. *Something I didn't deserve.*

"Call him again," Veronica urged, not for the first time, and I stared down at the phone in my hand and hedged.

"He's probably out on a call," I said. "He'll call me when he gets –
"

My phone, buzzing insistently, the photo of us together in front of the Liberty Bell lighting up the screen, cut me off. Veronica made an annoyed sound. I answered the call, self-conscious.

"Hi," I said lamely – and the voice on the other end wasn't Backdraft.

"Lil?"

"Yes?" I felt the color drain from my face and my mouth go dry in sheer terror.

"It's Brody."

"Oh, my God, what's happened?" I felt tears spring to my eyes in a rush of emotion as I thought to myself, *Please no, not this, I can't take anymore.*

"Oh, shit! No! It's not like that. He's fine – er, physically fine, unharmed..." he trailed off and let out a frustrated breath. "Look, it was a bad call, Lil. A real bad one. With what's going on with you, he's not taking it well. He doesn't even know I've called you. Angel and Lind are downstairs to smuggle you out. Can you meet them in your lobby?"

I turned to Veronica, who looked at me like I was being dumb. I smiled weakly and said into the phone, "Absolutely, Brody. I'll be right down."

He let out a rush of breath and said, "Good, that's great, we'll see you soon."

We ended the call and Veronica, who was standing close enough to hear everything said, "Smuggle you out how?"

Turns out, it was "in the back of an ambulance as a patient from the garage level," as was the building's protocol. The paparazzi didn't even stir, which was a plus for us and as soon as we reached the firehouse, they backed into one of the bays and shut the doors before letting me out. Lind gave me a helping hand out of the back, and I spied Backdraft's bike parked at the back wall.

"Where is he?" I asked, and the Captain waded through the guys gathered around and sighed.

"We are breaking so many rules, right now. He's in the showers; we'll stay out here. Don't rat us out to the brass, girly."

"I would never," I said, and took off my jacket, laying it and my purse over the back of his motorcycle seat. One of the guys held a tiny kitten, rubbing over its head with his thumb.

"What happened?" I asked, frowning at the sight. Something was totally off about how somber everyone was being, and how reverent they were towards the little tabby kitten with white feet. Angel answered me.

"Little girl," he said with a sniff. "Maybe five or six. Kitten lived, she didn't. Backdraft was the one to pull them out."

I felt my shoulders drop at the unfairness of it, and my eyes drifted back to the tiny cat.

"What are you going to do with him?" I asked.

"Seems to me he'd make a good mouser. We've been in need of a good housecat," the Captain said and smiles broke out among the crew. I nodded. Jaspar and Marigold would have been pissed, but I would have taken him if they said he was going to a shelter. Poor tiny thing.

I turned to the locker-room doors and squared my shoulders, unsure of what I would find inside, scared that maybe they were putting entirely too much faith in me. At the same time, any and all embarrassment had fled in the face of knowing Backdraft was in pain and that I needed to try and fix what I could of it, even though I might be a majority of the root cause of it.

Sorrow welled fresh out of the laceration on my soul that the media shitstorm the lies of Backdraft's ex had inflicted. While Mark wasn't precisely a liar about our relationship, he was totally lying about the mechanics of it. I hadn't known about her. I hadn't even suspected. *God what a mess.*

I took a deep breath at the locker-room door, and let it out slow before pushing the door open and stepping inside. Steamy vapor hung low on the air, and through it I could see his muscled back. The shower was going full blast, but he wasn't really using it. Instead, his forehead was pressed to the tile and his massive shoulders shook. Every line of his body echoed the overwhelming weight of that little girl's death bearing down on those shoulders, and tears immediately sprang to my eyes.

I didn't stop to think, I didn't care about my clothes or the water, or anything but doing something, anything at all, to make it even just a little bit better. I went to him and wrapped my arms around him, hugging myself to his back as the water from the shower soaked through my sweater and I cried with him. I couldn't not.

He jerked, startled, and, realizing who it was, settled again, one of his massive hands engulfing both of mine over his stomach as he tried to pull it all together.

"Don't," I said. "You don't have to. Not with me, not ever."

I felt the tension in him leak out and he turned in the circle of my arms and looked down at me, the water hitting his back, dripping off his nose, hiding his tears, but for the redness around his eyes which could have just as easily been from the smoke. The acrid smell of it hung on the steam and clung to the back of my throat.

"I missed you," he said, his voice unsteady. "It'd only been a couple of days but..."

"I missed you, too, Backdraft, but I – I'm not good for you," I said, unhappily.

"Bullshit," he said harshly. "You're everything I need, and this proves it."

His mouth crushed down over mine and I honestly couldn't resist him even if I wanted to, which – I didn't. I fell gratefully into his kiss and let him pick me up, his arms around me in a tight hug, my arms around him like I could never let him go, either.

I don't remember my clothes coming off, but they did, flung into a soggy heap near the entrance to the showers. He backed me up against the cool tile wall but I couldn't care. I needed something to quench the fire in my blood and the cool tile and warm water were helping. What I really needed was Backdraft inside of me, though.

Our mouths locked in desperation as he held me aloft. We weren't quite lining up, with our height disparity, and to do so we would lose our ability to kiss as easily as this, but I didn't care. I didn't care about anything but having this man inside me. I was fevered and flushed and he was pretty much the only cure I could think of. He lowered me enough and slid his cock along the lips of my sex and I moaned, writhing against him, drawing in a sharp breath when the head of his dick penetrated me, slipping just inside. I groaned and he eased all the way in, hitching me up, shaking with the effort before pressing me back into the wall and thrusting up into me with a satisfied grunt.

It was the first time we fucked rather than made love and I think it was precisely what we needed in that moment. With every hard thrust, he grunted and I panted. The illicitness of it seemed to work out some of our mutual frustrations at the current circumstances we found ourselves in that were wholly beyond our control. At least, it did for me. I didn't know if it was helping him at all, but I certainly hoped it was.

He bowed his forehead to mine and squeezed his eyes shut, just concentrating on the feel of me and I ran my fingers through his hair, slicking it back from his forehead, thin runnels of gray water seeping from it and running down his face. He hadn't really scrubbed clean from the fire and my heart broke for him all over again.

I tipped my head back and gasped, overcome by the feel of him running over that spot inside me, the heavy weight of orgasm taking up residence low in my body, just waiting to drop and take me plummeting with it. I held off, tried to make this last, wishing that I could stay like this forever, but alas... all good things must come to an end, right?

I loved how in tune with my body he was. He knew just as surely as I did how close I was and when I tightened around him, he moaned and said, "That's it, baby, come on," as he eased his way in and out of me, expending the effort to keep the pace that'd brought me to the brink in the first place. I pressed my mouth to his skin and bit gently but firmly as my last vestiges of control were ripped away and I was sent hurtling out into the ether. I was vaguely aware of him making a triumphant noise, before burying himself into me completely.

"Hold onto me, baby. That's it. Hang on tight."

I clung to him, locking my legs around his lean hips as he carefully lowered us both to the shower floor, sitting with me in his lap as the water beat down on us both. He laughed slightly and I smiled at how he seemed lighter, whatever weight of sadness he'd borne when I'd arrived lessened, but not completely gone.

He brought my forehead to his as we panted in the shower spray, and closed his eyes, like he was silently communing with me, absorbing my essence as if it would be the last time for a long time that he would be in my presence.

I instantly felt guilty. I'd walked away from him, disappeared. I always did that when I was wounded or hurt. I locked myself away to internalize it all and suffer alone and in silence because that was the way things should be. You didn't share your problems. You didn't spread your misery around to poison the lives of the ones you loved. You handled your shit. On your own. Like an adult. Right?

"I'm gonna fix this, babe. I'm gonna fix it, I promise you," he panted against my skin and I leaned back, capturing his face between my hands.

"There's nothing for you to fix, Backdraft. These are my problems, this is my mess, and I need to clean it up. Not you. I'm just so sorry you were dragged into it."

"No way baby, this is our mess and I'll help deal with it. You aren't doing it all alone anymore. I'm here now, and I'm not going anywhere."

I felt my shoulders drop under the weight of what he was consigning himself to and I couldn't let him do it. The urge to protect him and nurture him entirely too strong.

I felt my expression fracture and shatter into lines of pain. I couldn't stop it. I just hurt so badly for the both of us and I needed to put a stop to his crazy talk.

"I don't want to fight about this," I whispered, scratching my nails gently along his scalp as I smoothed back his hair. He closed his eyes and melted a little under that touch and I smiled faintly, loving that I could bring him even a tiny amount of peace while the storm raged all around us.

"Then don't fight me," he said pointedly, opening his eyes and fixing me with a somber stare.

I shook my head and sighed.

"The PR firm is handling it. They've advised me to take a break. I shouldn't even be here but I couldn't stay away..." I closed my eyes as he took one of my hands and reverently kissed the palm.

"Let's get cleaned up and you some clothes, and talk about this with our clothes on?" he said and I smiled.

"I kind of like having the home-field advantage here," I said rolling my hips a little, even though he'd gone soft some time ago and he'd slipped out of me.

"Yeah, well, we know it can't last forever, I guess," he said and it held a bitter edge.

"I hate living there now." I blurted the confession unexpectedly, even to me, and some of the burden I carried lifted; the tightness in my chest loosening slightly.

"Ah, shit, yeah," he muttered and gathered me close. "I could literally kill a motherfucker for that." His words, though all bravado and we both knew it, were still comforting. There was nothing more violating than being photographed in your own bedroom by someone outside it. That was something I didn't think could or would happen to me, let alone on the forty-fourth floor. I mean, did no one believe in privacy anymore?

I clung to Backdraft and took the shelter he offered, knowing it was fleeting and that all too soon I would have to go back to reality. He got up, helping me up, and we showered for real with soap and shampoo. He bundled me up in a large towel and I wrapped my hair in a second. He dressed in a clean uniform from his locker, kissed me soundly, and took my wet clothing out of the room in search for something dry for me to put on.

I blushed furiously, knowing that I was bound for yet another walk of shame through his coworkers. Although, compared to the last one? This was going to be a cakewalk.

I sat hunched on the end of one of the benches in front of the locker banks outside of the showers and felt my anxiety rise the longer Backdraft was away from me. I was slightly frustrated but not surprised at how much I had grown to rely on him in such a short amount of time. My mother had pretty much raised me to be co-dependent and though I usually had a better handle on it than this, with recent events, I honestly just wanted to find a better adult, an adultier-adult than I was to just fix the situation.

That's why you hired lawyers and PR people, dipshit. I thought at myself savagely. I wasn't completely helpless, I just felt that way. I had reminded myself of this no less than a dozen times when Backdraft came back.

"Sorry about that," he said, setting a pile of clothes beside me.

"Took me a minute to find things that might actually fit you but I wanted to load your clothes into the dryer first. These are Angel's, but they're the closest thing we've got to fit you." I smiled and blushed a bit but he'd already propped one of my feet on his knee. He unrolled a ball of socks and I laughed. They were huge.

"These, unfortunately, are mine. Just going to have to deal."

"I don't mind," I said softly, in a bit of wonder, as he rolled one down on itself and slipped it over my toes and over my foot. He was actually kneeling, at my feet, dressing me. I shook my head to dispel some of that wonder and said, "You don't have to do that."

"I want to," he replied gruffly, and I could see it was somehow important to him, taking care of me right now, so I let it go. I mean, I knew I was perfectly capable of dressing myself, but this was really nice. I'd never had anyone do anything like this for me before.

He continued administering his sexy brand of care and I let him, confessing quietly, "You're really turning me on, right now." He laughed and it was genuine. The icy layer of bereft sadness cracked, some of it falling away. Somehow, despite how awful his night had started out, his heart was already on the mend.

I wished I could be half so remarkably resilient and vowed at some point, to try and learn his secret.

He didn't stop with the socks, either. He dressed the rest of me with the same level of care, occasionally pausing to press a light butterfly kiss to various points on my body, finding erogenous zones I didn't even know I had. Each time he elicited a reaction a tiny smile raised the corners of his mouth, as if he were carefully taking notes. I marveled at him in disbelief, that there could be a man as perfect, as heartfelt and soulful as one of the heroes in one of my books. Not only that he was real, but that he'd found me and wanted me, despite the awful cloud of bad luck that seemed to follow me.

"Talk to me, baby," he murmured and I shot a look to the locker-room door. He sighed, nodding and said, "No one's listening. It's just you and me, and I need to know what's going on in that head of yours."

"Take me somewhere," I begged quietly. "Somewhere where it's just you and me and no one else." I hated how it sounded like I was pleading, like I was begging for something unfathomable.

"Captain is going to send me home anyways. A guy has a rough call like that, this close to the end of his tour, it ain't no thing to do it. I have plenty of time-off built up to cover a few hours. Let me grab your clothes in a bag and we can get out of here."

"You're sure?" I asked, barely wanting to breathe.

"I'm sure. I think you need me as much as I need you right now."

I nodded and he slipped back out, only this time, it was with my hand in his and me following. I wasn't about to let him face anything else alone tonight. I mean, I'd come here to comfort him and instead, here he was taking care of me... *or maybe you're doing something new. You know, like acting as one half of a healthy relationship. Maybe you're taking care of each other.*

Wasn't that a thought?

I called Veronica and told her I was going somewhere with Back-draft while he talked with his Captain and a few of the guys. She was on the fence and I felt instantly bad about putting her in such a precarious position.

"On the one hand," she said with a long-suffering sigh, "I'm glad you guys are doing you, and getting some time together."

"On the other?" I asked, slightly amused, knowing what she was going to say.

"Don't get caught by the media, please?"

"I'll try not to."

"Where are you going?"

"His place, I think. Lord knows, I really don't want to be in mine."

"I hear that. Good lord, the only place I feel safe changing is in the bathroom, now." She sounded as creeped-out as I felt, and I sighed.

"I hear you. I want you to put the condo up for sale."

"You're sure?" she asked, stunned.

"I have had nothing but rotten luck since moving into that obsidian tower." I shivered. "I'm sure, and no, I don't know where I want to go. Maybe something subterranean like a hobbit hole or something."

She laughed. "You need windows," she said flatly.

"You're right, I do, with lots of light."

"Come to New York," she begged, and I stared from where I leaned against one of the trucks up into the loft where Backdraft talked with the rest of his crew.

I shook my head, realized she couldn't see it, and said to her, "Indigo City is my home now, and I won't be run out of it completely. Besides, New York is great for a visit, but would drive me even more nuts than I already am."

"You're not as crazy as you think you are," she said softly. My personal assistant was gone, my best friend was in residence. "You've just been through a lot. I don't think anyone would be taking any of this well."

"Feed Jaspar and Marigold for me?"

"Do you one better, I'll give them lots of love from their momma."

"Thanks."

"No problem, you be careful."

"I will."

"Bye."

"Bye."

I ended the call and when I looked back up, Backdraft was gone and there were a whole bunch of curious and sympathetic stares in my direction. I felt my face flush, but the loud sound of boots hitting concrete made me jump. I turned and Backdraft was striding in my direction from the brass fire-pole.

"Ready to go?" he asked and I nodded. I put on my jacket, and braced for a cold ride. A bunch of the guys came down and the garage doors started to go up.

"Hang on, they're going to run interference with the trucks and sirens," Backdraft said.

"They have a call?"

"Naw, grocery run."

"This late at night?"

"Welcome to the city, baby. Got twenty-four hour just about everything."

I huddled against his back and put my arms around his waist, trying to make myself as small and inconspicuous as possible. I winced as the lights and siren started on the rig nearest us, the blare of the horn going off as Backdraft started his bike. The trucks drowned out the sound of the bike starting up and when they turned out of the driveway we hid behind them and turned the opposite direction.

I realized, belatedly, that I'd actually never seen Backdraft's place and I had no idea where it was or what it was like. I smiled and held on, looking forward to seeing this new piece of his life.

He took several turns to get us going in the right direction and wove through city streets. It wasn't a very long ride, even with the added turns to get on the proper track. He pulled off to the side and signaled for me to jump down. I did and stood on the curb in front of a stretch of old brownstones as he backed the bike into a space between two cars just big enough to fit the bike and leave them ample room to get out without hurting it.

I'm not going to lie. I was really hoping that it was one of the old brownstones that he lived in, rather than the rundown, tired old apartment tenement across the street. He reached out and took my hand, the bag of my still-soggy clothes, that he'd pulled from one of his saddlebag storage-things on the bike, in his other one.

"Which one is it?" I asked and he grinned.

"Don't get too excited," he said. "It's that one up there." He pointed.

"You really live in an antique brownstone?" I asked.

"Yeah, restoring it myself, outside has a lot more curb appeal than the inside, babe. I'm almost embarrassed to bring you inside."

"Really? Why?"

"You'll see."

He stuck the key in the lock of the weathered front door and twisted. I wanted inside and off the sidewalk before we were caught, before we were seen and I am afraid I may have crowded him a little.

He depressed the latch and swung the door in and let me go through where I stopped.

"Oh, wow…"

It was like a literal bomb had gone off in here. Holes in the walls revealing the skeleton of the building, insulation dripping from them like ticking from a stuffed bear. There was no rhyme or reason to any of the wallpaper or paint that still clung to the walls and the wood floors were in dire need of sanding.

"Is that even legal?" I asked, but I couldn't help but smile. He followed my gaze toward the ceiling and the exposed electrical dribbling out of it where a light fixture used to be.

He laughed and said, "First story has no power running to it currently."

"How long has it been like this?" I asked, but my eyes were no longer seeing what was but rather what could be.

"I've owned it around two years, started on the third floor and am working my way down." His voice was soft, careful, and I dropped my eyes to his face.

"It has so much potential," I said. "What are you going to do with it?"

His smile broke out across his face and was so infectious I felt an answering one of my own blossom out of my awe at the place. He drew me closer by the hips and considered me a moment, his expression growing serious, the smile he had fading.

"I want you to do me a favor," he said.

"Of course," I murmured.

He stood aside and looked around and said, "I want you to tell me what you see for this place."

I swallowed hard and asked, "How do you mean?"

He swallowed hard and searched my face in the dark, but the streetlights shining through the windows was plenty to see by. I saw him lose his nerve and I didn't want that. I didn't want him to and I didn't want to second guess everything. I wouldn't. I mentally punched my mother and the way she raised me in the face and grabbed onto the moment with both hands, clinging to it for dear life.

I put a hand on his chest and asked for him, "You mean if I were to live here? Like, our future together?"

He smiled and it was different. So timid and shy for him and I realized just how precarious we were, how fragile this moment was and I ached so fiercely. Like we were back to being 'just friends' when I honestly hated it. I didn't want 'just friends'. I wanted him and a chance to explore a life with him and what that would be like. I didn't want these assholes or my neurotic mess of anxiety to win, and so I sighed and put my imagination to good use.

"Give me the tour, let me see the whole thing."

"Bottom to top?" he asked.

"Yeah."

He took my hand and led me gently up the hall to a door and opened it: the stairs leading down to the basement. I smiled and he took out his phone and used the flashlight function. I went down the stairs to the first landing and looked out over the wide-open space down here. He went all the way down to a nook behind the stairs and I heard him open a dryer. I drifted down all the way, until my boots settled on the gritty concrete of the basement floor.

"Man-cave," I said and he laughed.

"Seriously?"

"Oh, for sure! A bar over there, a pool table over there with the red felt, not green, and a big-screen TV for all the sportsball your manly hearts could desire."

He straightened and twisted the knob on the dryer and hit the button. It started to tumble and he came back to me, drawing me back against his chest.

"What do you think?" he asked, looking up at the ceiling. "Finish the beams or just drywall it?"

"Mm-mm, neither! What about pressed tin or copper? Like the old-time saloons?"

"Expensive shit," he said.

"Not if you know where to look, and plus, if we're pretending that I'm doing this with you, money isn't exactly an object. I've invested carefully. Even if my career goes down like the Hindenburg at this point, I could sustain us beyond these remodels. Plus, I was making fairly decent money as a transcriptionist in the medical field before I turned full-time author."

"I never knew what you did," he said thoughtfully. "You know, before Timber." I sighed and leaned back into him, holding his arms around me.

"There's still so much we don't know about each other," I said unhappily.

He kissed the top of my head and whispered into my hair, "Got nothing but time, babes. That's the only remedy for that."

I twisted in the circle of his arms and looked up into his face, searching it. All I could find was love and commitment there, and I would be damned if I would let my fear of pain, for him or for me, torpedo this before it got started.

"I am so scared for you," I confessed and he touched the side of my face.

"Now, we're getting somewhere," he murmured.

I bit my lips together and rolled them out, smoothing them against each other and came clean.

"I'm terrified, actually, that something like this or even worse than this is going to happen and you'll be so hurt or get so sick of me and leave." I couldn't look him in the eyes. It was too hard when I was baring the darkest fears and parts of my soul. Everyone disappointed you or left eventually; I'd grown up abandoned by anyone and everyone that made a difference to me – my father, my grandparents, my own mother. I was naturally skittish from a childhood filled with false constructs of relationships, paper thin, yet so starved for love it was all I could seem to find as an adult – more of the same.

Until now. I felt it down to the very bottom of my heart that this, with Backdraft, was something different. The old myths of soulmates, that I'd made so much money writing about, were suddenly very real. I didn't want to let go of that.

He gently touched the side of my face, the light from his phone's flashlight illuminating things from where he'd rested it on the banister around the little landing. I looked up into his eyes which were just dark down here, the light leeching all the color away from them. Still, the one thing that it couldn't take or steal was the sentiment in them. The resolve he looked at me with made more of my insecurities fall away.

"I told you. I'm not going anywhere, Lil. You don't find this shit every day, babe, and I know it's moving at warp speed, but none of what is happening to us makes me feel any less about you. Makes me feel a whole lot less about the world in general, but I still love you, and I still want a shot with you. I'm not letting those assholes take that away."

"You really think that, don't you?" I asked, my voice faint with wonder.

"What?" he asked.

"Us. That this is happening to us. Not you or me, but us."

"Damn straight."

He smoothed a thumb back and forth along my cheek and I closed my eyes and swore, "Fuck." He burst out laughing.

"What?" I demanded, but I was smiling, too. I couldn't help it. His laugh had that effect on me.

"I've never heard you swear so hardcore before!"

"Shut up!" I said laughing, smacking him lightly in the arm. "I swear!"

"Yeah, okay, sure," he said getting it together. "What was that for?"

I sighed and told the truth, "This whole time, the last few days, I've been taking this all on myself. Like it's all me. My fault, my problem, 'my'. 'My.' 'MY.' When it's not. I've been shutting you out, and I feel really bad about it now."

"Don't," he said leaning back to look at me. "You've been all alone, on your own, for a real long time, Lil. That's a tough habit to break. This is all still real new."

"I don't deserve you," I breathed and he frowned.

"Stop that, you're long overdue for someone to take care of you instead of the other way around, babe. Now I'm here to do that, so relax for me, okay?"

I pressed my lips together and nodded, the tension easing from my body. I thought to myself, *Dear god, I need therapy,* and made a mental note that maybe that wasn't such a bad idea, that maybe I needed to look into getting some.

"Show me the rest of the house," I murmured, and he grinned and nodded.

The second floor was still as much a disaster as the basement and first floor, but the third floor was like stepping into another world.

"Oh, my god, this is beautiful!" I said and he flipped on a light. The classic light fixture hanging from the high ceiling cast a warm golden glow over the room. It was spartanly furnished, just a bed and tired old dresser but everything else looked smooth, polished, and brand new.

"You like it?" he asked, and I turned in wonder.

"You did this all yourself?"

"Yeah, had some help here and there from a bunch of the guys."

"Fire or Indigo Knights?" I asked.

He smiled and said, "Both."

"They did you proud," I said softly.

There was a fireplace up here, and the room was all white and full of light. Pristine in a modern yet classic sort of way.

The bathroom was huge; the tub, an old clawfoot; the shower, glassed-in and modern, with a dual his-and-hers sinktop made of the same stone as the shower stall's tiles. The floors were a white marble or granite and reminded me of a white sand beach.

Still, the bedroom and bathroom both, while beautiful, looked mostly unused and unfinished somehow. I realized there was no art on the walls. Nothing personal. As if it were finished, and a beautiful house, but had yet to be made into a home.

"You need a bigger bed," I said softly and he grinned.

"I think your king would look better in here, don't you?"

I debated telling him I put the condo up for sale tonight but finally decided against it. Scared that it would seem like I was moving myself right in here, which wasn't what we were doing, I mean, right?

"I think you're right," I said, a little breathy when he moved back into my space and hooked his fingers into the hem of the borrowed

Indigo City Fire Dept. tee shirt I was wearing, lifting it up, over my head. I raised my arms and let him have it, saying, "I think this room needs a king."

"Hmm," he said, smiling, the sound a slight laugh, like he found me cute. I was okay with that, the whole 'him finding me cute'. He kissed me, his warm hands sliding against my skin and I closed my eyes, grateful that my mind was going into that pleasant, blank place of just feeling rather than thinking. By this point, I think I was thought-out, and yeah, even felt-out a little bit, mentally and emotionally wrung-out from this crazy yo-yo, this insane back-and-forth along my heart strings from everything. The media, his ex, Mark, the lawyers, the paparazzi, the readers and publishers, and movie producers, and, and, and, and, *and...*

It was too much, and I shoved it all away, off my mental desk and onto my mental floor so Backdraft could put me on it and give me the only fuck I cared about right now.

Bless him and his never-ending patience with me.

23

*B*ackdraft...

She slept like an angel and it gave me a funny feeling, watching her do it in my bed. I loved that she was here. I loved that she hadn't judged when she'd walked into the disaster that was my place. I'd gotten it dirt cheap as a foreclosure; I'd envisioned Torrid and I refurbishing and building it to our liking, but boy, had I misjudged that one. She'd been pissed. Too diva to even consider getting her hands dirty. I sighed, a heavy thing, and thought to myself, *But you thought you loooved her!* I hadn't known the meaning of the word until my eyes had met Lil's stormy ones.

I'd gotten her laundry out of the dryer, had folded it neatly, and put it on the dented metal folding chair I'd brought up from downstairs. She'd slept like the dead. So tired, mentally and emotionally, and who the fuck could blame her? People had gone fucking crazy over Torrid's bullshit and I couldn't say I was surprised. The bitch was first-class at one thing and one thing only: crazy-making.

I stared at Lil, sleeping peacefully, the weak sunlight from the overcast day filtering through the water-spotted bedroom window and falling across her face in neat lines from the blinds. I'd promised her last night that I was going to fix this shit and I meant it. She'd rejected the notion, sure, trying to keep me safe and take all the hits, but, fuck that. What kind of man would that make me, hiding behind my woman? I shook my head and bowed it, gripping the back of my neck and trying to rub out the tension in it.

The short answer to the question was *Not much of one* and I wasn't about to go down that road. I left a folded note on the vacant pillow and took myself quietly back downstairs and out the front door. The paparazzi motherfuckers were across the street, shouting their questions at me. I gave them the finger and got on my bike, sticking the key in the ignition and giving it a twist, thumbing the ignition switch.

She started up like a dream and I smiled, flashing back to last night and the same thumb on Lil's clit as she rode me in my bed and how it'd elicited the very same reaction. Which did I like better? The curves of her body or the curves on my bike? It was a tough call, which told me this was true love. The fact I would even have a hard time between the two told me that what was up with Lil was the real fuckin' deal. I laughed at myself and carefully pulled out onto the street.

I took myself across the city to a different station house than mine and parked off to the side, out front. I would only be a few minutes. When I went inside, I was met at the door by some of the guys, one of them saying, "Look, man, we all know you got a beef, and with good reason, but not in the house, okay?"

I put up my hands in surrender and smiled a crooked 'suck my dick' sort of grin and said, "I'm here to make peace, not war, guys. Ackley on shift?"

"No, you just missed him. It's his day off."

"Could you call him up for me? It's important."

They exchanged a look and one of them shrugged, asking, "Where you want to have him meet ya?"

Good question. I thought about it a second and said, "Neutral ground, the 10-13?"

"Not sure that'd be classified as 'neutral', bro."

"Fine, fine," I grumbled. Fair enough, though. "How about the coffee house across from the courthouse?"

"We'll tell him. When?"

"Now," I said. "I'm headed that way."

The guys nodded and one asked, "What's the deal?"

I laid it out for them and they exchanged a look and nodded, indicating they'd let him off the hook if he went through with it. That's what I wanted. He and I would probably never be good, but this would definitely make things better.

I went to the coffee place Aly worked at and found a table. She looked up from behind the counter and I remembered, it was Friday, so of course, she'd be here. I sighed when her shoulders dropped and empathy flickered across her face. She knew Torrid, and she knew it was all a load of bullshit. She came around and gave me a hug, leaning back to look me over.

"How is she?" she asked and I smiled.

"Sleeping."

She raised her eyebrows and jerked her head over to a free table by the window. I sat and she sat across from me.

"So what are you doing here, instead of there?" she asked gently.

"Tryin' to fix this shit, once and for all."

"How?" she asked, her brow wrinkling.

"We'll see. He's should be coming any minute," I said, eyeing the text that'd just come through from the guys in his house.

"Two coffees?" she asked.

"Yes, please."

"I'm glad she's got you," Aly said. "If you've ever read her books or any of her blog posts, you'd know she's led a pretty lonely life."

"I actually have read a couple of her books, but thanks for the pro-tip about her blogs and that. Of course, I think we're in a place now that I could just ask." I gave Aly a wink, and she blushed to the roots of her dyed blonde hair.

"We can't all be so lucky," she muttered and I laughed.

"Better get used to her being around, number-one-fangirl," I called after her she rolled her eyes.

"Please, I'm number-two-fangirl. Over half of what I know about her I learned from Dawnie. She has cyber-fangirl-stalking down to an art form."

I laughed and looked at my hands which I had folded on the tiny round table top. I actually wished I'd had one of her books to read right now while I waited. It was like I could hear her when I read her words and it'd been a nice way of having Lil with me even when I couldn't be with her.

Aly set down two coffees in front of me just as the door popped open against the bell dangling above it and Ackley stepped through. He kind of froze up at the icy look of contempt on my face, but I had to give the man props. He didn't tuck tail and run. Instead, he pulled out the chair across from me and sat down.

"So what's the deal?" he asked, without preamble.

Oh yeah, he'd give just about anything to get back in the department's good graces.

"You go on TV with me and tell the fuckin' truth."

He stopped, his eyes gone wide and said, "You're shitting me, right?"

"Either that, or you can always be watching your back by your damn self."

"Fuck me," he muttered and bowed his head and shook it. He thought about it and looked back up at me, skeptical-like.

"You're serious?"

"As a heart attack."

"I never in a million years thought that bitch was that crazy, man."

"Well, you know what they say," I said, with a blasé shrug that I totally didn't feel.

"Don't stick your dick in crazy?" he asked, squirming in his seat.

"Or, you know, one of your bro's women, but yeah. That would be the one."

"What's your excuse, then?" he asked, trying to lighten the mood. I gave him a flat, cold look and he put up his hands in surrender.

"Okay, okay... How long is the offer good for?"

"Ten more seconds," I said, giving no quarter.

"And if I do this, we're good?"

"I wouldn't say 'good'," I said. "But yeah, we're as close to it as we're gonna be, which is a hell of a lot better than where we're at right now."

He nodded slowly in that way that said he was still half-thinking and yet was halfway on the hook. I jerked on the pole and started reeling.

"Two more seconds."

"All right, all right, I'm in. When and where?"

"Gimme your number, and you better not call her or screw me on this."

"Call her? Hell, motherfucking no! She's batshit fucking crazy with this shit."

"Who you tellin'? Gimme your number."

He gave it to me and looked down at the cup of coffee asking, "Is this for me?" I gave a curt nod and he sighed. "This new girl of yours, the author, she doing okay?"

"That's really none of your business," I said and he nodded, picking up his cup and sipping. My anger was quickly cooling, but he didn't need to know that.

"What Torrid did, that wasn't right," he said. "Is any of the rest of it true, though? About her and that other guy?"

I told him and his eyebrows went up. He shook his head in disbelief. "Shit," he said and sighed. "Sounds like Tori and this Mark guy are cut from the same cloth and totally made for each other."

I barked a bitter laugh and said, "Wouldn't that be some fuckin' Karma?"

Ackley smiled and nodded, "Yeah, it sure would."

We finished our coffee in silence, but the peace accord had been made. He still needed to follow through, though, before I put the word out over the wire to the rest of the guys. I wasn't born last night and I didn't trust him or anyone attached to Torrid as far as I could throw them.

Phase one complete. I thought. *Now for phase two.*

24

$\mathcal{L}$illi...

I woke up alone in Backdraft's bed and sucked in a breath. I pushed myself into a sitting position and rubbed the sleep out of my eyes, and when I put my hands back down to the mattress to prop myself up, one of them came down on a piece of paper that had slipped off his pillow. Only two words were written on it but they were two of the most important words that had ever been imparted to me...

Us.
Always.

I CLOSED my eyes and pressed the page to my chest, closing my eyes and sighing. My phone started buzzing on top of my clothes, which were on a metal chair by the bed. I reached over and snatched it up, answering it immediately.

"Where are you?" Veronica asked immediately.

"Backdraft's," I said.

"Where is he?" she asked.

"Not here, I woke up by myself."

"Ooookay." She drew out the word slowly, and my heart seized with dread. "Can you get a car back here?" she asked.

"Yeah, why, what's up?" I swallowed past the lump in my throat and thought to myself, Oh *god, now what?*

"Tell you when you get here, just hurry, okay?"

"Sure, um, what's going on?"

"Nothing bad, I promise."

My chest loosened and my phone beeped, that low tone of a call waiting, in my ear. I looked and sighed, frustrated. I was going to ask her if it was nothing bad, then why couldn't she just tell me, but instead what came out was, "Veronica, that's Backdraft. I'll be home as soon as I can."

"Try and get out without being seen?" she asked.

"Yeah."

"Okay, bye."

I accepted the waiting call.

"Where are you?" I asked.

"Had to draw the paparazzi away. They saw me leave, they should be gone if you can go check."

"Yeah, hold on, I need to get dressed. I'm going to put you on speaker."

I put him on speaker and got out of bed, deliciously sore from the night before. I worked on getting dressed, pulling on my jeans once I had my underwear in place.

"Veronica wants me home, like, right now; I don't know what it is."

"I called in some favors; it's nothing bad, I promise."

"Why can't you guys just tell me what it is, then?" I asked impatiently.

"What, and ruin the surprise?" he asked, and I was glad one of us was back to our old selves. I couldn't help but smile ruefully, though.

"I think I've had enough surprises this week, thank you very much."

"Lil. You trust me?" he asked and I paused.

"Of course, I do. Why would you ask me that?"

"I just need to know."

"What are you doing?" I asked.

"Want to give you some plausible deniability when it comes to your business, babe."

"Okay, now I'm really worried," I said, tossing my sweater over my head.

"So, you don't trust me, then?"

"Backdraft, that's not fair."

"Okay, you're right," he said with a gusty sigh. "Let's just say Tori's fighting dirty and I'm fighting fire with fire." I swallowed hard.

"And you don't want to tell me because it may, or may not, piss off my PR firm, publisher, producers and what have you, and if it does, you know I'm Miss Goody Two-shoes and I'd sing like a canary."

"Pretty much, babe, yeah." He was laughing now, but I didn't mind. The sound raised my spirits and put my heart a little at ease. His laugh had that effect on me.

"You vastly overestimate my goodwill when it comes to them," I said. "But thank you for thinking of all of that."

"What you don't know won't hurt you. Just trying to spare you from having to lie."

He had a point. If I didn't know, then they couldn't get it out of me and I had no way of getting in any kind of trouble. So I guess the question was, did I trust him?

Answer? *Yes.*

"I love you," I said.

I heard his smile through the phone, "I love you, too."

I pulled on my last boot, swung into my jacket and picked up the phone off the bed, turning off speaker.

"I'm headed downstairs now; I need to call for a car to come get me."

"Text you my address. I'll talk to you soon, babe."

"Okay, I'll make sure security knows that you aren't someone I consider a guest so much as a necessity. I'm sorry they denied you entry."

"I'm sorry I threw a tantrum and busted my phone."

I laughed and said, "You had a good reason. I'm sorry for thinking you didn't care and for the thing with security."

"You had a good reason, too, babe. You had a good reason, too."

"Okay, I'll talk to you later."

"Okay, bye."

"Bye."

I sighed and felt edgy and nervous. He texted his address and I texted the car service. I went to put my phone in my jacket pocket and came out with a set of unfamiliar keys. I frowned and then it dawned on me – they were for his brownstone. He'd given me the keys to his place.

I clattered down the stairs and went to the front window, peeking out the ripped edge of the paper he had covering them from the inside. I let out a relieved breath. The coast was clear. The paparazzi had cleared out.

Thank god.

I watched for the car to pull up and bolted for it, after locking up.

"Antonio, hi,"

My familiar driver said, "Hi, Ms. Banks, how are you doing?"

I gave a shaky laugh and told him the truth. "I've been better, Antonio. I've been better."

"Yeah, it's a real shame what they been saying about you on the TV. Breaks my heart, actually. You're such a nice lady."

"Thanks," I said softly. "That actually means a lot."

"Anytime, Ms. Banks. Any time."

The rest of the ride went by in a blessedly tranquil silence and, without being asked, Antonio pulled down into the garage for me so I didn't have to get out in front of the cameras. I tipped him handsomely and he tried to give it back. I insisted, he thanked me, but before he could get out and get my door, I got it for myself. I went up the garage elevator to the lobby and then took the elevator up to my floor.

When I let myself in to my apartment, Veronica was waiting, serving tea to two unexpected guests, one of them familiar, the other, new to me.

"Yale," I said, shutting the door behind me. "What are you doing here?"

He gave a tight-lipped smile and bowed his head. His lips continued to twitch with amusement when he said, "Ah, not today I'm afraid, Ms. Banks. Today I'm here in an official capacity. Please, call me Mr. Parnell."

I eased across the polished wood of my floor and said, "Official capacity?"

"Yes, I need to take your statement."

"About what?" I asked.

The woman with him arched one dark brow and said, "Ms. Banks, I'm Christina Marie Franco, a prosecuting attorney with the Indigo City District Attorney's office. Mr. Parnell agreed to accompany me as a courtesy, but your case is actually my case."

"I don't understand."

"Lilli, come sit," Veronica said. "Listen to what they have to say, they're here to help." My assistant and best friend pulled out a chair for me and I drifted over to it, hanging my jacket and purse off the back. The two attorneys sat across from me and Veronica took a seat beside me.

"Mr. Parnell, Ms. Franco, if you're worried about saying anything in front of Veronica here, because she's my employee, don't be. She's also my best friend and I'd really prefer if we could all skip being so stiff and so formal in front of each other. It's really not necessary."

Everyone exchanged a look and visibly relaxed which made me feel ten times better.

"Let me just start by saying, believe me, Ms. Banks, I know precisely what you're going through."

"It's Lilli or Lil, and you do?" I asked, and searched both hers and Yale's faces.

"I do. I went through something similar just last year."

That's when things clicked, "Oh, you're –that– Chrissy, and you're here about the pictures, aren't you?"

She smiled and bypassed the shortened version of her name and said: "The drone footage, yes."

I paled. "Footage?"

"Yes, Lil, footage. Those were stills from a video," Veronica said, and I closed my eyes.

"Well," I said, leaning back in my chair. "I guess I should be fine with it, I mean, I'm a porn author after all, am I right?" I asked bitterly. I wasn't, but there were a lot of people out there that didn't see a distinction between romance novels and pornography. It all depended on your level of prude.

"May I ask why you didn't contact law enforcement when you were made aware of the images when they aired on..." Christina trailed off and flipped through some notes on her legal pad, "*Celebrity Beat*, this last Monday?"

"I didn't even think about it being illegal, Lil. I should have, I'm sorry." Veronica said quickly. I shook my head.

"No, it's all right. I didn't either, to be honest. I just passed it to my civil attorneys." I sat in silence for a moment and said, "Wow, revenge porn. I guess she got way more than she bargained for out of selling her lies to that gossip rag."

Yale sat up straighter and exchanged a look with Christina. "What did you say?" Yale asked.

I shrugged and said, "It was Backdraft's ex-girlfriend, some woman named Tori, goes by the name Torrid. She lied and told *Celebrity Beat* that Backdraft was cheating on her with me. She's the reason, I think, that that footage even exists. Isn't that almost the definition of revenge porn? Just because it was a woman doing it to a man doesn't make it any less so."

He looked impressed and jotted things down on his legal pad. Christina took up the line of questioning.

"Where was the footage taken? What hotel?"

I looked at her and frowned, drawing my head back in confusion. "It's not a hotel; that was my bedroom."

"Excuse me, what?" Yale demanded, and I could tell he was totally out of the loop and not happy about it.

"Yeah, come with me." I stood and they stood with me, I took them down the hall and into my bedroom. Yale looked a deeply-dark level of pissed-off I don't think I had ever seen on someone before.

"I don't even know who took it, the footage I mean." I said unhappily. "But yeah, it happened here. From the angle of the pictures, likely from out that window." I pointed up and out the window and said, "I didn't think I needed blinds on the forty-fourth floor; didn't think anyone would be looking, or even be able to look, way up here. I never even thought someone would be so depraved as to use a drone, but that's the only way they could have done it."

"What do you think, Damien?" Christina asked softly.

"I think this sucks," he said. "Celebrity Beat isn't going to give up the source of the images willingly but they can be forced to. It won't be fast, and your civil attorneys have a better position to work from than we do."

"Can I just ask?" They both looked my way. "Did Backdraft call you?"

They both exchanged a look and smiled, "We are here in an official capacity after receiving a call from a concerned citizen who saw the *Celebrity Beat* segment. Due to your celebrity status and the delicate nature of the images that were displayed on the show, we thought it best that the DA's office pay you a visit personally," Yale said and I nodded and waved him off. He laughed slightly and said, "Actually, Aly's been bugging me about it since she saw it. I just couldn't do anything until someone called me in. Backdraft did just that around an hour ago. It's been a big game of telephone. I didn't see the segment myself, I've just gotten hearsay from Aly."

"Okay," I gave a solid nod, because fighting back in any capacity felt a lot better than sitting around sullen and silent doing nothing. "What do you need from me?"

"First, we would like to know if you're okay," Chrissy said.

"I'm not, really," I said with a nervous laugh. "It was, and still is, pretty violating. I can't stay here, too much bad blood, too many bad things in too short of an amount of time. I'm selling it."

"I'll be drawing up some restraining orders and an order of protection," Yale said. "Any of those paparazzi out there get out of line, you call me and we'll put their name on them. I'll save the order of protection for Torrid. Backdraft is right: she didn't get what she wanted out of this, which was a reaction from you guys. Your keeping quiet is probably driving her up a wall, which is a bad thing when it comes to her."

"How illegal is what this person did? You know, whoever took the video." I asked.

"Well, we're going to have to do some digging. At the very least, depending on who was operating the drone at the time, they could face a charge of voyeurism in the second degree, which is, sadly, just a gross misdemeanor punishable by some jail time that's not nearly enough for something like this, and a fine anywhere between five hundred and a thousand dollars," Yale said.

"That doesn't include what your lawyers are going to do to them," Veronica said.

"She's right," Chrissy said. "If we secure a conviction or even a guilty plea, even if they don't serve any, or just minimal, time, your civil attorneys will have them dead to rights. Financially, you could ruin them for life."

I felt my shoulders drop and looked out my bedroom window, up past the platform my bed was on, at the swatch of overcast sky where the drone must have been.

"Ruining someone's life financially isn't going to give me my dignity or sense of security back," I said honestly.

"Trust me, I know," Chrissy said softly. I exchanged a look with her and we both heaved a heavy sigh at the same time.

"Why just a misdemeanor?" Veronica asked, and I knew it was because she wasn't nearly as nice as I was, deep down inside.

Yale nodded, his hands stuffed into his slacks pockets. "Truth is, the laws just haven't, and won't any time soon, catch up to technology like this."

"It sucks, but it's true," Chrissy said. "There was some seriously fancy lawyering that had to happen when it came to my case which was mostly cyberstalking and using the media like a weapon."

"I can't even imagine," I said.

"Trust me, you wouldn't want to," Chrissy said flatly.

"Let's be real, here please?" I said. "What's the actual likelihood you can even catch who flew that thing? I mean, I know drones have to be registered, but there's no telling when or where they fly. I mean, it's not like it's something that can be tracked, right?"

"No, it's not," Yale said. "In fact, the more I think about it, the more I'm seeing that the only way that we're going to find out who took those photos and sold them to *Celebrity Beat* is through your lawyers. I would suggest making that information part of whatever settlement you are seeking."

"Okay," Veronica interposed carefully, as she searched my face. "Say I pass that little tidbit along to Timber's lawyers and they get the information. Why is it only a misdemeanor? Isn't there anything else you could charge them with?"

Chrissy sighed and gestured out into the hallway. I nodded and led everyone back up the hall to my dining room where we could retake our seats and, my hands shaking but needing to do something, anything, right now, I poured four cups of tea from my little teapot. I didn't really care if anyone drank them.

"Like Yale said, the laws surrounding situations like this are woefully inadequate to begin with," Chrissy said unhappily.

"Right," Yale agreed. "In order to stick a felony charge, we would have to prove the videographer's intent."

"His intent was to earn a buck, at the real cost of my humiliation," I said, frowning, and I felt my nose start to tingle in that familiar way that meant an ugly cry was coming. I didn't want to give in to it, so I tried my hardest to force it down.

"Right," Chrissy nodded. "And that's the problem. From a legal standpoint, the way the law is written, that's just a misdemeanor."

"If I may continue to be blunt?" Yale asked and I nodded. I actually preferred it because I could tell, for him, that 'blunt' really meant

'If I may continue telling you the un-sugarcoated version of the truth' which, in my line of work, was becoming harder and harder to come by. He went on.

"To be considered a felony, the person would have to be a stranger to you and the intent behind the video would have to be proven to be that he filmed it in order to get himself, or other people off."

"You're joking?" Veronica looked a mixture of angry and aghast. In fact, if she were a cat, her ears would have been plastered flat back to her skull. The image made me smile affectionately at my friend.

"I wish I were. If this had been filmed and released on a porn site rather than sold to the gossip show, this would be a whole different set of charges with higher stakes."

I'm pretty sure it looked like I had sucked a lemon when I said, "Doesn't matter, though. The same end result was achieved either way."

Chrissy's face crumbled into lines of sympathy and I remembered what Backdraft had said to me. That Chrissy's best friend had died and that she'd been shot during her situation. I had the brief thought that things would be so much easier if Backdraft's crazy ex-girlfriend had tried to kill me, instead.

"Look, I know it's bad news from a criminally-legal standpoint, but there's a reason for that," Yale said and I looked him in the eyes. His jaw tightened and I could tell I really wasn't going to like what he was going to say as much as he wasn't going to enjoy saying it.

"Just say it," I said.

"The law, as written, is classist as hell. It's mostly inadequate, in my opinion, because people like us, with money, don't really need criminal charges to even the scales. As a civil matter, you pretty much have everyone over a barrel here. Your lawyers are more than welcome to use my office as leverage. Even saying that the Indigo City District Attorney's Office is looking into this might be enough to shake-down a settlement in a civil suit."

"That's great for me," I said bitterly, "but what about when this happens to someone without money? Something like this to an underprivileged or even a middle-class girl trying to get in to a good college?"

"Hence, why the law is classist. For a 'normal'," he used air quotes around 'normal', which only made sense to me, because most people didn't have the kind of money to burn on something like this, "person, there's little or no recourse."

I scrubbed my face with my hands and sighed, heavily.

"What about Backdraft, then?" I asked. "This happened to us, not just me. I mean, I believe he's added to the suit per my request, but at the end of the day, even if we win, where's the justice? The person really behind this is Torrid, not even Mark, really. I mean, he's complicit, but he never would have done this and outted himself on TV like that, without her somehow being involved. He was pretty much home free." The bitter bite of anger flooded my mouth and I realized something about myself as I sat there.

That people like Torrid, like Mark, were used to getting their way. That they were used to people like me, who were too nice, too forgiving, letting their bad behavior slide and that they counted on it. *Maybe I need to rethink some things, here.* I thought.

"The justice," Veronica said derisively, "Is when they can't get a car or an apartment because their credit is so bad from not paying the judgment against them in your case. The justice is in them having to think about what they did to you every time they sign their name on the check paying out to you, to get out from under the mountain of debt you drop on them."

"She's right," Yale said. "It would take years to pay off the court costs and whatever fines are levied against them."

"And they would have to think about that, about why they were in the predicament they were in, every single day, for as long as it took to crawl out from under it," Chrissy added. I raised a hand and nodded, indicating they'd made their points.

"In short," Yale said, "jail would honestly be shorter and easier."

I leaned back in my chair and sighed. I looked over at Veronica and said, "I know I'm too nice..."

She gave me a flat look and interrupted me saying, "Honey, you're a doormat. Let's be real."

I laughed, a genuine smile crossing my lips and nodded, "I am what my mother raised me to be," I agreed. "So, let's do this. You are not a doormat and you will do the right thing by me and the situation at hand, so you call the lawyers and give them the new information and marching orders accordingly."

"They're coming straight from you," she said.

"That's right. You know how this is played."

"I surely do. That's why I am absolutely indispensable to you," she said lightly and she was already halfway across my apartment to the door leading into my office.

Yale chuckled and Chrissy was smiling. I couldn't help but smile, too.

"Thank you for coming," I said and they exchanged another look and smiled wider.

"You're part of the Indigo Knights by proxy, now," Chrissy said.

"It's how we operate," Yale agreed. "We help each other where we can and keep it above legal board at all times."

"I like that," I said.

Yale gave a tight lipped smile and said, "Well, we like you. Those of us that have had the opportunity to meet you. Otherwise, we wouldn't be here."

I smiled and blushed under the sentiment murmuring and awkward, "Thank you."

"A piece of unsolicited advice?" Chrissy asked.

"Of course," I said.

"As someone who's sort of been there, with the media dogging my steps, don't play into their hands. Don't hide. Just go out and live your life accordingly and eventually, they'll get bored. You and Backdraft staying strong, staying solid as a couple, will do more to make this die down faster than anything. There's no scandal, no drama, and no story there. You go out and live your lives and your truths, and don't let these assholes stop you."

I sat and processed what she was saying for a moment, really thinking about it, and finally nodded.

"There's absolutely nothing normal about my life anymore," I said with a strange, nervous sort of laugh. I lost the battle with fighting back my tears and a couple got free. I wiped my eyes with my fingers and sniffed.

The looks of compassion from across the table leveled me and I struggled even harder not to just lose it and cry.

"I think you know that's not true," Yale said with a wry grin and I blushed a bit. I mean, he was right. Backdraft and what we shared was definitely a nice, normal, and the happiest thing, oh, my god... They got up, and I rose with them to see them out.

"When you're club, you're family," Chrissy said softly. "You need anything, even if it's just a girl's night, you just call. Backdraft knows how to reach everyone."

I nodded, "Thank you. Um, Yale, can I send you out of here with some things for Aly and Dawnie?"

He smiled and shook his head gently, "I'm afraid not. Considering I'm here in an official capacity, being seen leaving with any sort of gifts could be easily misconstrued."

"Oh, I didn't even think of that. I'm sorry."

"Don't be, it was the thought that counts and I appreciate it more than you could know."

"Tell you what," Chrissy said, flipping to a blank page on her legal pad. "Why don't I get all the girls together and you meet us at the 10-13 later this week? You just name a time."

"Um, how about the day after tomorrow, around eight?"

"Saturday at eight, it is," she said with a warm smile.

"Sounds good," Yale agreed.

I opened my front door and they stepped out into the hall.

"Thank you for coming, and thank you for trying," I said.

"Believe me," Chrissy said. "I wish we could do more."

"Agreed," Yale nodded, the look on his face one of frustration and futility.

"It's the thought that counts," I said using his own words. I smiled wanly and he nodded slowly.

"Ball is in your civil attorney's court," he said.

"I'll see what we can do."

"Keep us posted."

"I will."

They turned and went for the elevator and I closed my front door, letting out a harsh sigh. Veronica sighed behind me in echo, and I jumped.

"Sorry," she said. "Spoke to our lawyer's paralegal. They're on it."

"Thanks."

"Go get a shower," she suggested softly and I nodded.

"I could use one," I murmured, even though I was mostly clean from my shower at the firehouse the night before, I wanted the hot water to see if I could loosen up my muscles and my own shampoo and conditioner to get my hair under some control.

"I was really hoping there would be more they could do from a legal standpoint, you know?" she said, and I nodded.

"Me, too, but I'm not surprised. Welcome to my life and what I was accustomed to, before I fell face first into all this money."

Veronica's face fell and she lowered her arms from where she had them crossed over her stomach. She and I, despite having vastly different upbringings, still managed to work well together and were like two peas in a pod. Still, there were some things that her affluent upbringing didn't prepare her for and this, unfortunately, was one of them. There was a reason she hadn't thought to involve the police, and that was just as Yale had said it was. The rich were used to dealing with problems like this through civil attorneys and the private sector.

I guess it was a mark of how much I was changing that I hadn't thought to contact the police either. That, or, deep down, I knew it wouldn't have made a difference. There was a lot more gray area where the law was concerned than anyone really recognized.

"That wasn't a knock, by the way," I said, worried I may have hurt her feelings.

"Yeah, no, I know that, honey. I guess it was just kind of a shock. A sort of wake-up call that there are some vastly different realities out there between people."

"Welcome to the class system, still alive and well."

"Unfortunately," she muttered. She sighed and said, "Go get your shower. It's not perfect, but maybe if we try and face down some things that that still need to get done despite this sideshow, it will get you back into the groove of things."

I nodded and slow-walked my way to the bedroom; I didn't think I would ever see it the same way again.

25

*B*ackdraft...

"Thanks for trying, Yale," I said into my phone.

"Hey, it's no problem. I just wish that you had thought to call me sooner."

"It's been a fucked-up last few days, dude," I said, scraping a boot against the pavement.

"I hear that, but we're your brothers. We can't help if we don't know what's going on."

I laughed a self-deprecating little chuckle and said, "I am duly chastised."

"Yeah, well, Chrissy is getting together with your woman and mine on Saturday at the 10-13, just so you know."

"Yeah?"

"Yeah. Might be a good time to spill to your brothers what the plan is, you feel me?"

"Yeah, and right now, it's not much of a plan. I'm trying to get in touch with that *Celebrity Beat* show's main competitor."

"What the hell will that serve?" Yale asked.

"I got Ackley on board."

Silence on the other end of the line.

"Oh, you're more devious than I gave you credit for. I like it."

"Yeah, we'll see what shakes out."

"Good luck on that angle. I wish there was more that I could do," Yale said.

"What about the pictures?" I asked.

"You mean 'footage'. It was taken by drone and is pretty much a dead-end. *Celebrity Beat* isn't going to give up their source just for the asking. But they'll throw Tori under the bus fast enough if it comes to a libel or defamation suit."

"Shit. While that's good to know, it's going to take them a while, though." I leaned against my bike and huddled in my jacket as the wind ruffled my hair and tried to go down the back of my collar.

"Best thing you can do now is go back to Lil," he said. "Her lawyers are going to try and get the information as part of a settlement with *Celebrity Beat* but, you're right, that's going to take time. Maybe even years. By the time any sort of settlement is reached the statute of limitations could be out for any criminal charges," he sighed and it was a weary one. I knew the feeling.

"Well, that's balls," I said bitterly.

"She's put up her condo for sale and I can't say that I blame her," he said.

"She did what?" I asked, frowning, worried that she could move away from Indigo City, a flare-up of desperate panic going up in the center of my chest at the thought.

"Guess she hasn't had the chance to tell you."

"No, but you know what? That's not surprising. This week is going by at warp fucking speed. Feels like it's been a month since this shit went down."

"Well, as Oz likes to say, pump the brakes there, Turbo. Why don't you go see your lady and try and get some quiet quality time in?"

"I will, after I do this one thing."

"All right, man. See you on Saturday?"

"Yeah, I'll be there."

"Okay, take care. Call me if you need anything or think of anything else."

"I will, thanks for being there."

"It's a brotherhood, that's what we do."

I chuckled. "Too right."

I ended the call and shot a text to Lil's phone.

Me: You up for some company tonight?

I got on the front of my bike and was halfway through buckling my helmet on when a return text came through.

Lil: Depends, is it just you?

Me: Just me, babe.

Lil: Then when can you be here?

I smiled.

Me: On my way.

I went to start up when my phone started ringing in my pocket. I sighed and pulled it out and realized it was a number I didn't recognize, a New York number. I answered.

"Hello?"

"Mr. Calder?"

"Yes."

"This is Marion Adler, with *Your Stars Tonight*."

"You guys are fast," I said, flatly.

"You stated in your email you were interested in coming on the show."

I felt a feral grin cross my lips and said, "You're damn right I am."

"That's great, when can we set that up?" she asked.

"How about now?" I asked.

I got up off my bike and went back up the steps to my brownstone, letting myself back in, cursing my over-eagerness in the back of my mind. Lil was expecting me and I was going to be late, something I hated doing to her.

The conversation was shorter than I thought it would be, but still lasted longer than I would have liked. I'd sat on the edge of my bed, writing everything down and was sort of happy the show was springing for our airfare. I'd told them how this was going to go and told them basically 'Deal or no deal, choose'. I can't tell you how glad I was they didn't call my bluff and hang up on my ass right then and there. They'd heard me the rest of the way out and Marion was pretty much speechless by the end.

I guess our version of the story had the right amount of drama to it to make for some juicy ratings. The thought was enough to make bile rise in the back of my throat as I thought of poor Lil and everything she'd had to go through up to this point, which, let's face it, hurt her a hell of a lot more than it hurt me. I was used to Torrid's crazy and I should have seen it coming that she'd go completely off the deep end when I hooked up with someone new. I'd buried my head in the sand and had completely believed that we were done. Over. Never to return. That I would never see or hear from her skank ass again and that I could just get on with my life and that she'd get on with hers.

I should have known better. Nobody, and I mean nobody, told Torrid 'No' and got away with it. I'd seen her be crafty before. She always had a way of getting what she wanted, usually through manipulation or by pulling a fancy end-run around the situation. I guess I kind of figured she would come at me directly, show up at the firehouse like she had a thousand other times, screeching. I never thought she would go after me through Lil. That was a low blow but that's also what I get for expecting honor out of the honorless.

I went back downstairs and got on my bike, riding over to Lil's and pulling down into the garage. I pulled my ticket, parked in the motorcycle-only stalls they had provided, which I liked a lot, and went for the bank of elevators.

In the lobby, I approached the front desk with trepidation. I was afraid the last time I had tried to swing by, after busting my phone six ways to Sunday, I was more than a little hard on the security guys for just doing their job. Apparently when Lil had told, or had Veronica tell them 'No visitors', they took that as literally as possible and even excluded everyone on her pre-approved list.

I walked up, with my ID out, and said, "Hey, guys, here for Lillian Banks," and slid it across. "Also, I wanted to say I was sorry for being an asshole the last time I tore through." The guy at the desk raised his eyebrows in surprise, and I kind of laughed. "Not used to apologies?"

"Not around here, Mr. Calder," he said, keying some things into the computer in front of him. His eyebrows went up a second time.

"Okay, just a moment," he said, opening a drawer in a little cabinet built under the desk wrap in front of him. He let his fingers do the walking along a stack of little white envelopes that were suspiciously the perfect shape and size of the RFID cards used to get into the building. He pulled one out with my name on it, a dash, and forty-four-oh-three written beside it and slid it along the wrap in my direction.

"Thanks," I said, and he stopped me from taking a step back with, "Hold up, not done."

He pulled an apparatus out that looked like one of the pulse-ox monitors Angel used.

"Put your thumb on here, please?"

I obliged and he had me do it several more times, like you do for your phone's fingerprint scanner, then repeated the process on the other thumb.

"Okay, you're all set, sir," he said when the computer chimed at him that everything was accepted for the second thumbprint. He handed me back my license and said, "No need to stop at the desk anymore."

"Thanks," I said, still a bit taken aback.

Just because I'd given Lil a set of keys to my place, didn't mean I expected her to return the favor, not at all. I went to the turnstile and used the RFID I'd tucked into my wallet by pressing my wallet to the reader. It worked, the lights switching direction to allow me to pass through. I tapped my wallet against the elevator and it lit up to floor forty-four.

I boarded the elevator car and hung onto the rail as it swept up off the ground and hit her floor in just a few seconds. I had to admit, I sort of hated how fast and smooth the ride was on these new elevators. It made my stomach drop out.

I went to her door and sort of stood there for a long minute, staring at the handle. I mean, it felt a little weird, just letting myself in. I reached out and pressed my thumb to the reader, the lock beeped twice, and I heard the tumblers roll back with a mechanized sound, the catch depressing from its locked position and the door swinging inward on smooth oiled hinges.

"I'll be damned," I muttered, and let myself in.

Veronica looked over the back of the couch at me, brow furrowed, brown eyes sparking fire behind her reading glasses.

"Took you long enough," she said simply, and I smiled, shutting the door tight behind me.

"Something came up, had to take a call. Lasted longer than I wanted it to."

"Ah, well, she went in to lay down a little while ago."

"Cool, cool," I said, and pulled a folded square of computer paper out of my jacket pocket.

"What's that?" she asked, her eyes narrowing.

"Just an idea I had," I said. "I mean, it's not up to me how she spends her money, but I think it would go a long way toward her peace of mind."

I handed it over and she unfolded it, looking down her nose through her glasses at the printout.

"Wow, that's a really good idea. I know her well enough to know that she'll be all about it." She redirected her attention to her open laptop in her lap and said, "I'll get it ordered up."

I smiled and gave a nod starting off down the hall.

"Shut the bedroom door, please," she called at my back. "I don't want to hear it."

I chuckled softly and passed the guest bedroom and bath on my way up the hall, pausing at the portal that led to Lil's bedroom. I didn't even know she had a bedroom door, but sure enough, there was a hidden slider in the recess of one side of the alcove. I slid it all the way over and latched it behind me, and it was suddenly just me and Lil in her fishbowl of a bedroom.

I looked up and could just see a curve of her shoulder and hip peeking above the edge of her mattress. I shrugged out of my jacket and hung it on the modern, brushed-aluminum coat tree where her purse hung, on the side of the door opposite the doorway from the dresser. I pulled off the rest of my clothes a piece at a time, folding them neatly and leaving them atop the dresser itself. I climbed the set of stairs on the other side of the bed from where Lil lay and found her tucked in carefully, sound asleep, her hands tucked under the pillow below one cheek.

Her back was to me and, not wanting to disturb her but wanting to be near her, I carefully lifted the blankets and sheet on my side of the bed and slid between them, cautiously inching my way up to her back so I could spoon her. Yet, when I got to her, I couldn't resist. I pressed my lips to the soft skin of the cap of her shoulder. Once I started, though, one wasn't enough. I pressed another, cupping her upper arm with my hand and smoothing down toward her elbow even as my lips trailed one slow, perfectly placed kiss at a time along the sweep of her shoulder up along the side of her neck.

It took three, maybe four kisses, my hand smoothing carefully up and down her arm for her to stir. She sucked in this tremulous breath and shuddered beneath my palm, gasping when my next kiss touched lightly over that spot on the side of her neck that drove her wild. It was one of my most very favorite erogenous zones on her to exploit.

"Backdraft?" her voice lilted in that way that said she still wasn't quite awake, and I smiled to myself, lifting my lips from her skin and murmuring near her ear.

"Yeah, babe."

"What took you so long?" she asked, cuddling back into me and I was instantly hard. I let my hand jump from her bare arm to her satin-covered hip beneath the covers and smiled when I found the nightgown she wore was as short as it was. Dipping my hand beneath the hem, I smoothed my hand up her thigh and had to smile when I found no panties.

"Unexpected phone call," I answered and buried my nose in her long hair, beneath her ear, pressing another kiss behind it.

She gasped, holding her breath for a heartbeat, then three, before it escaped her in a shuddering sigh.

Christ, she was sexy.

Her palm found the back of my hand along her hip and she thrust her perfect ass back into me, dragging that hand to the mound of her sex and pressing my fingertips against her clit. She turned her head and found my mouth with hers and I groaned into it. We kissed and she ground that ass into my cock.

I couldn't stand it. Moving from sensual to passionate in the blink of an eye, I curved my arm under her neck, bracing my forearm against her chest above her perfect breasts and dragging her back against my body. I dipped my fingers between the folds of her labia and found her growing wetter by the moment.

She tore her mouth from mine and let out this sexy little gasp and I took my hand from her pussy, shoving my boxers down in front to free my dick. I returned my hand to the top of her thigh and lifted her leg, back over mine, my cock jutting at just the right angle to rub against her slick folds, my hips working back and forth trying to find the right angle for penetration. It took two or three tries, but I got it, the head of my cock drawn to her entrance like a magnet. I eased into her slowly, pushing deep and deeper until I couldn't go any further.

She cried out softly, her hands gripping my arm over her chest, hugging it to her as she writhed on my dick, and I fucking loved it.

"God, I love you, Lil," I gasped into her ear and she cried out again, her pussy giving a little pulse around my shaft.

I moaned and worked myself back and forth, careful to keep my back to the windows and the blankets up.

Personally, I could give a fuck who watched; I just wasn't keen on any potential voyeurs sharing these intimate moments with my woman with the rest of the goddamn world.

I closed my eyes and breathed her in deep, that mix of exotic fruit and spicy vanilla intoxicating and sweet. Her breath came in those deep and even gasps and pants brought on by good sex and I loved that I could give it to her so good. She reached back with her top arm and dug nails into my hip and ass and I thrust harder but no faster.

She was on that brink, I could feel it with how she gripped my cock with her puss and goddamn, I wanted to keep her there as long as possible. I wanted to keep her there forever, where nothing else mattered except her and me and the passion between us, raging like a fire I didn't even want to control.

God, I loved her like this. God, I just loved her, period.

26

*L*illi...

Backdraft had this magic about him when it came to me that he could make me forget about everyone and everything else. It was the kind of magic I had sorely needed over the last week, and I was glad he was here, now. He kissed the back of my shoulder as we showered the next morning, and though the last few times we'd made love without protection, with the media and the crazy and the stress right now? I was glad I was on birth control injections every three months. I took those more to regulate my cycle and lessen their duration than for birth control, but as of right now, it was a really nice added perk.

We had a discussion about it while the water sluiced down our skins and I could tell he felt better about things. We were on the exact same page. Kids someday, but not this year and maybe not even the next. 'Not ever' might be okay, too. We were in no rush.

It was unbelievably good just even having the talk, though. I'd never been with anyone to this point where I'd felt comfortable planning any sort of future together and it just showed me that Backdraft, unlike any that'd come before, was indeed the man for me.

"Lilli," Veronica called through the closed bathroom door.

"Yeah?"

"Delivery out here, hope your guy is handy, because 'Some assembly required'."

"Delivery?" I asked and frowned.

Backdraft laughed a little and called back, "I am, and thanks, Veronica, be out in a bit."

"What did you do?" I asked him.

"My homework," he said and turned me to face him. He planted a quick kiss on my mouth and said, "Take your time finishing up."

"Okay."

He got out and pulled one of the towels down from the rack, running it quickly over himself and his hair. I watched, forgetting I was supposed to be finishing up myself, mesmerized by his ass as he walked out of the bathroom with the towel around his shoulders. I shook myself out of my lusty dream state and stuck my face under the water.

I made quick work of finishing up myself and went over to the makeup and dressing table in my bathroom suite. I picked up my brush and hairdryer, towel secure at my chest and quickly got my hair from wet to barely damp, my curiosity eating me alive.

What did he do? I wondered.

I dressed quickly in a pair of comfortable leggings and an over-sized boat neck tee, forgoing a bra for the time being. I didn't really have any intention of leaving the house. Veronica and I had some things to go over to get me back on track with the book I was working on. I was beginning to worry I wouldn't meet my deadline, but only because I had belted out a novel different from the one I was supposed to be writing first.

When a story demanded your attention that badly and tore out of you and onto the page like the side project had, well, any writer knew that it couldn't and wouldn't be denied, no matter what any publisher said. I'd gotten it done and pushed off to the side but still had at least three-quarters of the one I was supposed to be working on left to do.

I was thinking I would need a carrot on a stick to get any kind of decent word count down. Maybe instead of chocolate, I could get

Backdraft to deny me sex until I met a certain word goal. That would certainly motivate me to get my ass in gear.

"Oh, my god," I said and choked on a laugh at the long, flat boxes that Backdraft and Veronica were bringing into my bedroom. "What is this?"

"His idea, I just executed it. You can thank me later," Veronica said flatly.

I laughed and they set it down at the bottom of the steps up to my bed.

"Grab the other one?" she asked.

"Yep."

I went over to the box, frowning, and ran my eyes over it trying to see if there was anything identifying what was inside. The words 'canopy' and 'frame' stood out and I straightened.

"No!" I cried, delighted. "You guys!" I was suddenly very excited to get the boxes open.

"You and Ronnie go," Backdraft said. "Go do whatever work it is you need to do. I'm going to get this unwrapped and figure out what tools I need, and run home."

I felt happy tears spring to my eyes, and went over to him and wrapped my arms around him. He laughed and folded his arms around me, kissing the top of my head.

"Don't do that," he said. "No crying."

I sniffed and managed to rein them in without any spilling over.

"You're too good to me," I said. "The both of you."

Veronica looked at her nails and said, "Oh, trust me, I know."

I laughed and she jerked her head out toward the rest of my apartment.

"Now, to the office, we have shit to do."

I turned my face up to Backdraft's and he kissed me soundly, saying, "Go to it, babe."

The rest of the day was both the most productive and harmonious I'd had since moving to the Echelon. It was certainly the best day I'd had all week. I found myself smiling more and laughing. We ordered takeout for lunch and listened to Backdraft's power tools and cursing from the bedroom while we kept working at the dining room table. The true highlight, though? When Backdraft came out and put his hands over my eyes and whispered in my ear, "It's time."

"Oh, yay!" I cried enthusiastically, and tried to pull his hands away.

"Nope, uh-uh, come on, now."

Laughing, I awkwardly got up from the table and, his arm around me, one hand over my eyes and the other across my chest, cradling me in his body protectively and doing this awkward gait to keep me safe, we moved up the hall.

"Oh, wow," Veronica said, and his hand moved from over my eyes.

I blinked, waiting for my eyes to adjust and had to agree.

"It's beautiful," I murmured and drank the sight in.

It was a brushed-aluminum frame, simple in design and matching the simple modern feel of the rest of the room. What made it, though, were the sheer cream curtains, matching the cream comforter and light peach sheets on the bed. Over the cream sheer drapes, gathered at the corners to keep the view intact, were deeply off-white lace curtains to further obscure things. A bar rested atop the framework, material draping down at the head of the bed artfully. Slide the bar to the foot of the bed, that material created an instant roof, let down the curtains and there were four walls. Privacy restored. It was perfect.

"I love it," I said, turning in Backdraft's arms. He smiled down at me, hazel eyes alight with love, and bent to kiss me. I kissed him back with everything I felt in that moment and more and he sighed against my mouth, a happy and contented sound.

"Stay tonight," I urged and he sighed again, a very different sound from the one before.

"I can't."

I groaned, whining a little. He smiled and pecked me on the nose, stepping back just a bit and I knew there was no convincing him.

"Why not?" I asked, pouting out my bottom lip.

"Can't tell you; plausible deniability, babe." I nodded, and he said, "In fact, I need to go now."

I wrinkled my nose and asked, "When will I see you again?"

"Soon, I promise."

I nodded again and reluctantly let him go.

"Take care of my girl, Ronnie," he said and she winked.

"Like it was my job," she said and he and I laughed.

He packed up his tools, kissed me one more time and left. I confess, I stood at the door and watched the Indigo Knights logo splashed across his broad back float up the hall with every stride he took. He gave me that cheeky little salute of his before he stepped on the elevator and I gave a little wave, heaving a big sigh once he was gone.

"You are totally sprung," Veronica said from the kitchen, working open a bottle of wine.

"Can you blame me?" I asked and she scoffed a laugh.

"Not at all, honey. Not. At. All."

27

*B*ackdraft…

"I think I'm gonna be sick," Ackley said and I shook my head.

"Suck it up, buddy. You walk on me now, you can kiss your ass goodbye as a fireman."

"I know, I know, it's just when I agreed to this, I knew it would suck, but now we're here and staring at the cameras and shit, I'm well aware I'm about to go on national TV and tell the world what a fucking dickhead I was."

"Yeah, yeah, you are," I said and I have to say I felt zero sympathy.

"Most guys get to step off a situation like that and pretend it didn't happen," he muttered.

I snorted. "Yeah, rich guys, maybe, but guys like us? Not so much, man. Not so much. As much as I still want to punch you in the nuts for what you did, you're still one of us. You're still one of the good guys, and for some reason the good guys always face the music."

He stared me in the face for a few heartbeats as we sat across from the hostess in the old school canvas-and-wood director's chairs, which were uncomfortable as fuck. She had a whole pit crew fussing with her hair and makeup, doing last minute touches.

I gave Ackley a nod as the guy behind the camera started counting down and he let out a slow breath and nodded back. We faced the hostess and she smiled bright, the lights intensified and she said, "Welcome, gentlemen."

I gave a curt nod and Ackley murmured a thanks. She turned her attention to me.

"For those in our audience that don't know, you're Emmet Calder, renowned author Timber Philips' new flame, right?"

I cleared my throat. "If she wants to keep me around," I said.

"There has been quite the scandal surrounding your relationship after *Celebrity Beat's* scorching interview with your girlfriend, Victoria Russo."

"Ex-girlfriend. That's why I'm here, to set the record straight."

"Please, do tell," she leaned forward, all ears.

"I broke up with Tori over four months or so ago. You see, she cheated on me, and I took her back, but then she cheated on me again."

"With me," Ackley said, owning his shit.

"Wow," the hostess said. "And who are you?"

"I'm Cameron Ackley, and I met Victoria through Calder here."

"You use his last name."

"We're firemen, it's just something we do. You get enough Johns, Daves, and Franks in a house, it can get complicated real fast, so we just use last names."

"I see. How did you meet Timber?" she asked me.

I cleared my throat and shifted, this was the part that was hit or miss on if Lil would ever forgive me.

"I was at a bar and grill hanging with some buddies and I saw her and that Mark Schumer guy at a table. I was shamelessly eavesdropping and figured out pretty quick he was breaking it off with her. He was telling her about how she wasn't the first girl he'd been with. That she was, in fact, the other woman. She had no idea. I heard him tell her that being with her made him realize how much he loved his wife or girlfriend and that it was over. She was humiliated and I couldn't deal, so I went over and stepped in. Asked if she needed a ride home."

"Oh, wow, my hero," she said with a light fake laugh and I gave a nod.

The interview went on for around ten minutes more and I was sweating bullets under the lights. By the time we wrapped it up, I could see a spark of something in Mindy, the lady interviewing us. She was pissed. The revelation that the drone footage wasn't taken through a hotel but Lil's bedroom window struck a chord with her somehow, although, why it made a damn bit of difference, hotel room or not, was beyond me.

The camera man yelled cut, and I started pulling microphone wires right away. Mindy came up to me and said, "I had no idea this went as far as it did."

"Well, now you know," I stated.

"I'll make sure they don't edit too much out," she assured me. "This needs aired."

"No offense intended, ma'am, but I really just wish the lot of you would stop airing a whole bunch of shit. Namely, I wish you'd all just leave us alone. Lil's a good woman, she just wants to write her stories and make people feel good and in return? You all tear her the fuck down."

She rocked back on her heels a bit, and her expression went from nonplussed to not-surprised as she processed what I said. She gave a nod and asked, "Is there anything we can do for you to make your stay in New York tonight more comfortable?"

"Yeah," I said. "Get me on the very next flight out of it and back to BWI. I don't want to be here. I want to be with Lil."

She gave me a sharp look and barked out, "Hal!" and one of the studio hands came scurrying over.

"Get Mr. Calder on the next available flight out if you please?" She looked at Ackley. "You too?"

He gave a sad grin. "If you don't mind, no. I'd like to try and get one last shot at getting laid before that airs and I can never get a woman again."

I laughed, and she gave him a slightly dirty look but nodded.

I guess I was going home a little early. I might even be able to catch Lil at the 10-13 with the girls.

28

illi...

    I was glad to see no paparazzi when we arrived at the 10-13. Veronica wrinkled her nose and said, "I thought we were going someplace called the 10-13."

"That's just what Backdraft and his club calls it, something about a radio call-sign, and it's the address, too."

"Weird."

"It's actually a nice place and has really good food."

Antonio, our driver, opened the back door to the towncar and I got out first. Veronica and I both said thank you and I tipped him generously. He smiled and nodded and told us to just holler when we wanted to be picked up.

I pushed open the door and we went inside. Aly squealed excitedly and I laughed. Veronica was somehow included in Aly's enthusiastic hug and Christina laughed from behind her.

Dawnie said, "Down, girl! Jesus," from somewhere off to our right.

I heard a male voice say, "Mm, that's her? I expected her to be taller."

"Don't be salty, Pasquale," Chrissy admonished.

"Girl, you know I have to have some salt in with all this smooth caramel."

"Oh, Jesus Christ," Dawnie said, but she was standing from her perch on the tall bar stool and had her arms open for a hug of her own. I went to her and gave her one and got a look at the man with them, Pasquale.

'Outrageous' didn't even begin to cover it. He was slender and wore shiny black vinyl pants held up by a black punk rock belt, the kind with rows and rows of those square silver pyramid studs. The tee shirt had been cropped to show his flat stomach and the neck cut away so it hung artfully off his shoulders. I kid you not, it was a white Lisa Frank tee shirt with a white kitten on it surrounded by a pink halo to make it stand out. His hair was sprayed or waxed into a faux-hawk with equally pink product, and his makeup was just as ostentatious. Big, pouty, matte-pink lips, pink eyeshadow fading to white at the brow bone and black liquid liner making the smoothest cat's eye I'd ever seen. He looked completely outlandish but carried himself with such a confidence he worked it into the next century.

Martine has nothing on this guy, was my first thought upon seeing him and I realized we were standing there measuring each other up.

"So you're the one to steal my man, Backdraft, hm?"

Chrissy rolled her eyes and said, "Pasquale thinks all the men of the Indigo Knights are his."

"Oh honey, they so are, they just don't know it yet."

Veronica laughed and he leaned back and gave her such a look. Waving his hand up and down in front of her he said flatly, "You look like the help," and even though it was rude as hell, Veronica and I couldn't help but exchange a look and laugh. He just had such a way about him.

"All right, ladies! Oh, and Pasquale." The bartender had come around the bar and had a pad and pen.

"Oh, nuh-uh, Skids! You don't get to do me like that. I am a lady and you are gonna hurt my feelings!" Pasquale was looking at him and if looks could kill! I tried valiantly not to giggle.

"All right, all right, don't get your panties in a bunch. I'm sorry," Skids said, smiling. "What are you ladies drinkin'?"

Pasquale harrumphed and stuck his straw between his lips, sucking down the last of what looked like a mojito out of his pint glass.

"Another mojito, *por favor,* baby."

"Right, and counselor?" he asked Chrissy, and she held up her drink, which was half full.

"I'm good right now, thanks."

"Aly Cat?"

"Um, I don't know, ask me in a sec."

"Okay,"

"I'll have a beer," Dawnie said and he wrote it down.

"The usual?"

"Yeah."

"Righty-o, one Blue Moon, extra orange," he said, and turned to Veronica.

"I'll have a glass of wine."

"White or red?"

"Red, a Merlot if you've got it."

"What about you, Lil? Riesling?"

"Actually, I'll do a Cosmo, if it's all right with you."

"You want it I'll make it," he said. "Be right back with these. You gonna want food?"

"Yes, please," Veronica said, and he gave a nod and wandered off.

"Oh! Skids!" Aly bounded off after him, walking with him to the bar.

I loved it. The only thing I would have loved more was if Backdraft were here. I slid up onto a stool next to Dawnie, Veronica took up my other side, and Pasquale sat across from her and Chrissy across from me, leaving the empty seat for Aly across from her blind best friend.

"Oh, did you get the audio books, Dawnie?"

"I did! Thank you."

"You're very welcome."

"You really write porn?" Pasquale asked and I laughed.

"Some people think so."

"Pretty good, huh?"

"A lot of people think so," Veronica supplied and I laughed.

The conversation flowed back and forth naturally in the crowded restaurant and bar. We sat at one of two tall bar tables set side by side as you came in the door. Beyond them were two dart boards and beyond them, a pool table. There was a raised, glassed-in room with a gentle ramp that swept back and forth leading up to it for wheelchair access.

There were several Indigo Knights watching the fights in the glassed-in room while a local station played football silently above the bar, the black closed-captioning boxes rolling underneath. I found myself really enjoying the company and not doing what I usually did, which was hide in my phone or in the closed captioning. Reading had always been my refuge; even if it were only a cereal box that were handy, it would suddenly become the most engrossing piece of literature ever written to my eyes.

I was dying to know what Backdraft was doing, but was surprised that I wasn't worried at all. I really did trust him. I couldn't tell you the number of times I had said it but didn't mean it, but with him, I really did.

"Well, fuck me!" Pasquale said, his voice clipped. "I'm not getting that one back." He let out a dramatic sigh and took a drink of his mojito through its straw.

"What?" I asked, frowning, and turned around, following his gaze.

Backdraft was coming through the door, a cab pulling away from the curb. He had a backpack slung over his shoulder and a bouquet of flowers in his other hand, white lilies, which were not only my namesake but my favorite. I'm not going to lie, I lit up from the inside out.

"I thought you weren't coming!" I cried, slipping off my stool and going to him. I folded myself against his chest, slipping my arms beneath his jacket and around his waist. He was so warm. He hugged me, smiling and kissed the top of my head.

"You meet the guys yet?" he asked, and I shook my head.

"Not yet, the girls and I have mostly just been out here doing our thing."

"Hmm, 'k. Come on, I'll introduce you. Ronnie, you coming?"

"Naw, I'm good," she said, laughing at something Chrissy had said.

I laid my flowers on the table really quick and Veronica gave me a nod to indicate she'd watch them and my purse.

"I'll bring her right back, I promise."

"You do that, stud," Dawnie said dryly, an amused smile on her lips.

"Ah, hmm!" Pasquale choked off a laugh and hid behind his mojito.

"Never gonna win me back that way, buddy!" Backdraft called back over his shoulder at him. I laughed and hugged his arm, just happy he was here.

"I'm glad you made it back from wherever," I said as we went up the four steps at the end of the bar to the glassed-in room. The door opened and some of the guys were being rowdy at Backdraft in greeting.

"Oh, shit! It really is a fuckin' party," he declared.

"Yeah, buddy! You were the only hold-out this time."

"Youngblood! Good to see you, man." I let go of his arm so he could go around hugging and whatnot.

"Yo, who's the chick?" Angel asked and I frowned and realized it must be his twin. My suspicion was confirmed when Angel nudged his way in behind me.

"Shit, went to the bathroom and look what I missed."

"Hi," I said laughing and gave him a quick hug.

"Boys, this is Lil. Lil, meet the guys."

"Hi," I said again, much louder, and gave a shy wave.

Oh, my god. There were like a dozen of them! I didn't know how I would remember them all. I mean there was Yale and Angel who I'd met already, and Golden would be easy to remember because he was Angel's twin brother. Then there was Blaze, who had used my bathroom at my apartment, and then a whole host of new faces!

Narcos and Driller looked the roughest out of everyone, and Backdraft whispered in my ear it was because Narcos was full-time undercover and Driller also had to be from time to time. Reflash came out from the kitchen to meet me briefly, and Skids was behind the bar. Then there was a muscular, bald, black man they called Oz, and another youngish, police officer called Poe, who was related to Edgar Allen Poe, which is how he got his name.

We chatted for a while before one of the guys, Oz, kicked out a chair and told Backdraft to cop a squat. I kissed him goodbye and said it was nice meeting everyone and went back out to the girl's table, where they were all laughing at whatever Pasquale had said. I smiled and rejoined them just as the food we'd ordered arrived.

I looked back to the fishbowl and caught Backdraft watching me. He winked and I was suffused with warmth and good feeling. My spirits buoyed by his surprise arrival, I had a damn good night, even if it was back to work for him in the morning. It was made even better when he took the car back to my place with us.

29

*B*ackdraft...

I was antsy, eagerly awaiting Lil's arrival. I didn't want her home alone when the interview aired tonight, and the crew seemed cool with pulling a do-over on dinner, so that's what we did: invited my lady to dinner at the firehouse. She arrived much as she had the first time, though when she stepped out of the back of the car I was pleasantly surprised.

Instead of her typical jeans, boots, and a nice sweater, she'd done her hair and makeup, and a clinging sweater-dress that accentuated every curve in a bright cream hugged her body. I could even swear it shimmered when she walked towards me. Her high-heeled brown boots that came over the knee clacked sharply against the pavement.

Down, boy, I thought at my sudden and raging erection but I knew the futility of it.

"You look incredible," I said low, my voice full of heat, and bowed to kiss her perfectly-glossed and sparkling lips. She wore this lip gloss stuff that the color took an act of God to remove and all she had to do was keep reapplying the clear glossy topcoat to bring it back to life. Whoever invented the shit needed a Nobel Prize, I'm telling you.

"Hey, you," she said gently, softly smiling.

"Ready to do dinner with the crew, take two?" I asked.

Her smile grew and she nodded happily and I gave her my arm. We went inside and I fucking loved following her up the stairs, her hips swaying that ass in front of me like a pendulum and holy shit, I was firmly under her spell, hypnotized into happy by just her being here.

She was warmly greeted by the crew and that made me both love and appreciate the people around me even more. It was the Captain's night to cook and he was hard at it in the kitchen. Lil stepped over and asked if there was anything she could do to lend a hand and I took her coat and purse, which I had failed to do downstairs. He put her to work, and I leaned on a counter nearby to talk and just generally sucked up all the warmth and good vibes we had going on.

Midway through the meal, Lil and I facing the living area this time, Barnaby sounded the alarm.

"Hey, yo, yo, it's on!"

The Captain picked up the remote by his plate and unmuted the TV.

"There has been quite *the scandal surrounding your relationship after* Celebrity Beat's *scorching interview with your girlfriend, Victoria Russo."*

Lil's head came up sharply and she chewed slowly, carefully, riveted to the television set.

I set the record straight, that's for sure. Her back straightened when the text logs from my phone company came out. The studio had done a good job recreating screen captures of them, even though my phone had been obliterated and the messages had been lost. My new phone started buzzing across the table, my brother's name on the screen. I'd already had a conversation with him and my parents after the first show had aired with all the dirty pictures.

Of course, it'd been more like an ass-chewing from my brother about not calling them and giving them the heads-up. I rejected the call and shot a text back.

Not now, with Lil.

My asshole brother surprised me and shot back, **Good deal. Proud of you. Mom and dad, too.**

Okay, so maybe he wasn't as much of an asshole as I'd first declared. I know my folks had been worried and so it made me feel pretty good that things were calmed down on the home front. With everything happening in the here-and-now in Indigo City where I was located, unfortunately my immediate biological family, and even my club, had taken more of a back seat. I figured part of that was still a symptom of Torrid. They'd all hated her and I'd been a stubborn shit and wouldn't give up when I really should have put that relationship out to pasture.

As a result, most of them had done the right thing, which was to step off and let me make my mistakes and crash. As soon as the crash had happened, they'd stepped back in, which I'd needed, but when it came to this new thing, with Lil, I'd gone back to some old habits; I had cut everyone out. I recognized it now, I didn't want to hide Lil or keep her my secret. There was no shame in my relationship with Lil like there'd been with Tori, so I was determined to redirect my course and make things right with everyone. Just, one thing at a time. I let them all know I wanted to settle into a new normal with her, establish a routine over the next few weeks before we ventured out and started meeting family and shit.

I'd already remedied the club situation, which was geographically easier, the night before last.

Lil trained glassy storm-swept eyes on me and I smiled, all thoughts of the tangled mess of club, family, workmates and the aftermath of Torri swept clear out of my head when she blew me away with the gratitude in that gaze of hers. Still, I needed to check...

"Hope you're not mad at me," I said softly.

"Mad at you? Why would I be mad at you?" she demanded. She sniffed and dabbed beneath one eye with the back of her knuckle, trying to keep her careful makeup intact.

"I put a lot more about us out there than I really wanted to," I said.

She smiled and it was bursting with pride. "I don't know," she said. "Sounded to me like you spun one epic love story. Couldn't have written it better myself."

The table broke out into laughter and a chorus of 'Awe's, and I couldn't be mad or even start to feel embarrassed because I held onto Lil, who was holding onto me like she never, ever, wanted to let me go.

"Think it's time to let ol' Ackley off the hook," Captain Walden said, and there was a chorus of agreement around the table.

I nodded and said, "Yeah. Yeah, it is."

"I don't want to go back to my old house, I like it here," the new guy, Rice, called out and we all laughed.

"I wouldn't go that far," Barnaby said.

"Me, either," Lind agreed.

Her radio crackled to life on her shoulder and she and Angel exchanged a look.

"They're singing our song," Angel said with a sigh.

"Let's roll," Lind said, and they got up.

"Keep your plates for you," the Captain said, and got up himself to get the cling wrap for them.

Lil let me go and leaned back into a proper sitting position in her own seat. People resumed eating, laughing, mostly at Torrid's expense, and Lil worked on fixing her runny makeup some by wiping it away from beneath her eyes with her napkin, laughing at the gentle ribbing she got from some of the guys.

My phone started blowing up a second later. Torrid. I just ignored her. She was old news, anyway. I looked at the TV, which was in the middle of a commercial break, and thought to myself, *So five minutes ago,* and laughed at my own joke.

It felt like life was about to get a whole lot better from here on out; Victory, for once, was mine when it came to her. It was like she hadn't thought I might actually fight back in some way. I may have patience, I may put up with a lot of bullshit from her, but once I really realized that I didn't have to, it was game over. Once I met Lil and realized that wasn't how any of the whole love and relationship needed to be, that you shouldn't have to fight, that it really could be as natural as breathing, she'd completely lost any hold she may have ever had on me.

I looked at Lil now, and I couldn't imagine ever going back to anything less. Life was just so much better with her in it.

This is real. This is what love really is.

*L*illi...

He'd been absolutely perfect on that show. He had been cool, calm, and collected the entire time, never losing his temper. The only evidence of his displeasure had been his clenched jaw and the smolder in his eyes. Which, if you didn't know him, you could completely overlook. He'd been articulate, had backed up his statements with truth, fact, and most importantly, proof. He'd cracked his life like an egg and let it spill over national television for everyone to see.

It was probably one of the most selfless things I'd ever seen anyone do for someone else and he'd done it for me. I loved him, so much that all I could think about was how we could weave each other more completely into the fabric of one another's lives.

I let myself into my apartment and closed the door, Jaspar and Marigold trotting out from their hiding places to greet me. I smiled, they weren't fooling me; they wanted fed. I rushed through opening them a can of wet food and portioning it out between their two plates, my mind working a mile a minute and jumping between things I needed to do like a hummingbird on crack.

Mostly, I really thought about what I knew was important to

Backdraft, and, of course, the first thing to come to mind was his beautiful old brownstone, so full of potential. I picked up my phone from where I rested it on the counter and committed completely to what I was about to ask.

I called him. He picked up on the third ring.

"Hey, babe. Sorry, you caught my hands in a sink full of dishes. You home okay?"

"Safe and sound," I said.

"I miss you already," he said and I felt my smile grow.

"Feeling is mutual," I told him and sighed.

"Uh-oh, that was a big sigh, what's going on in that gorgeous head of yours?"

"I want to ask you something, but at the same time, I'm a little scared to." I moved from the kitchen and traveled slowly up the hallway toward my room, mostly to get away from the sounds of my kitties noshing on their food.

"Shoot, babes. You can ask me anything, you know that."

"I want to do something meaningful, something with us, for us," I said and I could hear the smile in his voice with what he said next.

"I like the sound of that. Any ideas what you want to do?"

"I'd really like to help with your brownstone. I know you said that you were doing the renovations by yourself and that money has been the main obstacle holding you back..." I sighed again, frustrated. "You know, for an author, you'd think I would have the words and articulate this much better!"

He laughed and said, "Relax, babes. Take a deep breath. It's your nerves getting in the way, and they shouldn't, because I'm liking what I'm hearing so far, if it's where it's going where I think it's going."

"If you think it's going that I want to help build your house into our home, then, yes," I said, bouncing nervously on the balls of my feet. "I don't mean hire a bunch of contractors to do it, I mean take our time and do it ourselves. I mean, obviously, there are probably some things we'll need contractors for, but I'm saying I want to build a life with you."

"Thank fuck, because I never want to spend another day without you, and what you're offering is pretty much all I've ever wanted in a partner in life."

"Yeah?" I asked, voice breaking with emotion.

He laughed slightly and said, "Yeah, Lil. I meant it. Us. Always."

"I love you," I murmured.

"I love you, too."

"So, when do we start?"

"You know my schedule, baby. I get off Friday morning. I think, for now, the best thing is for you to work from the condo while I'm stuck here at the firehouse, but if you can meet me at the brownstone Friday, we can work on it during the day and be home to feed the kitties at night."

"I like that plan," I said softly.

"I just like planning things with you. Feels good," he said.

"It does," I said with a laugh, much lighter for not being on the verge of more emotional tears anymore. I was so glad, so grateful that he felt the same and wasn't insulted about using my money to get us going. There were so many men who weren't so easy-going about the kind of money I was worth. Some were resentful, some were all too happy to spend it for me; Backdraft had never made a thing about it. He'd always either paid or went halfsies, but never once bore a grudge where my net worth was concerned.

We talked about smaller things, that were still no less important, as I changed and got ready for bed until he asked me, "You're sure you're good with how much I said on that show?" I could hear his nerves shining through with the question and smiled.

"Absolutely," I murmured. "You did beautifully, you didn't over-share but didn't hold back in confronting what had been overshared already. Not to mention, you looked really hot up there."

He laughed and I smiled, glad I could make him.

"Shit, I've got to go," I pouted, listening to the grating alarm in the background. "Be safe!" I told him as a farewell.

"You know it," he said and the call ended.

I smiled and lowered the phone and moved about my closet and bathroom, putting up what I'd worn and getting the makeup off my face, generally just getting ready for bed.

THE NEXT FEW weeks flew by as we settled into a new routine. I would work from home while he was at work at the firehouse and it was nicely motivating for me to get my self-imposed daily word count in. If I didn't, I would have to cut my nightly conversation with Backdraft short, and if I didn't he certainly would. He was so incredibly supportive and motivating and it was like we fueled one another, sparking a drive in each other to be the very best versions of ourselves we could be.

It was Thursday and I had blown through my word count for the day, partially the night before and the rest early this morning, so that I could meet with one of the contractors and with an interior-design firm about my very own secret-squirrel project at the brownstone.

Backdraft and I decided to work our way from the top down, and the first step had been deciding together what the bedroom and bathroom that were already accomplished would look like. Our first weekend working on the brownstone had been deciding those things, giving the top floor a finished and polished look.

The second floor we'd started dreaming about that weekend, too. The next weekend we had started in on it. There were two rooms on the second floor. The front room we had decided to make into a library and reading room, while the room toward the back, overlooking the back garden, we'd decided would be my office.

I'd called the contractor for the basement, though. Upon further inspection, I'd realized from the outside that something wasn't right. The basement wasn't actually the basement at all, but rather the ground floor, but I could have sworn there was something about a basement in the paperwork Backdraft had shown me on the place.

I was really excited now, because I'd been right. The windows of the first floor had been bricked up and there was a basement below it.

In talking to some of the neighbors, I'd discovered this was a Prohibition thing, that the building did indeed have basement levels that were actually old, narrow garages meant for horse-drawn carriages; there was even a curb cut in front of each one. They'd been bricked up for a speakeasy to be put in down there. It was a huge renovation project, but I had the money to open them all up and I aimed to do just that.

The ground floor would then become Backdraft's man-cave, while the basement would become a functional garage for his motorcycle and tools. Meanwhile, I could be guilt-free about taking up the entire second floor for office and library space.

The top floor would remain our bedroom suite, plus the guest room, while the first floor would be living, dining, and kitchen, the front door leading down the front steps and out onto the street, and the back door out to the small terrace and down into the garden. When the ground floor/basement renovation was through, the ground floor, or man-cave, would also open up out into the back yard.

He had no idea about my plans expanding to the whole building, but I didn't want him to build his own man-cave space. I wanted to do that for him and this, this was a lot more than he was going to be able to take on. He may be good at contracting, after all, that's what his brother did, carpentry and construction work. Still, he'd told me where his skills ended and the professionals needed to be called in, and this was only his second passion. His first and foremost would always be firefighting.

Now was also the time to do this, while most of the building still sat empty. We only had two neighbors in the block of eight in the row, and it made things a lot less complicated when you factored in that most of the units were owned by a real-estate company intent on flipping them. I had lawyers involved and was pretty much looking to become an investor of sorts. I should see most of my money back with the increased values and sales of those empty units.

I was so excited about this and Veronica had been, too. We'd postponed putting my condo on the market until this could all be done; it would tap my pretty considerable resources, so by the time it was done, I would need the condo to sell, but I wasn't worried. This all felt so right. Plus, real estate was pretty much a sure thing. Indigo City was only growing.

After the contractor and decorator had left, I went back up to the third floor and took a hot shower and settled into bed with my laptop to get some more writing in. There may have been no internet, but that never stopped me from doing my job.

I had my nightly call with Backdraft and he said he would be a little late getting to the brownstone in the morning. The next shift had some sort of in-service training and so his crew was holding over four hours later than they usually did for the next shift to get through it.

I went to bed feeling good about life, but I was in for a rude awakening the next morning. I got up and decided to get a shower but hadn't slept exceptionally well. It was tough still, sleeping in the brownstone without Backdraft there. I was far closer to street level and could hear things out there. It wasn't as quiet as the Echelon.

When I got out of the shower, I thought I heard something downstairs, out front, but dismissed it at first until I heard a definite crash and a 'Woomf' sound.

"Backdraft?" I called, knotting the belt on the satin robe I'd brought with me. I took up my phone off the card table we'd set up in here and I unlocked it, creeping to the top of the stairs.

"Hello?" I called, lightly taking the stairs and pausing on the second floor. I could smell it, then. The smell of campfire and burning plastic. I frowned and rushed to the top of the stairs to the first floor and let out a short scream. Smoke was creeping in underneath and between the cracks between the two front doors; flames were licking the outside of the frosted decorative glass panels.

I dialed 9-1-1.

"9-1-1 what is your emergency?"

"Yes, fire, I'm at eight-three-zero, Twenty-Third Avenue, Indigo City."

"Okay, slow down, what's the address again?"

I repeated the address and shouted "Please hurry!"

"Are you inside the residence?" the male operator asked and I shouted, "Yes!"

"Can you get out?"

"Through the back garden, I'm trying to get there now."

I rounded the banister and the glass exploded in one of the doors. I jumped and let out a little scream and ran further up the hall to the kitchen, but froze.

"Oh, my god!"

Backdraft's ex looked in the back window and gave me a savage grin. She backed away from the back door and there was shattering glass and that sound, as flames engulfed the back door.

"Ma'am? Ma'am are you still with me?"

"I'm trapped!" I cried. "She threw something, she set the back door on fire. Please hurry!"

"Who, ma'am, who threw what?"

"Um, this is my boyfriend's apartment." I coughed and covered my mouth and nose with the sleeve of my robe, choking on the rising smoke which stung my eyes. I squeezed them shut and went back for the stairs, skirting the flames eating their way up the door frame and chewing through the front door, the heat intense and unbearable.

"You can't get out?" the operator asked again.

"No!" I wailed. "I'm going to try the second floor back terrace. I'll jump if I have to!"

"No, ma'am, don't do that, help is on the way."

I got to the second floor just as something crashed on the stone of the second floor back terrace.

"Shit! She threw something up there. There's no way out. Please, please, hurry! I don't want to die."

"You're not going to die, ma'am, just stay with me. Help is on the way." I shut myself into the third floor master suite and went into the bathroom up here, wetting a washcloth in the sink and putting it over my nose and mouth.

"I wish I could believe you," I said, coughing, my chest tight with fear and smoke, my eyes burning with tears.

"You can, are you sure there's no other way out?"

I heard glass shatter down below and sniffed.

"No. I'm trapped inside and the building is burning."

"The fire trucks should be there any minute, just stay on the phone with me."

"You're recording this, right?" I asked.

"Yes ma'am."

"Then I've got some things to say," I said, my chest hurting with every rushing heartbeat.

"You just say what you need to, just stay on the line with me."

31

*B*ackdraft...

"Look alive, boys! Structure fire, one trapped inside!" Captain Walden yelled, as was his custom.

I was halfway into my gear when Ripley called out, "Wait, I know that address. Why do I know that address?"

"What is it?" I shouted up to him over the blaring alarm.

"Eight-thirty, Twenty-Third."

"Shit! That's my address, that's why! Lil! Lil's there!"

The truck fired up and I took my seat, my heart pounding in my chest. I dropped the communication headset onto my head. Barnaby's voice came through as he looked at me from across from where I sat and said, "You're fuckin' kidding us, right, Backdraft? This is some kind of a fucked-up joke."

I glared at him, and sternly grated, "You better fuckin' move your ass, Ripley. This is no joke. I wouldn't, not about that."

The sirens wailed, we took turns at break-neck speed, and my heart sank when I saw the smoke pouring out of my front door.

"Shit!"

"Engine, get water on that, get water on it right now!" I screamed, and jumped out of our truck, ripping open the locker containing my gear.

"Calder, slow down, brother!"

"Don't tell me to slow down! The love of my life's in there!" I screamed back and ripped my mask down over my face, made sure it had seal, and put my helmet on. I grabbed down my axe and, Barnaby on my ass, climbed the steps to the burning front door. I didn't even wait for them to put water on it, I hauled back and kicked the charred wood open, and trusted they would get it wet while I was inside.

Fuck, it's already climbing the walls! I thought in a panic. I could see smoke pouring up the hall and went for the stairs.

"We got flames in the back," Barnaby said over the radio.

"Stay with Calder!" the Captain came back.

"Lil!" I bellowed and someone muttered, "Goddamn," over the comms. I didn't care. I took the stairs two at a time and kicked open the doors to the back terrace. There was black on the stone, evidence of charring, but whatever accelerant was used hadn't caught the doors or frame.

I went back, blowing past Barnaby, who cursed but stayed on my six. The smoke was thick, the visibility shit but not zero, not yet. I could still get around. I heard water down on the first floor blast the entryway and swallowed hard. It was bad in here for anyone without gear. Someone like my Lil.

"Lil!" I cried and busted open the door to the master suite on the third floor. It was smoky up here, by like, a lot, smoke traveling upward like it did. I ripped open the bathroom door and found her crouched and coughing through a soaked rag she looked up and lowered her phone from her ear, tears streaming down her face.

I crouched and broke protocol. I ripped off my helmet and took a deep breath, then, pulling off my mask, I gave her some air. She took three or four deep breaths and I said, "I got you, babe, I got you. Deep breath, deep. One, two, three, gonna take it back now." She nodded and took a deep breath and I pushed the rag over her nose and mouth. I put the mask back on, threw my helmet back on and pulled her into my arms. She clung to me sobbing and I hooked an arm beneath her knees and hauled us both up onto my feet.

"I got her," I said into the radio.

"He does, he's got her; we're coming down." Barnaby affirmed. We went back down the stairs for the front. The guys had drug a hose down the hall through the ruin of the front door and were putting out my kitchen.

I had her, though. She was in my arms, I had her.

I went out the front door to a smattering of applause from some of the neighborhood and some relieved cheers from the guys and went straight for the waiting gurney, Angel, and Lind. I set her down and grabbed the oxygen mask from Angel. He let me, hovering, concerned. Lil took the soot stained washcloth off her face and I put the mask in its place. She took deep and even breaths, staring at me as I nodded.

"Here, man," Angel said, stepping in to do his job. "Get your gear off."

Lil was shaking like a leaf, but I let Angel step in, dropping my helmet on the gurney next to her and pulling off my mask.

"Baby, babe, I got you, you're okay," I said as she broke down. She dropped the oxygen mask and I put my arms around her, holding her tight as she let loose a torrent of tears in the front of my thick fire jacket. I ripped off my gauntlets behind her back so I could touch her.

"You hurt? Baby, you hurt?" I demanded, running my hands over her.

"N-n-n-o!" she got out before she broke down in more uncontrollable sobbing.

"What the fuck happened?" Captain Walden demanded from nearby us.

"I don't know," I said. "I don't know yet."

I held her tight, like I would never let her go, because I wouldn't. *Close. Too fucking close. What the fuck happened?*

"Backdraft. Yo, Backdraft?"

"What?" I snapped.

"I want to run her to Trinity Gen, just to make sure she's straight,"

Angel said and I nodded and pried Lil back so I could get a look at her, smoothing her tangled hair out of her face, strands of it clinging to her snot and tears, as she was in full-on ugly cry.

"Babe, baby, calm down for me. Breathe, just breathe," I said and took some exaggerated breaths, looking her in the eyes, showing her what I wanted her to do.

She nodded and mimicked me and she managed to calm down some and I put my forehead against hers, closing my eyes, just grateful she was alive.

"Angel's going to take you to the hospital, get you checked out, but babe, you gotta tell me: what happened?"

"It was Torrid," she said, and hitched a shuddering breath. "She threw something. Set the front door on fire. By the time I got to the back, I saw her through the window. She threw something again, I heard glass breaking, and then it was on fire, too. I couldn't get out, I was so scared I wouldn't get out." Her voice grew higher, strained, and she broke down into fresh sobbing. I felt my face shut down into grim lines and looked at Angel, who looked as pissed as I felt.

"Take care of my woman," I said and all the fuel in me had been used up. All my patience, all remaining thought, feeling, or emotion that I had for Tori was used up. I didn't feel anything. I just wanted Lil safe. I shook my head and said, "Get her to Trinity Gen, don't let her out of your sight, and make sure she gets back to her obsidian tower and that she stays there. You feel me?"

"I'll call the club. We got you," Angel said, and I nodded.

It took me a moment to pry Lil off of me and when I did, it was to capture her soot-stained face between my hands.

"I'll see you at home, babe. I love you," I said, looking into those storm swept baby blues of hers.

"What? Why? Why can't you stay with me?" she asked startled.

"Protocol, babe. I'll be with you as soon as I can." I kissed her forehead and she nodded against my lips.

"Okay." The one word was tremulous, her voice so fragile it made my heart give off this fractured ache.

"I love you," I repeated.

"I love you, too," she said, and let Angel and Lind take care of her.

"Thanks, man," I told him and he shook his head.

"Not for this, not today," he said and I jerked a nod. He handed my helmet back to me and I took it.

"What're you going to do?" he asked.

"What I should have done a long time ago. Get that crazy bitch put away where she can't hurt anybody anymore."

"Amen to that," he said and Lind called from the rig, "Let's go, partner." She shut herself into the back with Lil, who was laying back, oxygen flowing, and Angel jogged to the driver's seat of his rig.

I looked back at the smoldering wreckage of my front doors and cursed.

"We get back to the house, you go take care of business," the Captain said and I nodded.

"Thanks, boss."

"Don't mention it."

~

Too many hours later, I was standing outside the bar Torrid tended. I heaved a breath. They weren't open yet, but she'd be there. I knew her routine. Apparently she knew ours, too. I pushed my way into the dimly-lit interior and she turned from where she was sliding a bottle back onto a higher bar shelf. She lowered herself down flat on her feet and turned with a wicked grin.

"Surprised you called," she said and I ground my teeth.

"Like I said, we need to talk."

"Figured out Little-Miss-Perfect fantasy author isn't cut out for this life?" she asked and I knew the smile that curved my own lips wasn't friendly.

"What makes you think that?"

She laughed and it was a haughty sound. I slid onto one of the bar stools across from her and she leaned on the bar, squeezing her breasts together with her arms to make them pop in her low-cut top.

She had her palms flat on the bar top and she worked herself back and forth on them, studying my face.

"Why'd you do it?" I demanded.

"What? Set your place on fire? Hell hath no fury like a woman scorned," she said and the bitch was so smug. I wondered how, for the life of me, I could have ever loved her, even for a minute.

"You've got some brass balls," I ground out.

"That makes one of us. I'm guessing she went running back to the west coast? Make you feel like a man for a minute? Rushing in there to save her?" I clenched my fists.

"You listen to me," I started, but I was cut off by her sharp laugh.

"No, you listen. That was punishment for making me look like an asshole on TV. You either leave the little bitch or stay single for longer than a minute, or I'll do a lot worse."

"What, like kill me?"

"Not you," she said and straightened up. "Wouldn't want to damage what's mine."

"You're sick, Torrid. You need some real professional help," I stated and stood up.

"Oh, please. You promised forever," she spat and I turned back from where I'd been about to walk away from her completely.

"That's before you decided to fuck other men, Tori!"

"Would it make you feel better if I found you some hot chicks to bang?" she asked.

"No! What will make me feel better is you, leaving me and Lil the fuck alone!"

"Mm, not gonna happen, lover boy. Might as well get used to it. I'm not going away."

"We'll see about that."

"Not like you have any proof, Backdraft. I'm not stupid."

"Lil saw you, Tori."

"And what physical evidence is there? That's right, none. It's your guys' word against mine, so you just go on now and break it off with her."

"Fuck you," I snarled.

She vaulted up onto the bar, sitting on it, and spread her leather-clad legs wide, leaning back on her palms.

"Ready when you are. You always give it to me best when you're angry, why do you think I keep pissing you off?"

"Jesus fucking Christ," I grated and walked away for real that time.

"You'll be back!" she called at my retreating back. "You always are!"

I stepped back outside and put my wraparounds on, pulling my phone out of my pocket. I turned off the recording app, and pulled up my contacts.

I dialed out and was connected on the first ring.

"Yeah, Youngblood, meet me at the 10-13," I said, before he could even say hello.

"See you when you get here," he declared and I kept walking down the block for my bike because fuck Torrid. I wasn't going to get angry, not this time. This time, I was going to get even. She didn't fuel my fire anymore and I'd used all of it up where she was concerned anyways. Lil was my food, my life, and I wouldn't roar back to life completely until I was with her and I'd be damned if I let this consume us.

I rode to the 10-13 and Skids unlocked the door for me. It was before opening and the guys were in the fishbowl. He clapped me on the back and dug thumbs into my knotted shoulders as we walked back there. I took the steps and went in first.

"What have you got?" Youngblood asked.

"Got her dead to rights," I said and set my phone in the center of the table and hit play.

The guys around the table listened in stony silence.

Yale looked pretty disgusted. "I can't use it," he said. "Not unless you get the investigating officers to sign off that it was a result of a legally-procured wiretap. One my office signed off on."

"You boys have all the pieces, but it's a slippery fucking slope," Skids said.

"Sounds like a no-fucking-brainer to me," Narcos said, licking a line along his rolling paper to seal his cigarette.

"You been under too long," Reflash said, arching a brow at him.

"Man, I don't like it either, but bitch be batshit fucking cray-cray," Oz said.

"I say we do it. We don't and she's gonna kill somebody," Golden chimed in.

"I showed you mine, now you show me yours," I demanded and Youngblood sighed. He slid his phone out onto the table and hit play. Lil's panicked voice filled the room.

"You're recording this, right?"

"Yes ma'am."

"Then I've got some things to say."

"You just say what you need to, just stay on the line with me."

"If something bad happens to me, if I somehow don't make it out of here, I need you to play this back for Emmet Calder of the Indigo City Fire Department. Promise me."

"Nothing bad is going to happen, ma'am. I promise you. The ICFD is on their way, they should be there any minute."

"Promise me!" Lil snapped savagely.

"Yes ma'am, I will do my best."

There was a bunch of muffled choked coughing and Lil's voice came back on the line.

"Emmet, Backdraft, I just want you to know I love you, you have given me the best weeks of my life and if this goes badly, it's not your fault, baby. None of this is your fault. I don't want you to blame yourself. I want you to live for me. Okay? I love you so much..."

"Ma'am, do you hear the firetrucks? They should be there now."

"Yes, yes, I hear them. Tell them I'm on the third floor, in the bathroom."

"Turn it off," I said grimly and Youngblood shut off the recording. Skids cleared his throat.

"All in favor of doing this thing, raise your hand."

Every hand went up and no one looked happy about it, but every damn one of us looked resolved.

"I'll get the paperwork started, have your officers come see me," Yale said, getting up.

"Investigation is out of the ninth," Youngblood said.

"That's us," Driller said and dropped the front chair legs to the floor. "I've got it."

"I gotta get back out there," Narcos said. "Doesn't sound like you need me for anything."

"Nope," Driller affirmed. Narcos grunted and I nodded.

"Thanks, you guys."

"This isn't by the book, but sometimes everything ain't in the books," Skids said with a sniff.

"Doesn't make any of us feel any better about it," I said.

"Fuck that," Oz said. "Hell, naw, getting that hooker off the street is gonna feel great."

Laughter broke out around the table. Youngblood nodded.

"It's true. It may not be by the book, but I think we can all agree, we're on the side of the angels with this one."

"Here, here," Reflash said and we all knocked on the table top in agreement.

I send the audio file to Youngblood; he'd know what to do with it.

"I need to find out if Lil is still at Trinity Gen," I said standing up. Golden picked up his phone and shot off a text.

"Angel says naw, she's gone home."

"Then that's where I'm headed. Thanks, you guys."

"Don't thank us yet. Thank us when the bitch is locked up," Golden said and Oz held out a fist to him. Golden knocked it with his.

"Alright, I'm out," I said.

"Take care of your woman," Skids ordered.

"Ain't gotta tell me twice, Captain."

Ain't nobody got to tell me twice.

32

*L*illi...

The police found me in a curtained-off area of the emergency room. I'd been given a breathing treatment and had coughed up some nasty phlegm with grey and black streaks in it. They'd given me some IV fluids and some medicine to calm me down, too. I guess they were concerned I would go into shock.

My robe was toast, soot-stained beyond saving and reeking of smoke. My hair, too. I had black smudges on my feet, chest and hands. I was assuming there was some on my face, too, but I couldn't see it so, yeah. I was in a hospital gown and one of the nurses said she would scare me up something to wear home.

The police came into my little curtained-off area before she came back, one of them peeking into the curtain saying, "Knock, knock. How you feeling, Ms. Banks?"

"Okay, I guess."

"Up to talking with us?"

I nodded, and he slid into the little area with me, a female officer behind him. They were both in uniform and I wondered if that was normal.

"I'm Officer McKernan and this is Officer Hart, we're here to take your statement."

I told them everything and they were patient with me when I found myself tearing up again. They told me that they would pass my statement along and if there was anything else needed, someone would contact me. I swallowed hard and nodded, keeping it to myself but thinking, *That was it?*

The nurse came in as they were finishing up and set a set of folded green surgical scrubs and a pair of those hospital socks with the grippy bottoms on the end of the bed.

"By the time you finish putting these on, I'll have you ready for discharge," she said kindly.

"Thank you," I said hollowly. My throat hurt, but they assured me that was normal and would go away.

I put on the clothes on offer and was surprised they fit. When I pulled the curtain aside, I figured out how they managed to know my size.

"Y'okay, baby?" Pasquale asked me.

"Been better," I said and was fishing through the plastic personal-effects bag looking for my phone.

"I have to get back up to the upper floors now, but I heard through the grapevine you was here. What happened?" I told him and his face, strangely ordinary devoid of makeup, fell into lines of 'You can't be serious'.

"Fucking bitch," he said flatly and I smiled, but it held no humor.

"I just need a ride back to the Echelon."

"Well, your chariot has arrived," he said and waved behind him. I looked up and blinked in surprise as much to see if I was seeing things right. Everyone from Backdraft's firehouse, his whole shift, was standing around the nurse's station looking at me expectantly.

"Wow," I said, blushing hotly. A collective laugh swept through them and I went forward.

"Don't suppose I could get a ride home to the Echelon tower?" I asked meekly, taken aback by their presence.

"You surely can; c'mon, this way," the captain said, and steered me toward the emergency room doors.

"Your discharge papers!" my nurse called out and ran forward. She got my signature on a couple and I let Backdraft's team take me home.

Security let me up to my apartment. I thanked them, and they assured me they would have new keycards made for me and brought up.

I threw my ruined robe down the garbage chute and took my phone with me into my condo, grateful for the biometric locks. I paused at the laundry in the hall and tossed what I was wearing directly into the washer, pausing only to set my phone on the dresser as I made a beeline to my bathroom. I just wanted the stink of fire and near death off of me.

I don't know how long I huddled in the bottom of my shower in the corner, crying, but it was a good cry, cathartic, and that was where Backdraft found me. He didn't even hesitate. Just opened the glass door and got in with me, fully clothed, sitting on the tile floor with me and pulling me tight to his chest. I huddled there and let it out and it was the perfect thing. Just what I needed.

He tipped my face up to his and I gripped his face between my hands, surging up to press my mouth to his. He kissed me back, his arms crushing me to him, our tongues lashing against each other, the desperation we both felt, the fear and gratitude, mixing into a heady cocktail, carrying us both away on a storm surge of passion.

"Off, off!" I ordered between impassioned breaths, and he hauled his wet shirt over his head while I worked at his belt and the button fly of his standard issue indigo-blue uniform pants.

He had his back against the wall and lifted his hips for me so I could pull his pants down. His cock sprang free of its wet cloth prison and I straddled his hips, rising up on my knees. He pushed his cock down so it was at the right angle and I settled over him, moaning as I took him into me in one single, hard fluid thrust.

It was too quick, almost too rushed, too much, but it was exactly what we both needed. I rode him, rising and falling steadily, and dropped my forehead to his, murmuring in a breathy voice, "You saved my life."

"I saved our life," he growled, kissing me. When the kiss came to its natural conclusion, he drew back to look me in the eyes and said, "My life is nothing without yours, Lil, so I saved our life, baby."

I bit my lower lip and closed my eyes and let the power of his words renew me. They shook me to my very core, unmade me, and then carefully put me back together again into a new, better, stronger whole. Our mouths met again and his hands found my ass, gripping, pulling and pushing, rocking me on his cock. I got back into the swing of things and cried out, close, so very close, ready to die the little death for him, with him, with absolutely no regrets.

33

$\mathcal{B}$ackdraft...

She was wildfire moving above me and I was consumed, *gladly* consumed. I held her soft body as she writhed like dancing flame; beautiful, exotic, hypnotizing, and I felt like her air to breathe, her fuel. It wasn't totally one-sided, either. This? This was a fluid exchange. For now I fed her flame, and when I needed it, she fed mine.

I'd never felt a part of something so completely, and to be honest, I never thought I would. Her mouth worked mine and she tasted of life itself. Her body worked mine and I could feel she was close, so very fucking close and when she came above me, I went with her, falling, hurtling back to earth a ball of wildfire, devastating everything around us like an active fucking volcano burning every bit of doubt and fear to fine ash.

We slowly came back to ourselves, limp and spent, clinging to each other as the warm shower water pattered around us. She gasped, and slowly pushed off my shoulders so she could look at me and I let her, loosening my hold around her back.

"That was," she swallowed before she could finish. "That was, wow."

"That was, wow," I said and she laughed. I felt a slow smile, full of life and full of light, bursting with joy and love overtake my lips and I was suddenly laughing, too.

We sat there, for the longest time, both laughing, that laughter bouncing off each other and the glassed-in shower walls, until all we could do was sit there and laugh, clinging to each other, joyous and free.

I was never, ever letting go, either.

It was us; forever and always. *Us.*

EPILOGUE

*L*illi...

Victoria had been arrested and booked into the Indigo City jail. She was still awaiting trial and refusing to take a plea. Yale said he was confident he could and would get a conviction on attempted murder charges; we would just have to wait and see, though. I didn't take anything for granted anymore. Especially not one single moment with Backdraft.

There was extensive damage to the brownstone, enough that Backdraft and I talked it over. With the discoveries that I made about the building, we decided it was just better and easier, to let the professionals handle it and with Veronica's help, her dad being in real estate, I became an official investor on that end. The neighbors who were in the other two occupied brownstones were more than happy with my generous offer to relocate them to a hotel for the duration of the remodel to open up the basements and garages. All the work on our unit would take months, but when it came to opening those basements and garages, we started with theirs so it would only be a matter of a few weeks until they were able to come back in.

In the meantime, Backdraft moved in with me, full time at the Echelon. In the intervening weeks between then and now, I never did run into Mark, and I could only assume his fiancée took the right course of action and kicked his ass to the curb.

Now, it was Christmas Eve, and Backdraft's parents and brother were due to arrive any minute. We'd unfortunately missed Thanksgiving with them this year, partially because Backdraft had drawn the short straw and had to work that night and partially because I just wasn't ready to meet them.

"They're downstairs," he told me and kissed me quickly.

I dusted off my hands even though there was nothing on them and smoothed them down the front of my sweater dress.

"Okay, I'll see you all in a few."

"I love you, don't be nervous, they'll love you too."

I gave him a look that said he wasn't helping my nerves at all saying something like that and said, "I love you, too."

"Us. Always," he said, walking backwards to the door.

"Us. Always," I said back, gravely.

I took the plate of appetizers I'd been plating over to the table and set it down.

"Don't even think about it, you two," I said to Jaspar and Marigold, who eyed the table speculatively, one from the back, the other from the arm of our couch.

The front door opened right as I took a fortifying sip of wine and Backdraft piled in with his parents and brother in tow, calling, "Babe, come on over here."

I swallowed my sip of wine carefully, tried valiantly to shove my shyness to the side, and turned to face the music.

I had no idea what I had to worry about. Of course, the family to produce a man like Backdraft would have to be everything he embodied. Warm, welcoming, funny, and kind. We made it all the way through dinner when his dad turned and asked, "Well, son, when are you going to ask her to marry you?"

"Dad!" Bryant, Backdraft's older brother admonished.

"What?"

Backdraft laughed and reached over, taking my hand. I smiled and he stared at me, saying, "No rush, pops. We have all the time in the world and in the grand scheme of things, it's all just fine print."

"Well, I, for one, am glad to see you so happy," his mother said.

His dad looked at me and winked saying, "I have to agree."

I laughed and said, "Thank you."

"Welcome to the family, Lil." Backdraft's brother leaned back in his seat and smiled at me. "It's nice to have you here."

I looked over at Backdraft and he pursed his lips in a phantom kiss. I rolled mine together and blushed furiously.

"It's nice to be here," I said and it was. It so was.

The End

<u>**A Special Note from the Author**</u>

If you want to read Hallowed Be Thy Light by Timber Philips, the book does exist and can be found on all platforms.

ALSO BY A.J. DOWNEY

1. I Am The Alpha

2. Omega's Run

3. Hunter's End

ABOUT THE AUTHOR

A.J. Downey is the internationally bestselling author of The Sacred Hearts Motorcycle Club romance series. She is a born and raised Seattle, WA Native. She finds inspiration from her surroundings, through the people she meets, and likely as a byproduct of way too much caffeine.

She has lived many places and done many things, though mostly through her own imagination...An avid reader all of her life, it's now her turn to try and give back a little, entertaining as she has been entertained.

Stalker Information:
www.ajdowney.com

www.ingramcontent.com/pod-product-compliance
Lightning Source LLC
Chambersburg PA
CBHW070622170726
48291CB00003B/831